The Last Wizard is a work of fiction. Names, characters, places, and incidents are either the product of the author's imagination or are used fictitiously. Any resemblance to actual persons, living or dead, locations, or events is entirely coincidental.

2021 First Edition

Copyright © 2020 by John Bachkosky

Cover by Anthony Celli

All rights reserved.

Published in the United States by John Bachkosky through Amazon Kindle Direct Publishing services.

ISBN: 9798985813005

This edition is dedicated to Kevin and Greg.

Kevin is a stellar storyteller through both music and written word. His commitment to his craft is both motivating and inspiring.

Greg is the brother I never had. His ability to be honest, in a way only a brother can be, is one of the main reasons this novel is as good as it is.

Introduction

I went to school for engineering. My life revolved around Greek symbols and page after page of mathematics that describe the marvels of both space and powered flight. As evidenced by the first edition of *The Last Wizard*, engineering school was not an adequate preparation for writing a novel. The 2020 First Edition was riddled with my technical shortcomings as a writer and showcased that, despite coming up with a good story, I had a lot to learn about telling it.

Thanks to the wonderful lectures of Brandon Sanderson, author of the Stormlight Archive and Mistborn series, as well as the many online resources that teach how to use a semicolon, (it is my hope that) this new edition is a smoother and more intriguing ride than before. Thank you to everyone who has already picked up *The Last Wizard* and enjoyed the story this engineer believes in. This one's for you.

Prologue

Heron could hear the soldiers approaching. There wasn't much time. She had to leave. Now.

As quietly as possible, she closed the back door to her house and ran across the wheat field into the woods. Arriving at the tree line, she allowed herself one last glance back and watched the soldiers set a torch to the dry thatch roof. The fire wasted no time as it leapt into the sky and began dancing whimsically on the building that could have been her grave. Heron stood watching the scene unfold while storm clouds rolled in above her.

Her pause proved costly as one of the soldiers noticed Heron and pointed his spear in her direction, shouting for the rest of the crew to follow. The knight ran towards her, followed by five additional suits of armor that clanked loudly as they gave chase.

Heron's heart pounded faster than her footsteps as she barreled through the woods. As she ran, she supported her infant daughter close to her chest while using her free hand to throw blue fire blindly over her shoulder at her assailants. Trees igniting behind her lit up the forest, casting shadows that made dodging thorn bushes and cutting back and forth between the large, sturdy oaks much more difficult.

The knights who pursued her were well-trained, superiorly fit, and had the added benefit of being able to run right through most of the underbrush in their armor. She wasn't sure how long she could stay ahead of them. While ducking a low branch, Heron tripped on an exposed root and stumbled but managed to keep her footing. The sky rumbled as the storm continued its mighty march. Her chances of escape were waning. She needed a plan. Heron ran until she came to a break in the trees and was met by cliffs that rose up and blocked her exit.

Heron cried out as an arrow ricocheted off the rocks just above her head and she took off, following the sheer cliff face. Her daughter looked up from underneath the blanket with bright blue eyes that matched her own, unaware of the life-threatening chaos surrounding them.

Heron knew the soldiers would not hesitate to kill them both. She continued to run as her eyes scoured the cliffs to the right and the woods to the left for a place to hide her child. Rain started to fall in large drops as a bolt of lightning cracked the sky in half.

Finally, Heron spotted an outcrop at the top of the cliff face. Time stood still as she looked down at her child for what she knew would be the final time. Heron's heart broke. Would her daughter ever know the sacrifice she was about to make? Would she remember her at all? Heron began to cry as she kissed her baby on the forehead.

"Good luck," she said as she woefully removed the bundle from her chest and, with the soldiers nearly upon her, sent the swaddled baby to the outcrop with a strong gust of wind.

As her child disappeared over the top of the cliff, an arrow sank deep into her shoulder. Heron cried out in pain and turned to face her pursuers. Blue fire enveloped her hands and did not waver despite the rain. Her eyes were ablaze with rage; rage that would not quit until every one of these bastards were dead. Strands of black hair fell across her face as the rain came down in sheets. Small waterfalls began to manifest on the cliffs beside her as streams of tears rolled down her face.

Unconcerned with the chaos below, her baby girl lay magically quiet, tightly wrapped in a red blanket.

~~~

"What do you mean, you're the only one? There were half a dozen of you and only one of her!" General Long yelled in frustration as he examined the soldier. The boy's chest plate was scorched and his eyes were wide with fear. "You mean to tell me that wench took out five royal guards on her own?"

"Y-yes, sir," the boy squeaked.
~~~

"Surprising for someone so unprepared, but at least she is dead. What about the baby?"

The general had gotten up from his chair and started pacing. His huge frame covered the width of the tent in about four strides. Muscular arms pushed out against his shirt as he folded them across his broad chest. He expected greatness and loyalty from each soldier; they had never failed a mission until now.

"What baby?" the boy asked, instantly regretting doing so as he watched the general's face contort into a fuming and terrifying expression.

"WHAT BABY? She had a child! Three actually, but we took care of the first two. You're telling me you did not kill the baby?!" The general did not blink as he stared the boy down.

"We found no baby, sir. Only her!" The boy cowered and started shaking as he defended himself. He did not know what punishment would befall him for failing this part of the mission, but it would not be painless. General Long turned his back on the boy.

"Such a shame; I had rather hoped that we could be permanently done with this hunt. All that hard work wasted. She was the last one, the woman. There were to be no traces of her in any way. Now her baby is…goddess knows where! You were supposed to do your job QUIETLY!" he bellowed. "Take them out. Draw no attention. Instead, you got into a wild goose chase with a wizard!"

"We didn't know she was a wizard, sir! We thought that the king—"

"Of course you didn't," Long interrupted the boy with an unsettlingly calm voice. "That is the whole point of this squadron. Do the job, no questions asked."

"I-I'm sorry, sir."

"You will be." General Long reached for the sword at his side.

Before the boy could protest, Long pulled the sword clear of its sheath and in the same motion, sliced the blade through the boy's neck. The boy gasped helplessly for air while clawing at his neck, a look of terror on his face as he realized that this was his end. Long wiped the blood from the blade, sheathed it, and left the boy to die alone in the tent.

Chapter One
Saros

The road glistened from a fresh coating of rain as Gant walked towards the herbalist's shop. It was the only paved road in town, the only one of interest, lined on each side with every shop they needed. The stone buildings of differing heights stood next to each other like silent sentries in the dawn light, their thick glass windows catching the sun's yawning rays.

Saros consisted of no more than three hundred residents, all of whom knew one another and most of their business; privacy was slim here. Travelers who came through Saros only had one choice for respite: the inn run by Bess, a stocky elderly woman with stark white hair and a sharp eye for drama that could coax a story out of any guest. She thrived on gossip like it was her lifeblood, and since most guests only stayed one night, she didn't waste the opportunity to offer a free drink or savory meal in the hopes of adding a new tale to her arsenal. More often than not, however, the inn was empty. This was fine by most of the other residents, as it kept the town quiet and free of any trouble.

Gant walked past the blacksmith, who had started his forge well before the sun started to rise. Most of the shop owners made their homes in the same building as their storefronts, save for the shopkeepers on either side of Sari's forge. Sari's early morning hammering ensured that the adjacent shops' owners lived in homes set in much quieter parts of the town.

"Good morning, Sari! Crazy storm last night," Gant called cheerily as he continued walking.

Sari didn't bother to glance up but acknowledged Gant with a grunt as he continued to prepare the forge; he was a stout, muscular man with a black beard and a complexion obscured by soot.

Gant kept walking past the shuttered windows of the butchery and tannery. He arrived at the herbalist at the end of the street; his mother had put her shop as far as possible from their home, a cabin set back in the woods, which had annoyed Gant when he was younger. Now twenty years old and equipped with much longer legs, he didn't mind the stroll into town, especially on quiet mornings like these.

Around the side of the single story building there was a locked door that led to the storage room. Gant unlocked it, stepped inside, and closed the door behind him, plunging the windowless room into total darkness. Pulling out a flask, he drained what was left of the potion he had been using the night before and placed it back in his pack.

With a snap of his fingers, the room was illuminated by a small orange fireball in his hand, crackling almost imperceptibly as it flickered and cast the shadow of his tall, thin frame on the wall behind him. The fireball caught the end of the long sandy hair that framed his face like curtains and began to eat its way up the strands. Gant quickly extinguished the rebellious flames but not before a woman half his height walked into the room. She held herself with a refined posture, and her short black hair was peppered with gray.

"You should be more careful when playing with fire. It's wild and unpredictable," the woman joked, knowing full well her son had years of practice with fire.

Gant and his brother were accomplished alchemists, creating and using potions to mimic certain aspects of real magic for brief periods. When they were young, King Gjanion had issued a decree stating that alchemy was dangerous and unpredictable. In his proclamation, he cited an event that had occurred at the castle, killing many of the most prominent royal alchemists. From that day forward, alchemy had been banned across Kyros, but that hadn't stopped the two boys from exercising their natural prowess at alchemy.

"I'm not playing, Mother," Gant said. He extended his fingers and the fireball split into streaks of flame that sought out the candles placed around the room.

"Why are you up so early?" His mother did not flinch as the last flame whizzed past her face into a lantern on the wall.

"There is tons to do before this evening, so I thought I would get an early start. I came to grab some supplies…where is the selaroot?" Gant began searching the many crates stacked around him.

"I'm afraid I'm fresh out. You'll have to go and get some."

"I went last time; I'll make Zhira go get it."

"Make sure you get enough for me too this time, you greedy boys," Fiona said as she walked through a door and out into the store. She began opening the windows so the plants could get their morning sunlight and any early rising villagers passing by could admire her display.

The front windows of Fiona's shop were filled with every color of flower and plant imaginable. Red roses, lilac lilies, yellow daisies, and more accompanied a variety of medicinal plants and roots that sprouted in various shades of green. Behind the windows, the main shop was framed by shelves on either side that sported smaller, individually potted plants along with bottles of prepared ingredients for any concoction or remedy a patron might need.

Centered on the back wall was the counter, adorned with a variety of bowls, a white marble mortar and pestle, and yet more bottles of various shapes and colors. Behind the counter was the door to the storage room, where Fiona kept the remainder of her supplies as well as extra inventory of the everyday items people came in for. Gant was gathering a few pebble-like berries into a small burlap sack when his mother came back into the room.

"Your brother has not been around to see me in some time! Does he not love me?" she asked as she brought out a feather duster and cleaned the vials on one of the shelves.

"You know how Zhira is, locking himself in the tower and meditating on the meaning of every change he sees in the stars."

"Always looking for a big revelation, that boy. But that is no excuse to not see his own mother! Make sure he stops by to smell the roses." She laughed a little to herself and watered a pot of vividly blue flowers.

"I will; I'll send him with the selaroot he picks for you," he said, gathering the rest of the items he had procured from the shop.

"For me? I think you mean for us!" she retorted, knowing full well that her sons used gathering supplies as an excuse to please their mother. Fiona had raised Gant and his brother Zhira alone after the death of their father, and despite their closeness, they were now of the age where she knew they viewed seeing their mother as a chore. She made them gather ingredients for her so she could check in on them every so often. Plus, that meant she didn't have to go out by herself and she always had more than she needed.

Gant rolled his eyes and chuckled on his way out through the main shop. "I'll see you tonight at the festival!" The little bell attached to the door frame rang as he pushed his way out.

The sun had cleared the horizon and was peeking through the trees as he made his way back down the street. Rays of sunlight hit the roofs of the shops, causing the previous night's rain to evaporate in steamy clouds.

The cabin where Gant lived with his brother Zhira sat alone off any known path or road; to find it, one had to know it was there. Built almost entirely of logs, it blended into its wooded surroundings and looked like nothing out of the ordinary apart from the stone tower that sprouted from the middle, the top of which just barely cleared the tree line. A wooden trap door existed where a roof would be so that it could be opened for a brilliant view of the night sky when the weather was kind.

Gant shut the front door, which groaned in protest, and turned to put away the ingredients he had collected from their mother's shop. The cabin had been a modest, one story home with two bedrooms, one for their mother and one for Gant and his brother, as well as a decent living space and a kitchen that always smelled like something was burning. Once Gant and Zhira had finished building the tower, however, there was barely any living space remaining, and only half of the kitchen was still usable.

It had taken them the better part of two years to build the tower, even assisted by potions enhancing their strength. Their mother, unable to stop her sons from defacing their childhood home, decided to permanently move into her shop on the main road. Zhira was fine with this and promptly moved into her room, though he spent so much of his time in the tower that his move hardly mattered and Fiona's room remained largely empty. When she left, he had told Gant that her absence meant that she would be 'less of a distraction from the stars' than if she had stayed. Gant worried that Zhira needed something to draw him back to the real world, or his brother's head would never come down from the stars.

Gant finished putting the berries in a bucket by the stove and turned to find his brother. He didn't have to look very hard; Zhira was exactly where he had left him late last night.

"We have so much to do. Can you please make yourself useful?" Gant asked as he walked into the room at the top of the tower.

Charts, maps, drawings, and books the two had written and compiled in their years of observations of the night sky lay scattered about the room. Zhira was sitting in the middle of the floor, eyes closed and apparently meditating. He was a fair bit shorter than his younger brother with hair as dark as Gant's hair was light. The flowing green robes he wore masked the weight he had gained from never leaving the cabin.

Zhira nodded and turned to Gant, "Today is an important day! Of course I shall make myself useful!"

"We need to gather more selaroot. Mother's run out and we need them for the festival potions."

"Yes, I have foreseen this!" Zhira said matter-of-factly.

"You…foresaw that we needed to gather roots?" Gant raised his eyebrow, amused.

"No…not that specifically, but-"

"Bring it to mother and be back by lunchtime. We have a lot to get done." Gant started back down the wooden spiral stairs.

"Gant! Wait! You must hear what I have read in the stars!" He hurried after his younger brother.

"Fine," Gant sighed, "let's hear it, Z."

"Right, well, last night I witnessed something special…I saw another star. A new star, right next to The Bright One!"

"A new star?" Gant asked, intrigued.

"Yes! It's red; I believe it to be a nova. It's a sign, Gant! We are meant to find new purpose."

"How did you deduce that? What new purpose?"

"I'm…not sure really," Zhira replied.

"Well, let me know when you figure it out," Gant said dismissively, "I'm sure you'll have plenty of time to consider it while you go out and get roots."

"All right, all right, I'm going." Zhira said as his brother pushed him towards the door. He slid on his leather boots and left, leaving the door open behind him. Gant closed it out of habit, accustomed to Zhira's absentmindedness.

~~~
~~~

Zhira packed his bag with as many of the purple roots as he could fit, making sure not to separate them from the stalks. Both were equally valuable, but once separated, the stalks would float off on the warm morning breeze. The sun was well clear of the trees but was still a ways off from the peak of its dance across the sky.

Ahead of schedule, Zhira decided to take the scenic route home. He found the path that wound out of the woods and onto the cliffs. Looking out over the dense forest below, he noticed something odd.

"Why are those trees burned?" he pondered aloud, a habit he knew Gant was not terribly fond of. He walked further along the cliff until he was level with a section of forest that appeared to have caught fire.

"Lightning from the storm last night maybe?" Zhira continued scanning the trees and examining the scene below. The longer he looked, the more he noticed. "There are some arrows…and a spear!" he exclaimed excitedly to no one in particular, or so he thought.

At the sound of his voice, someone started wailing. Zhira, caught completely off guard, nearly lost his footing. Two selaroots fell from his bag and went tumbling over the cliff. One hit a rock on its way down and split, sending its stalk floating away into the late morning sky. Zhira grabbed the nearest tree to prevent himself from falling as well. Regaining his balance, Zhira looked around frantically for the source of the cries until his eyes settled on a red blotch in a sea of green.

"What is this?" Zhira bent down to examine his new find. "Oh my goddess…"

Laying swaddled in a red blanket underneath a rosebush was a baby who looked to be about three months old with black hair and a tiny nose. The child went silent as Zhira leaned over her, the blue eyes staring back up at him large enough to catch the reflection of the trees above them. Zhira looked around, trying to find any sign of a guardian, then turned back to the baby. The small child continued to look up at him with curiosity, tears still on her face, as he sat down next to her.

From his bag Zhira produced a vial containing bright pink liquid and removed the stopper. He looked around until he found some white flowers growing upside down on a bush and resembling umbrellas. A few two-headed mice scurried as he plucked three of the smallest flowers, crushed them up in his hand, and added them to the pink potion. He tipped his head back, drained it, and focused on the child, whose attention had been won over by the discovery of her own hand. Zhira closed his eyes and waited.

Suddenly, he had a view of a dark sky flying by him through what seemed like black curtains. He heard distant yelling and watched an arrow pass over as a woman cried out. Moments later, Zhira felt as though he was falling…or was it flying? His view settled on the dark canopy of a forest, as if he was lying on his back.

Zhira opened his eyes and looked up. The same canopy was now bathed in sunlight. Something terrible had happened surrounding this child, and as he looked down at her Zhira felt the overwhelming need to keep her safe. He took one more look over the cliff at the scarred woods.

"Who are you, little one?"

Zhira adjusted his bag and bent down to pick her up. He hoisted her into his arms and began the walk back to Saros.

The baby fell asleep as he walked. Once Zhira had made it to the outskirts of town, he became more cautious; everyone knew everyone here, so to be seen walking with a surprise child would certainly arouse suspicion. He skirted the edge of town, staying among the trees until he could make his way to the alley behind the shops where nobody could see him. He walked briskly behind the buildings when suddenly the back door of the cobbler's store opened and out walked a boy carrying an empty sack.

"Make sure you come back with DEER hide!" A high firm voice called out.

"Yethur!" the boy said with a lisp and rushed up the alley towards the tannery, red hair bounding with every step.

"Zhira!" The cobbler, a miniscule man with a curled white mustache and shiny bald head, had noticed him. "It's nice to see you out and about! What brings you to the alley?"

"Oh, hi Litik, just…going to visit mother." Zhira tried to keep walking.

"What do you have there? A gift for your mum? That's a brilliant red color!"

"Yeah," Zhira lied as he shifted the blanket to hide the child's face. "It's a festival dress. We used a color changing brew on it; she didn't like the green we chose."

"How kind of you; I'm sure Fiona will love it!" Litik said cheerily.

"Indeed. Anyways I must be off, lots to do before tonight! See you later," Zhira said hurriedly and set off before Litik could get another word in.

He darted up the alleyway to avoid any more chance meetings. Zhira had no idea who this child was, but his protective instinct was kicking in and the last thing he needed was a villager spilling the beans to the wrong ears. Questions swirled in his head. *Who was this child? Why was she so important to the people who had been hunting her? Who had helped her escape?*

Zhira and Gant enjoyed a quiet existence in the woods that offered them secrecy to experiment with and create potions and brews for various purposes. The king forbade the study of alchemy, but the brothers had a knack for it. The people of Saros knew, and kept it quiet in exchange for the protection and assistance the brothers provided. It was much easier to have a bountiful harvest if you poured a multiplying potion over your crops.

Zhira closed the door to the storeroom, his mind swirling. Fiona was at the counter wrapping up some pink bulbs for a customer. She heard the door close, and when the customer left she went back to find her son standing with his bag and a red bundle.

"So you finally decide to visit! You've been eating well, I see." She pointed to his bulging gut.

"Hi Mother, I brought you the-" he was cut off by the baby waking, squirming suddenly in his arms, and surprising him for the second time that morning. Zhira nearly dropped her and the scare caused her to start wailing.

"What in the name of Eres is that?!" his mother exclaimed.

"I found her in the woods; I don't know where she came from, but nobody is coming back for her," he said before proceeding to tell his mother about the forest and the memory he had obtained from the child. "She's young, so her memory was fuzzy, but it was new enough that I got the gist," he finished.

"So what do you plan to do with her?" Fiona regarded the baby curiously.

"I'm not sure."

"Let me see her." Fiona took the baby into her arms. "Oh my…"

"What is it?"

"She has blue eyes."

Chapter Two
Beginnings

Captain Genda shot to attention as General Long threw the doors of the barracks open. Her and her co-captain, Orin, had not been expecting his arrival. She and Orin were in charge of the garrison located in Hawthorne, one of the many small towns that lay just outside the capital. Hawthorne was a quaint town nestled in a small thicket. The citizens kept largely to themselves, going about their days against the lush green backdrop that surrounded and permeated the town. Most days here were quiet, but recently, Long had received reports that the people of Hawthorne were disrupting the comings and goings of royal knights.

"General Long, what are you doing here?" Genda asked him.

"You know why I am here," Long said sternly.

"Sir, I don't understand..." Orin said quietly.

"You have lost control of this town. I am here to help you take it back," he said sternly, looking around the small, ramshackle barracks.

"General, we have not lost control." Genda feigned confidence as she stood a little straighter.

"We had a scouting party ride through here not a week ago, and they were assaulted by your people. How were they punished?" General Long asked in a way that indicated he knew the answer.

"We could not find who committed the crime," Orin admitted, head tucked down into his armor, resembling a turtle.

"You don't need to find them. Make them come to you." General Long turned towards the door. "Call a town meeting. Now."

In a matter of minutes, the town's square had been filled with close to one hundred residents. Long addressed the crowd while the two knights stood flanking him.

"My name is General Long, commanding knight of King Gjanion's royal army. It has come to my attention that a reprehensible act was committed against knights of the king's army, my army. I am here to see that justice is served for unwarranted aggression against keepers of the peace."

The crowd was silent.

"Captain Genda, bring him forward," General Long commanded the taller of the two knights.

With a blank expression on her face, she procured an elderly gentleman with white hair and a severe hunch. Murmurs began to bubble through the crowd.

"I do not believe that this man, who I am told is your presiding elder, committed the crime. However if nobody is willing to step forward, then it is the responsibility of your leaders to take the blame and suffer the consequences. Will none of you spare this man?" General Long asked as he drew his sword in a purposefully menacing manner.

The murmurs grew into concerned shouting, but nobody stepped forward.

"No takers? Very well," Long said and gave his sword to Orin.

"Do it." General Long stood looming over him.

Captain Genda looked directly at Orin but did not express any emotions. She held the old man in place and watched patiently.

Orin hesitated for a moment and then lifted Long's sword. As he swung the sword, time slowed. He watched his own arms bring the blade down for what felt like hours before it finally connected and severed the old man's head.

The crowd's shouting broke down into cries and screams as the general wiped his sword and placed it back in its scabbard.

"That is how it is done. These people will not cross you again. If they do, kill them," General Long said to the two knights before walking to the stables to retrieve his horse.

Genda glared at Long as he walked away.

"I didn't sign up for this," Orin muttered dejectedly once Long was a safe enough distance away.

"Nor did I," Genda replied, keeping her eyes squarely on Long until he disappeared into the stables.

"These people are going to kill us. All those knights did last week was ride through. We just killed their elder!" the short knight said as he began to panic.

"They won't. I promise," Genda said with resolve, reassuring him.

~~~

As General Long arrived back at the castle that evening, the sun began to set behind the trees leaving a smattering of orange and pink in its wake. Stars poked holes in the darkening sky; as it turned a deeper and richer blue, more and more stars found their place as if taking their seats for a show. General Long strode across the lawn of the castle yard and into the main hall. He entered the throne room, walked past the throne itself, and opened a door off to the left. He climbed the spiral stairs two at a time at a steady pace until he reached the top and knocked on the wooden door.

"Enter," a strong, smooth voice answered through the heavy oak.

Long pulled open the door and stepped into the study. The room was adorned with brilliant purple drapes that framed windows that stretched to the ceiling on each wall. The windows glowed as the setting sun's
~~~

rays shone through and illuminated the room in a brilliant orange. The walls themselves were lined with dark cabinets with all of their doors locked, concealing a wide range of books, bottles, and assorted vials. An ornate red and gold carpet covered most of the floorboards, and two high-backed armchairs upholstered in a purple pattern resembling the carpet sat in one corner. Standing in the center of the room was a long wooden table covered with a dark blue tapestry. Next to it, a tall man stood dressed in bright purple robes that looked like they were cut from the same cloth as the drapes.

King Gjanion was not as intimidating a presence as General Long, but was every bit as commanding. He wore a crown made of silver atop his long black hair, which was currently flowing down over his shoulders. The crown was simple yet elegant, containing a ruby, sapphire, and emerald in a triangle on the front. Gjanion's features were chiseled: high cheekbones, thick eyebrows, and green eyes that could bore through the thickest stone wall. He held himself with confident and rigid posture, arms behind his back as he regarded the general.

"I assume you have good news?" the king asked, snapping a fire into existence in his left hand. He flexed his fingers and the fire became many, quickly finding their places in candles around the room.

"Yes, Your Majesty, on both fronts," Long replied, standing at attention.

"And?" The King was impatient.

"My team carried out the mission. The woman is dead, but not without some difficulties."

"What sort of difficulties?" The king furrowed his brow. Long's team was efficient and effective. Gjanion had told Long not to inform the team about who they were truly hunting, but that should not have mattered. To hear of difficulties implied that someone had not performed their tasks correctly, a rare occurrence under Long's leadership.

"There was some cleanup necessary. The woman put up a fight and we weren't a total surprise like we'd hoped. She managed to escape before we could trap her in the house. After a brief chase, she was dealt with. The team suffered casualties, but it's done."

"Who messed it up?" Gjanion asked.

"A younger soldier who no longer has a head," General Long said so matter-of-factly that Gjanion decided to move on.

"As long as there is no more threat to my rule."

General Long stood there, mulling over the information he had not disclosed. He should have seen to this assignment personally, but what harm could a baby do? These people hid in the woods and kept to themselves; anyone who found the child wouldn't ever know its history.

"None, sir."

"Good. With this threat out of the way, I believe nothing will undo the secret we have worked so hard to maintain. Should anyone else find out I am not a wizard, my right to rule would become a sham. It would be a disgrace upon my grandfather's name if all he gave our family was ruined by a loose end.

"Agreed, sir. This will make certain that your secret is yours alone now," Long said.

"You know too, general. This secret is not my own."

"Yes sir, but I am the *only* other person who knows. Should the secret get out it will be little trouble to determine who let it slip."

"Indeed…anyway, what of the other matter?" Gjanion inquired, changing the subject.

"The small revolt in Hawthorne has been quelled. The knights in charge there were shown the proper way to handle aggression against our men," Long reported.

"Very good. It is imperative that we make an example of those who do not appreciate all we have to offer them."

"Agreed. Sir, I—"

Long was interrupted by a knock at the door.

"Enter," the king answered.

A man wearing light blue robes came hurriedly into the room. "It's your wife, sire! She's gone into labor. It's time!"

King Gjanion's unblinking gaze moved from the man still wheezing from his apparent sprint up the stairs to General Long, whose expression remained unchanged. Gjanion was rarely caught off guard, but he appeared totally shocked by this news.

"N-now? My child is coming…now?" he said much more quietly.

"Yes, now my king." The man's words were punctuated by heavy breaths. "She is with the midwife."

"Very well," said the king. With another snap of his fingers, a gust of wind came from nowhere and extinguished the candles. As they left the room, he pulled out a bronze key and locked the door.

~~~

King Gjanion followed the man to the bedchamber on the west side of the castle. As they approached the delivery room, they heard crying.

The king quickened his pace. He burst through the door and saw the queen, his beautiful wife, lying there holding a baby with a full head of golden hair that matched her mother's. The baby was wailing but the queen was smiling; she looked up at Gjanion.

"Say hello to our daughter," she said as she shifted the baby so he could see her face. "What should we call her?"

"Rylan, I think," said Gjanion, the only words he could manage to get out as he was totally overwhelmed by his new daughter. A deluge of emotions came over him: elation over being a father, excitement to teach her all he knew, and burning desire to care for her and to love her. She would be his treasure.
~~~

"It's a perfect name for a perfect child," the queen said as Rylan finally stopped crying. "She will be loved by all."

"We shall throw a celebration in honor of her birth. I will begin preparations at once. Tomorrow, we feast!" the king exclaimed, upsetting the new baby; she began to cry again.

~~~

Gant stood speechless in the storeroom of the shop, his arms still full of the fireworks he had put together that afternoon for the festival. He had not seen or heard from Zhira since his departure that morning and had assumed his absent-minded brother had gotten lost or distracted. When Gant had walked into the shop in a huff to complain to his mother, he had discovered her standing with Zhira who was holding a baby.

"You just…found her?" Gant asked, dumbfounded.

"Yeah," replied Zhira. "She was just lying there next to a rose bush."

Gant stared at the baby, who was currently trying to see how close she could pull her foot to her head. Fiona emptied a crate and padded it with the red blanket for the child to lay in.

"She has beautiful blue eyes," their mother said.
~~~

"I can see that," Gant said annoyed. "What I can't see is what we are going to do next! Do you see us taking care of a baby?"

"No, Gant, I think her blue eyes are important!" Zhira retorted, ignoring his brother's question as he laid the baby in the crate. "Have you ever met someone with blue eyes?"

"I… no I don't think I have." Gant gave them a confused look.

Fiona looked up from where she was kneeling next to the baby. "I've never seen someone with blue eyes before. Do you think it has to do with her powers?"

"I'm sorry, her *what*?" Gant was completely lost.

"Her powers, Gant. The baby is a wizard!" Zhira exclaimed.

Gant stared gaping at him. "You honestly believe that this child…this baby…has…has…magic powers?!"

The child successfully pulled her foot to her mouth and celebrated by feasting on her own toes.

"Yes, watch." Zhira picked up a metal bowl and dropped it, which caused a series of loud clanging noises. The baby immediately began to cry, and the candle nearest her went out.

"Don't play with me, Z!" Gant looked at him skeptically.

"It wasn't me. I swear!"

Gant turned from Zhira, not buying any of it, and looked to their mother. "You really believe she is a wizard?"

Fiona lifted up the baby and bounced her in her arms in an attempt to quiet her, and replied, "I don't see why we can't consider the possibility, but what does it matter? If she has powers, she needs to be protected. If she doesn't, she still needs a home. This town is safe for her, thanks to the villagers keeping your alchemy a secret, they should be able to handle one more. If someone's looking for her, this will be the last place they look."

Zhira gave Gant pleading eyes while his younger brother considered the implications. If the child was indeed a wizard, that meant she could be extremely useful to them in their alchemical endeavors. If she wasn't, Mother was right; she still needed a home. Either way if someone was looking for her, which seemed likely given the evidence of a significant battle Zhira claimed to have found in the forest, it could bring ruin to Saros.

"As far as we know, the king is the last wizard. What if this is his daughter or something?" Gant asked.

"He won't find her here," Zhira said, sounding more desperate than assured.

"Our whole world could be thrown out of balance if anyone comes looking for her. You found spears and burned trees just a stone's throw from where she was!" Gant said. "How do we know they aren't already here looking for her?"

"This town has kept your secret for over ten years. They can keep this one too," Fiona said confidently.

"You really think everyone will keep this secret?" Gant asked once more.

Fiona replied, "I do. The people of Saros have a lot to lose if you two leave."

Gant stared at the child. He knew there was no point in arguing any further; Zhira and his mother had already made up their minds. Besides, what was his goal? Did he want his brother to put the baby back? Abandon it in the forest?

"All right, let's raise a baby!" Gant said begrudgingly.

"You're not going to resent her…or me, right?" Zhira asked with genuine concern.

"No! No, of course not. I just don't know that we are prepared for this," Gant replied.

"I wasn't prepared when either of you came along either, yet here we are!" Fiona smiled at her boys.

"Okay, fair enough. We'll raise her together. All three of us," Gant smiled at his family, now one larger.

"So what do we call her?" Zhira asked his brother and mother excitedly.

"Wait, how old is she?" Gant questioned.

"Does that matter for naming her?" Zhira asked.

"No, but I feel like that's something we should know, or try to figure out."

"She can't be more than…three or four months old," Fiona observed.

"Works for me," said Gant.

"How would she know?" Zhira questioned him.

"Would you have a better guess? She at least has some experience with babies!"

"Fair enough," Zhira said, conceding.

"Why not name her after your grandmother, Mara?" Fiona offered, changing the subject.

"That's a pretty name—I like it," said Zhira.

"Me too," Gant agreed.

"Then it's settled! Mara it is!" Zhira beamed at Mara and she seemed to smile a little back at him, as best a baby could.

"Excellent," Gant said as he began to gather up the supplies he had brought with him, "Mother, can you keep her tonight during the festival? It would be odd if either of us were missing. We can tell the townsfolk you're ill. That will at least cover tonight."

"Sure," she said without hesitation, "Good idea. Be careful, as always!" their mother called out after them as they stepped out the front door into the cool evening air.

The brothers turned and walked up the street to the main square. Laden with fireworks and vials full of colorful liquid, they began setting up their display in the center of the open space. Residents from the village had set up stands selling all sorts of things: Litik was selling shoes and boots with stars worked into the leather; the glassblower Keylon, Sari's wife, had created little uniquely shaped trinkets that held candles and emanated star patterns on the walls, and Sari himself had forged a beautiful statue of Dazel, the goddess of magic, that stood just to the side of where Zhira and Gant were placing their fireworks.

Ten years ago, it had been Zhira who had discovered that the brightest star in the sky, known as the Bright One, didn't follow the same pattern across the black night as the rest of the stars. Over the ensuing two years, he had realized that it doubled back on itself, whereas the rest of the stars swept across the sky in the same lines and arcs over the years. Gant too had observed this anomaly and together the brothers took it as a sign that Dazel was watching over them and their alchemy. He had decided a celebration was in order, both for Zhira's discovery and to appease the goddess. Making it known to her that they had seen her sign of approval, the two of them founded the Festival of Dazel. With the help of Bess ensuring there were no visitors in Saros, Gant and Zhira used the festival to provide a night of alchemically enhanced revelry and enjoyment for the town as thanks for keeping their secret.

The two brothers had discovered their natural aptitude for alchemy by accident while trying to imitate their mother in her shop. As an herbalist, she was always mixing and concocting medicines and remedies for the people of Saros. From a young age Gant and Zhira spent their days mixing random things in the back room of the shop while their mother worked. One day

Gant had dared his brother to drink a particularly gross-looking mixture they had made. Zhira expected to throw the concoction up, but instead he had levitated briefly. The two frantically tried to recreate the experience and soon enough were both flying around the storage room.

They began to experiment over time with different ingredients and mixtures with varying degrees of success. Zhira kept meticulous notes of their trials and over time they developed a book of potions and other useful concoctions that Gant realized could be very useful to the townspeople of Saros. King Gjanion had banned alchemy not long before their discovery, so they swore the town to secrecy in exchange for their help and their education to anyone who wished to learn the art. Despite the ban, a few people attempted to learn alchemy but could never get the hang of it like Gant and Zhira, so the town left alchemical tasks to the two of them. The people of Saros kept their promise and word never got out about the brothers' defiance of the king's decree.

Gant finished placing the fireworks and began to tie a string dipped in oils between them so they would go off in the order he had planned, producing a vibrant display for the town. Zhira took the potions they had brought and divided them into tiny glasses no bigger than the size of his thumb. Each one would give the drinker a moment or two off the ground, long enough to have a good laugh and spin around, but not so long as to put the user in any real danger of getting too high off of the ground. The children especially loved these. Being so much lighter, they could get higher up before the effects began to wear off.

Litik walked over and greeted the alchemists, "Good evening gentlemen! What a lovely night for a festival!"

"Yes, it should be a good one!" replied Gant cheerily.

"Where is your mother? I'm sure she looks lovely in her new dress!"

"Her wha—" Gant began to reply but Zhira interrupted his brother with a jab to the ribs.

"Unfortunately, she is quite under the weather. Not sure what it is, but she won't be joining us this evening," Zhira lied convincingly.

"What a shame! I saw her out and about just today," Litik exclaimed. "I know how much she loves this festival."

"Yeah, a real shame." Gant side-eyed Zhira.

"Oh, the floating potions!" Litik became sufficiently distracted by the small thimbles as his eyes settled on the stand of levitation brew. He practically skipped over to the brothers' small wooden table and downed one of the thimble-sized glasses; instantly, his feet left the ground and he was hovering about three feet in the air.

"Yippee!" he cried as he began to do somersaults in midair. The sight of him drew people out of the woodwork and soon the stand full of small potions was crowded by dozens of eager participants.

Small children floated about five feet above the square, some spinning around, others flapping like birds, still more bounding into each other and having a laugh as they flew in opposite directions over other stalls. The adults were having a grand time as well, dancing to the music being played on small wooden instruments by some of the townspeople as the sky became littered with more stars than could ever be counted. Torches lit up the square and cast shadows every which way while the light gleamed off the life-sized statue of Dazel as the village danced and drank long into the night.

The moon set behind the trees just past midnight, and in the absence of the overpowering light, the stars began to twinkle. The Bright One dazzled and gleamed like a radiant diamond as Gant lit the string connected to the fireworks. One by one, they shot up into the sky and exploded in a brilliant display of color and light. No ash fell on the crowd, Gant made sure to use the proper ingredients, and they all cheered as red became green became purple became yellow. One of the children, the same redheaded boy from the alley Zhira had seen earlier that day, thought it would be a good idea to try and reach the fireworks. He took three thimbles of levitation potions and began to float up and up until he was above the trees.

Zhira, ready for this eventuality that occurred every festival, grabbed a lasso he had fashioned and threw it. It easily caught the boy's foot and foiled his attempt to become a firework himself.

"Awh, dang," the boy cried in disappointment as Zhira reeled him back down to the ground and tethered him to the stall until the potions wore off.

The fireworks ended in a cacophony of explosions, which was greeted by much whooping and hollering and cheering from the now drunk adults and overly tired children. Slowly, the residents began to trickle home, some stumbling, others carrying sleeping sons and daughters. Sari picked up his son who had fallen asleep eating a chicken wing under Keylon's stand. The stand, which had once displayed over two dozen miniature glass candelabras, was now empty except one that consisted of red, purple, and pink swirls.

"Another for the collection, sirs," she said, offering it to Gant as they packed up their supplies. "Thank you for yet another fantastic night of fun and celebration!"

"Happy to do it, Keylon." Gant took the glass piece from her with a smile. "You're too kind making these for us. Our home will look even more stunning at night!"

"I'm sure it is no match for that view from your tower, but it's the least I can do. It's nice to see you two out and about rather than closed up in that place. You should make it more of a habit."

Keylon was as open and kind as her husband was reserved and cold. Their son Kei had inherited Sari's black hair but had Keylon's soft features and kind smile. Keylon gave the brothers a wave and left with her husband and son. The torches in the square were burning low, offering little light in the deep black of the predawn darkness. Gant and Zhira gathered the empty potion vials and began walking back to their cabin in the woods.

"Wait." Zhira stopped where he was. "We should go to Mother, take Mara off her hands and bring her with us. It's dark and everyone is either drunk or asleep so nobody will see us."

"Better than walking her down the street in broad daylight," Gant replied, giving Zhira a knowing look.

"I was in the alley. I wasn't careless!" Zhira retorted.

"Clearly," Gant said, rolling his eyes.

"I was overwhelmed in the moment. I managed to hide her though! Litik had no idea I was carrying a baby."

"Barely! We need to be on the same page and be more careful," Gant said as they went to retrieve their new daughter.

Chapter Three
Broken

Mara ran as fast as she could. They were gaining on her. She didn't look back as she willed her legs to go faster, but there was no way she could outrun them.

I'm gonna get there first!" Zhira called out, his burgundy cloak flowing behind him as he ran after his little girl.

"Nuh-uh!" she yelled back in her high pitched voice as her little legs carried her up the paved street. She blitzed by Sari as he and his son, Kei, worked the forge, paying the antics no mind.

Suddenly, Gant popped out of the alley between the forge and cobbler's shop.

"Boo!" he yelled as he scooped Mara up. She gave a squeal of delight as Gant ran her the last fifty yards or so to the front of their mother's store.

"See, Daddy, I beat you!" she giggled as Gant set her down and Zhira caught up.

"You had some help! That's not fair!" Zhira said as he smiled and readjusted his cloak.

"You never said I couldn't!" Mara dashed inside the shop, followed by her two fathers.

Zhira had lost some weight since Mara's unexpected arrival eight years ago. Chasing around a child had him spending less time in the tower studying the messages in the stars and more time teaching his baby girl how to read, write, and draw. Gant was grateful for this, as he had worried his brother was going to be lost staring up at other worlds rather than enjoying their own. Discovering Mara had ensured that would not happen.

"Grandma, Grandma!" She ran behind the counter and gave Fiona's hip a huge hug.

"Hello, my rose," Fiona replied affectionately. Fiona had given Mara the nickname shortly after Zhira had explained the circumstances of her discovery eight years ago under the rose bush.

"Guess what! Daddy is gonna let me watch the stars with him!"

"Oh yeah? Which daddy?" she asked as she grinned, showing a few more lines crossing her face than in years past.

"Daddy! Not Dad, don't be silly, Grandma!" Her excitement caused one of the small green stalks on the counter to sprout a pink and white flower. Zhira stepped in front of it as a customer walked by, who was totally unaware of the small miracle.

"Mara, what did I tell you about getting too excited?" Gant asked a little impatiently.

"Oh, don't be so hard on her, Gant, she is only eight," his mother scolded. Gant hated when she did that. Ever since Zhira found Mara, his rigid demeanor and scholarly lifestyle had been replaced by a much more relaxed and excitable approach to life, as if something inside him had woken up after all those long days and nights in the tower. Gant appreciated the change in his brother, but by nature had become the sterner parental figure; where Zhira was playful, Gant was cautious, when Zhira bent the rules, Gant stiffened them back up. He felt it was up to him to make sure that Mara's secret remained that: a secret.

"It's important she doesn't give herself away!" Gant said. He paused, waiting until the customer that had been browsing Fiona's shelves left the shop. Once they were alone, Gant resumed his rant. "She needs to control her powers; all these folks know is that we found her in the woods. That's gossip enough without them knowing she can do real magic!"

"Even still," his mother continued lecturing, "you weren't so easily controlled at this age. Just be more gentle and understanding."

Gant just grunted and turned away, pretending to be interested in a vial of crushed blue cherries.

"Do you mind watching her today?" Zhira asked, changing the subject to avoid the impending awkward silence. "Gant and I need to go down to the gorge to collect more darkstone; our supply is low and

Keylon has asked for more Nightpowder. Apparently Sari is working night and day on a big project and the forge is bright through their floorboards."

"I'm always happy to watch my precious granddaughter. You two be careful down there," she replied, smiling at Mara, who was still attached to her hip.

"We will. Be good Mara. We will be back by dinner!" Gant didn't waste any time leaving the shop.

"Don't worry, Mom, I'll get him to relax," Zhira added as he chased his brother out the door.

Mara frowned. "I wish Dad wasn't so mean all the time."

"He isn't mean, my rose, he is just worried and wants to keep you safe. He cares about you a lot and wants to make sure you stay out of trouble."

"I won't get into any trouble! I'm eight!" she said, puffing out her chest defiantly. Several more flowers grew next to the white and pink one on the counter.

"Dad always tells me not to do things, but I like to do things! Daddy lets me do things! He lets me do magic on plants, and even change the color of his fingernails!"

Fiona opened her mouth to respond, but noticed the plants on the shelves behind Mara had begun to grow at a rapid pace. The intensity of the child's emotions was having an impact on the plants; they were soaking it in like sunlight, feeding off of it for energy.

"Mara, sweetie, you need to calm down," Fiona said in a gentle voice, trying to subdue her.

"You have an amazing gift, but it's important to listen to your dads. Have they told you the story of the broken planet?"

"No, what's that?" Mara's anger evaporated and now her blue eyes stared up at Fiona with nothing but curiosity.

"Well, the broken planet is what happens when little kids—"

"I'm not little!" Mara stamped her foot.

At that, several of the bottles on the nearest shelf fell and shattered as they hit the ground, their contents exploding across the floor.

"Excuse me then," Fiona smiled, grabbing her mop, "when *big* kids don't listen to their parents. Once there was a girl about your age, and she refused to do anything her parents told her to. She didn't clean her room, she didn't eat her dinner, and her parents got very angry. One day, the little girl threw a huuuuge tantrum and slammed her bedroom door in defiance. Well, the goddesses didn't think that was very nice." Mara's eyes were wide and unblinking as Fiona talked. The air in the shop was weirdly still.

Fiona continued. "The goddesses were so disappointed with the girl's actions that they decided they were going to destroy the whole planet! The ground shook beneath their feet and cracks began to form in the fields! Soon, the whole planet was cracked and broken!"

Mara gasped.

"The girl had to spend the rest of her life doing as much good as she could so that the cracks would heal and her family could farm and eat again."

"I don't wanna break the planet…" Mara stared at Fiona and started to tear up.

"Sweetie, you won't!" Fiona consoled the weeping girl as several plants drooped in response to her sudden sadness. "It'll all be fine! Listen to your dads and everything will be okay." Mara smiled and wiped away her tears. "Now, why don't you help me water all the plants?"

"O-okay," Mara said, still sniffling. She grabbed the nearest jug and began walking around with her grandmother.

~~~

"Why?"

"Because, Your Majesty, some believe that you don't care for your subjects. They believe that you only care for yourself. There are…rumors being spread that you hoard resources and they think that by overthrowing you, they can gain that wealth for the people."

"That's absurd!" King Gjanion snapped the quill he had been toying with in half. He, General Long, and the rest of his advisors were gathered around a long marble table covered with maps that showed the
~~~

surrounding villages. Reports had been coming in steadily that soldiers and guards were being attacked and stripped of their armor and belongings. The attacks had gotten more violent, so the general had sent additional troops to quell the insurrections.

Now, severely underpowered and outnumbered, the villagers had adopted a more guerilla style of disruption. They began attacking wagons of goods headed to the castle and raiding barracks by cover of darkness. Rebels were stealing directives, messages, and reports, intent on disrupting the information flow across the Royal Guard. As a result, the castle started using decoy methods of communication, leaving false reports and using multiple routes to deliver goods. Despite these efforts, things were not improving and King Gjanion was getting frustrated; he did not like to get involved in affairs concerning the Royal Guard. He had General Long for that.

Not wanting this disconcerting behavior to turn into an all-out rebellion, he had decided to insert himself into the fold and told Long to inform him personally at any hour when a threat had been discovered so they could act swiftly. Long had taken this order to heart and called the king out of bed to address a concerning report one of the spies had recently delivered. The fire crackled in the marble hearth of the meeting room, casting elongated shadows of the high-backed chairs. A battle axe hung above the hearth, and several torches lined the relatively bare stone walls, causing the shadows to dance.

"There are reports from Hawthorne suggesting that there will be an attempt on your life tomorrow evening," General Long stated. "We do not know who is behind this."

"Hawthorne is close. Send troops and crush them before they can mount their horses," said a woman whose brown hair had started greying at the roots.

"It's not that simple," the king said firmly. "We need to show restraint. We can't just go about killing all the commoners. Who would I rule if they were all dead? Who would respect the crown if all I did was kill anyone who voiced displeasure? This is still a salvageable situation."

"With all due respect, sire," an old, bald, wrinkled man wearing a sand-colored nightgown said, "this is more than voicing displeasure. This is your life! Voicing displeasure would be sending you a list of grievances. To attempt to take your life…that is far more dangerous. I would not allow this report to go unattended."

"Long, you've been to Hawthorne. Do you really think these people are capable of getting into this castle and taking my life?" Gjanion asked.

"Nearly eight years ago, I personally saw to the execution of one of their elders as retribution for attacking our soldiers, as you had requested. Since then, it has been a quiet, peaceful, and cooperative town. I think it is unlikely the people there would attempt such a daring plan."

"I still think you should send a contingent of knights to the town. You need to make sure the reports are unfounded at the very least," Geralith argued.

"I understand your concern, Lord Geralith, but if there is indeed an attempt to be had on my life, I do not want the castle to be missing a single knight, that would leave us vulnerable and—" King Gjanion was cut off by the door at the far end of the room flying open.

A guard, sword drawn, burst through. "Invaders! In the castle! Invaders, my liege!" he exclaimed.

General Long reacted immediately, drawing the sword from his hip before the soldier had finished his warning. "Sir, we need to get you to safety." The king stood up and grabbed the axe off the wall.

"They're in my castle, dammit, and I'll make sure they never leave," he said with conviction. His eyes blazing, Gjanion followed Long out of the room while the rest of the advisors clambered out of their chairs and back to their chambers.

Long and Gjanion followed the soldier to the main hall, where they saw two men dressed in all black dueling with two knights of the Royal Guard. King Gjanion turned to the soldier. "See that my family is safe."

The soldier took off back into the hall they had come from and up a set of stairs into the main tower. General Long looked at the king.

"Remind me to kill the spy who told us the attempt was tomorrow."

The king barely acknowledged what had been said and charged at the nearer of the men in black, who was occupied with the Royal Guardsman, and swung his axe with both hands. The axe struck home, audibly cracking through several ribs, and lodged its silver head in the man's side. Howling, he crumpled instantly, and the guardsman turned to challenge another man in black, who had come through the main door with three more companions, swords drawn and bloody.

Unable to dislodge his axe from the dead man's body, Gjanion pried the sword from his hand and turned to face the attackers. The other knight got the better of the short disguised invader he had been dueling with and ran his sword straight through the man's stomach. Together, the king, General Long, and the two knights turned to face the four new players. King Gjanion gripped his sword tightly as his purple gown now bore smatterings of red. General Long, always suited up in his dark green armor, pulled a dagger for his free hand, wielding his broadsword in his right. The knights bore their gold-hilted swords and shields with the king's crest on it: a white circle reminiscent of the moon with a purple lightning bolt across it.

Each man took on an invader, almost as if it had been choreographed. General Long parried the man's first swing and quickly spun behind him, driving the dagger into his side. Clearly the inferior fighter, the man screamed and swung blindly at Long, who easily countered the assault and drove his sword through the man's gut. The invader fell to the ground, a red pool spreading fast on the stone floor.

The first guardsman threw his shield at the charging attacker, surprising him with such a bold move. Taking advantage of the momentary shock, he severed the attacker's sword-bearing arm from his body. A blood curdling scream exploded from his chest as he grabbed helplessly at his side. Coming back across from the first swing, the guardsman did to the invader's head what he had just done to his arm. The screaming stopped as soon as it had started.

The second guardsman, much shorter than the first, didn't need a distraction to gain an advantage. He was surprisingly fast despite the metal armor he wore, and dropped his shield to enable the use of his second hand. Dueling a black-clad invader who was much taller than he was, the short but agile knight continuously utilized both hands, tossing the sword back and forth in a beautifully dexterous display. His agility made it appear as though he was using two swords.

The guardsman quickly overpowered the invader and gashed the back of his unprotected knees with one slash of the blade. The man crumpled, still attempting to hack at the knight who now stood above him. Now the Guardsman had the height advantage along with two perfectly working legs which he used to move around the invader and stab him, driving the end of the blade clean through his chest.

Meanwhile, the king dueled with the skill of a trained swordsman against the vigilante. He thrusted, parried, countered, and stepped beautifully around the man in a dance-like fashion. His opponent made a desperate plunge and tripped, falling to the floor and losing the mask. Gjanion looked upon the woman's face and frowned.

"You are a good swordswoman. I hate to see you die." The king held the tip of his blade an inch from her face, keeping her where she lay. "Why have you done such a foolish thing?"

"It was not so foolish, though we may have missed our mark. Your reign will end soon enough, you monster." She spat back at him.

"Captain Genda?" Long asked, genuinely surprised as he walked over to join the king.

"Hello, General." Genda glared at him.

"Why…why would you do this?!" Long's voice rose with each word as the realization of her betrayal hit him.

"It is your fault. That day you came to Hawthorne…that day you made us execute an innocent man…that was the day we vowed never to obey your commands again. The townspeople were ready to slaughter us if we did not denounce you and I don't blame them!" Hate fueled every word that she threw at Long and Gjanion.

Before Gjanion could reply, the soldier that had alerted them earlier came back through the hall.

"Sir…" he said a little too quietly.

"You're supposed to be guarding my…" but the king's voice trailed off. He knew before he had finished his sentence why the soldier was back. He dropped his sword and took off at a sprint down the hall and up the stairs, leaving General Long to tie her up.

When he arrived at the big wooden double doors of his bedroom, they were already ajar. Peacefully as if they had never awoken, his wife and son of not yet four years lay in bed; the red stains on the white sheets the only giveaway that they were not, in fact, sleeping. Gjanion fell to his knees a broken man. His head fell as he wept and he let out a shattering roar of rage that could be heard throughout the castle, echoing off of every wall, attacking every ear, signaling the fury and despair of a man who had lost everything. He knelt there, helpless until General Long came up behind him.

"My king…" His voice seemed to leave him as his eyes found the source of the king's fury.

"They didn't deserve this," the king said.

"No, they did not."

There was a pause, and after a moment, a realization dawned on Gjanion.

"Long, where is Rylan?" the king asked as he surveyed the room and realized his daughter was not there. His rage found new life. "IF THEY'VE TAKEN HER!" he roared again.

"Daddy?" came a tiny voice from behind a tapestry to the left of where he now stood in the room. His fury disappeared as soon as he saw the blonde curly hair of his daughter peeking out from behind the cloth.

"RYLAN!" he exclaimed as she came running towards him.

"Daddy, are you ok?" she asked as he hugged her tight.

"I will be, my beautiful girl, I will be." He wept as he held her. The soldier came up the stairs.

"Sir, the invader has been imprisoned. How would you like to proceed?"

King Gjanion stood up and held Rylan's hand in his. He addressed the knight, "I want to make an example of her. Get the executioner and have the stand brought out by dawn."

"Yes, my liege," the soldier and General Long said in unison. Together they went back down to the main hall to prepare for the morning as the king walked his daughter, now his only family, back to bed.

~~~

As the sun rose over the castle battlements, there was a stifling quiet that blanketed the grounds like a thick snow. A wooden stand with a sharpened blade atop sat in the middle of the square outside the castle gates, glinting in the morning rays. A small crowd had already gathered, but nobody said a word. More people made their way down the cobblestone streets and saw Genda, still wearing the black outfit she had charged the castle in, standing next to the beefy hooded executioner with her hands tied behind her back.
~~~

"This is your last chance. Where is your ally, the assassin?" Gjanion asked Genda as he walked up the steps on the side of the stand.

Genda said nothing, choosing instead to stare off in the distance past the king.

"Very well. If you choose not to speak, then you no longer need your head."

"Cut off my head and you will unleash a war you cannot hope to win. We've spent years spreading the truth of your misdeeds. You rule ruthlessly, cutting off the heads of those who defy you. You occupy any town that dares speak ill of you. You are a tyrant, a selfish and controlling man. Our story along with many others will spark a change in this kingdom. Go ahead, light the fire."

The king turned and slapped her. "You underestimate my power," he said, and walked the length of the stage to General Long, who had cleaned his armor of the blood from the evening's attack and stood at attention. "If only I had kept a bottle on me," Gjanion said quietly so that only Long could hear him.

"You couldn't have known."

"But if I did, they may still be alive."

"And how would you have known which potion to have on you?"

"Good point, but…" The sun cleared the walls, and a trumpet sounded, interrupting the king mid-sentence.

King Gjanion stepped forward in front of the crowd and raised his arms. His elegant royal blue robes fell from his limbs like shimmering curtains made of the bluest water.

"Last night," his voice boomed over the people, "an attempt was made on my life. Thanks to the quick reactions of my Royal Guard and our very own General Long, I survived unscathed."

A cheer went up from the crowd. General Long gave a slight bow.

"HOWEVER," the king said, cutting the applause short, "your queen, my beloved wife, and the prince…our son…were slain where they slept!" He drove the last word out with extra force and turned to the woman on the stand with them.

Boos, jeers, and taunts rose up from the masses, which King Gjanion allowed to go on for some time. Their energy gave him strength. Those that lived in the capital, the city that immediately surrounded the castle, loved him unconditionally. To them, he could do no wrong.

The surrounding towns were largely the same, filled with loyal followers that heeded his every word. The further his men got from the castle, however, the less people they found so devoted to the crown, Gjanion was not surprised by this. Life beyond the capital and its surrounding hamlets was far more difficult. His subjects that lived across the furthest reaches of Kyros were more concerned with their day to day life than the goings on of the castle.

Gjanion resumed his speech as the booing died down. "Let this be a warning to anyone who dares to try and challenge me…you will not succeed. This crown will remain upon *my* head for many years yet!"

As the king spoke, the executioner put Genda in the stock, locked it, and stood back. Cheers rose gradually from the crowd as he placed a basket in front of the woman and the king raised his hand high in the air, ready to give the order. The executioner took hold of the lever. Gjanion's hand dropped and the sun lost sight of the blade hanging above the stage.

The crowd roared. "I promise you that I will do all that I can to ensure the safety of this kingdom and the longevity of my family!" he bellowed over the still cheering masses. "I will not stop until every last threat to our beautiful realm is snuffed out!" The noise did not falter for minutes as the crowd supported King Gjanion with cheers and applause. They loved him, and he loved ruling them.

Chapter Four
Under the Stars

The candle had almost burned through its entire body; as the flame danced on nothing but a pool of melted wax, it sputtered and flickered. Gjanion hardly looked up from the book as he lit another candle next to him with a snap of his fingers and flick of his hand. General Long came striding down the hallway, passing shelf after shelf of old text.

"Sire, I think it might be time you got some rest."

"No, I think I'll stay a bit longer. This has to be the book, I can feel it."

"You've said that about half the books in this library." General Long gestured to the large tower of books to the left of the king, considerably taller than when he last checked on him. "I'm afraid I must insist. It's been nearly two weeks since your wife died, and you've been holed up in here without any real sleep. The doctor is worried about you."

"No," the king snapped, still not looking up from the tattered brown book his nose was in.

Gjanion rarely showed anyone the side of himself he was showing to Long now. His demeanor was usually nothing but regal, refined, and rigid in the presence of others, but Long knew there was a much more volatile man underneath the kingly facade. Long knew Gjanion to be short-tempered, headstrong, and unpredictable when nobody else was around. With the death of his wife and son, Long had watched the walls come tumbling down as more of Gjanion's true colors began to reveal themselves: anger and impatience chief among them. Despite all of this, Long knew the one thing that could break the sleep-deprived king from his current mood.

"Gjanion, please come with me. You need to rest. Tomorrow is Rylan's birthday."

At the sound of his daughter's name, Gjanion finally looked up at the general. His eyes were bloodshot and his face had a fair bit of stubble. He looked disheveled and exhausted, but Long knew the king was too stubborn to give up until he found what he was looking for.

"There must be something about him in these books," the king said helplessly, "I have to find something to help me get my revenge."

"The stories of gods and dead men are just that, stories," Long said, "If you want something you have to go take it for yourself. No amount of prayer to an all-powerful deity can help you there," the general said with conviction.

"You know I admire your lifelong dedication to your craft and your mission, Long. You are an example I hope every knight in our ranks emulates. But I feel I've reached the limit of my alchemy. My grandfather managed to overthrow the wizards and unite Kyros under his rule. He had power far greater than mine. I need to know how to tap into it."

"Why? You already have plenty of power at your fingertips," Long said in reference to himself and the many knights he commanded.

"That wasn't enough," Gjanion replied coldly. "If I had been stronger or had more control or knew how to do…I don't know, something else…maybe I could have saved them."

Long watched as his king began to spiral. The pain he was feeling was apparent in every word. Long knew the loss Gjanion had endured would change him forever.

"I think you'll find your own mind a better place for solutions than the ramblings of your ancestors," Long replied. "However, I do not think that your mind, in its current state, will be of much use to you. You are suffering a pain that cannot be put into words, and so is Rylan. Take a break. Be with her. These books are going nowhere."

The king sighed, "You're right."

"It is my job to protect you and your family until the day I can no longer lift a sword, and right now

I am protecting you from the wrath of an eight year old who will not be stopped until she gets to go out and ride with you, like you promised."

King Gjanion finally broke and smiled, "She's so much like her mother…caring…kind…but that temper she got from me!" he laughed, "Alright, Long, I'll get some sleep." He closed the book, grabbed a candelabra, and followed the general out of the library.

~~~

The next morning, the king was awoken by his daughter bouncing on his bed.

"Daddy, Daddy come ON!"

"Ry…" he said groggily, "is the sun even up yet?"

"Yes! …Well, no, not yet, but I am! I am, Daddy!" she said at such a rapid pace that Gjanion was sure he didn't hear all the words.

"I have a few matters to attend to today; why don't we meet at the stable after dinner, and we can go out," he said as he got himself up slowly.

"I have to wait ALL DAY?" she whined.

"I promise it will be worth it, go get your breakfast." He patted her head and sent her to bother the cook while he prepared for the day.

Gjanion put on a set of purple robes, placed his hair in a tight bun that sat inside his crown, and made his way down the stairs to join her. As he entered the
~~~

main hall, he crossed paths with Raynard Geralith, his top advisor.

Lord Geralith was the oldest lord in the castle by a considerable margin. His shoulders were so hunched that they were level with the top of his head, which sported a few wisps of grey hair still clinging on for dear life. He walked with a cane made of knobby wood topped with a beautiful amber stone.

"Good morning, my king. Your daughter flew through here as if she was the wind; she seemed quite excited for today," he said as he gave as much of a bow as he could manage, which was barely noticeable with his hunch.

"Morning, Raynard. Yes, 'quite excited' is one way to put it," he replied with a small smile.

"Have you found what you are looking for in the library?" Lord Geralith was one of the few people in the castle permitted into the library. His status as chief advisor to the king, as well as his contributions to the library's volumes over his long tenure with the family gave him that privilege.

"Unfortunately, no. Nothing I've read so far has given me any indication that my grandfather did anything more special than what I am capable of. I've searched for days and I fear it may be a dead end."

"I have been around since the time of your grandfather." He waved his knobby cane at Gjanion, "I may have something that could be useful for you. Find me when you return from your ride."

"I shall." King Gjanion nodded in thanks as Lord Geralith began his slow march out of the main hall.

The king entered the stable later that evening to find his daughter trying to carry a saddle almost as big as she was. He smiled and waved his hand, causing the saddle to float up out of her hands. The saddle drifted through the air and landed on the back of a beautiful white and brown mottled horse with blue eyes. Next to it stood Gjanion's grey mare, almost a head taller than his daughter's horse.

"Daddy," her little voice came from the other side of the beast where she had taken up brushing what she could reach of her horse's mane, "How come I've never met a person with blue eyes? Why do animals have them but not people?"

Gjanion's smile vanished as her question hit him. Before she had died, Gjanion's mother had told him that wizards were once a fairly common sight in Kyros, with special jewel-encrusted garb and dazzlingly blue eyes that denoted their connection to the many sources of magic around them. By the time Gjanion was born, the wizards had been nearly erased from the kingdom thanks to his grandfather. Now, more than half a century since his Radion's decade-long conquest to eradicate magic, wizards were little more than legend. Any that had survived were long gone, either in hiding or dead. On rare occasions, a rumor would surface of a wizard in hiding and Gjanion would send Long and his team to snuff it out, real or not. Hardly anyone alive remembered them apart from stories, details fading and changing with every retelling.

Gjanion perpetuated the changing details as he responded to his daughter, "Blue eyes aren't a human trait. We can only have brown, green, or sometimes golden eyes like yours. Animals are different, they can have all sorts of colors like the red of a basilisk, or the black of a strix."

Rylan frowned, "I want blue eyes like Neela."

The king knelt down to eye level with his daughter, "I think you have the most beautiful golden eyes in all of Kyros!"

She gave him a big hug and let him lift her up onto the horse. Neela had been a present on her fifth birthday, and she had climbed on with ease; though Rylan had grown, the horse grew faster. She had dubbed it Neela after a heroine in a storybook her mother had been reading to her at the time.

"Ready?" Gjanion asked as his daughter vibrated in her seat with anticipation.

"Yes! Can we go already?!" she asked impatiently.

"Of course, just one more thing…" and before she could get out another word, he took off out of the stable. Laughing, Rylan chased after him and they rode out into the rolling hills; the sun was setting behind the tallest of them, giving the fields an orange glow. As his hair whipped in the wind and fresh air filled his lungs, Gjanion realized just how long he had been hidden away with his nose in books. It was refreshing to get out and ride. He watched his daughter, who had handled her mother's death almost too well, move in her saddle like a professional.

Rylan was a natural rider. After having a few lessons when she had first mounted her horse, she had shown fantastic control and understanding. It was intuitive for her, and she loved being on the back of Neela; anyone who saw them ride was witness to the obvious connection they shared.

After galloping for some time, enjoying the cool evening breeze, they had put some distance between them and the castle. It was rare for the king to be without any guard or protection, especially in the wake of the assassination, but he had been adamant about coming out alone with his daughter. They slowed their horses to a walk and he turned to Rylan.

"I think they've earned a little break," he said as he stopped his steed and dismounted.

"Okay," she replied, patting Neela on the neck and hopping off into the grass. Above, the first few stars twinkled in the twilight.

The king pulled out a vial of red liquid. "Drink this, and whatever you do, don't snap your fingers." He handed her the vial.

"Is…is this going to let me be a wizard like you?" She stared at the vial, mesmerized by the vibrant red color.

"Yes, my angel."

"Why can't I do it like you? You don't need potions," she asked, looking up at him.

Poor girl, Gjanion thought. *She just wants to be 'like me'.*

"I'm not sure Ry. Just because I have magic does not mean you do as well. I hope you'll be a wizard someday. Maybe your powers just need some time to show themselves! For now you can use these, only under my supervision, and only when nobody is around. You don't want anyone to get hurt accidentally."

"Okay, I'll be careful," she said as she drank the vial's contents.

She grimaced at the foul taste of the potion and grabbed her flask to wash it from her mouth. *Am I doing the right thing by keeping her hopes up? I need her. If she doesn't think she will become what I am, or what she thinks I am, will she still love me?* Gjanion took a swig from his flask as well, then produced a candle from his saddle bag and placed it on a rock.

"Watch carefully and do exactly as I do," he instructed as he snapped his fingers, producing a small fireball that hovered in his hand. He watched her do the same; after a few tries, she managed to snap a fireball into existence, squealing as it sprung to life in her hand. Rylan watched it with excitement and nervousness, but did not lose control of the flame.

"Very good!" he said, impressed, "Now for the next step."

Gjanion faced the candle and splayed his fingers wide. The flame shot from his hand and lit the candle. He waved his hand and the candle blew out. Rylan watched, still cupping her little fire.

"Oh wow…" she said, "So I just open my hand and…" she flexed her fingers outward and the flame shot past the candle and lit the grass behind it. Gjanion drew the fire back to his hand before it could spread. The horses, uncaring, continued grazing.

"Not bad for a first try!" he said, smiling as he patted her head. "Let's try again."

Eventually a blanket of stars covered the night sky. Rylan managed to light the candle a few times, but still needed practice to do it consistently. Gjanion promised her that they would come back out again soon, and with that they mounted their horses and headed home. She fell asleep in his arms on the way up from the stable, exhausted from the exciting day. He tucked her in, checked in with the guard posted outside her door, and made his way to Lord Geralith's chambers.

Eager to see what the old lord had that could be so useful to his search, he knocked on the door. It swung open and the king entered.

"My liege," Lord Geralith greeted the king.

"What do you have for me?" the king asked impatiently.

"Yes, yes, over here."

The old lord's room was adorned with many different animal heads on its walls and strewn with books and scrolls. Geralith reached a bony hand underneath his bed and pulled out a trunk. He unlocked it, pulled out a threadbare red book, and handed it to Gjanion.

"I think you'll find everything you want to know in there."

"Thank you, Raynard, I will return it as soon as I am through," he said as he looked over the cover. In faded gold lettering it read:

The Book of Radion

"Do not let anyone else read this book. Your grandfather entrusted it to me for safekeeping after the uprising. It is imperative that only your eyes grace its pages."

"I understand," the king said, eyeing the book with extreme curiosity.

"You don't, but you will," said Geralith.

~~~

Mara sat on the floor, focused on making one of Zhira's books float in midair. Zhira meanwhile was opening the roof; it was a beautiful night and the moon was new, so the stars were plentiful. He climbed back down, sat next to Mara, and looked up at the sparkling sky.

"Whoa…" Mara said awestruck, "there's so many…how do you keep track of them all?"
~~~

"We make constellations. See those there?" He pointed to a cluster of seven stars that stood out among the rest around them.

"Yeah, the bright ones?"

"Yes, those are the Dipper constellations. It looks like a ladle pouring into the other."

"Oh yeah, it kinda does!" she exclaimed, tilting her head. "That one looks like a rabbit!" she said as she pointed to a bunch of stars in the eastern sky.

Zhira laughed, "You're right, it does!"

"And that one's a frog!"

They continued this for some time, him pointing out constellations and Mara making up new ones. "You see that one there? That's the constellation Censi; when we found you, there was a red star inside it. I told Dad I thought it meant we were supposed to find a new purpose, and then later that day I found you in a red blanket!"

"I was your new purpose!" Mara smiled.

"And the best thing to ever happen in my life," Zhira replied fondly, hugging his daughter close.

They continued watching the stars for a while until Mara's attention waned and she began making quills stand on their ends and spin. Zhira watched as Mara made the quills dance across the room, now accompanied by a few books. Her control impressed him, despite her youth. Eventually, she stacked books in a tower shape and eyed Zhira's globe mischievously.

"What're you…" Zhira began to ask as Mara used a quick flick of her hand to send the globe flying at the stack of books.

Zhira grabbed the globe out of the air just before it hit the tower and looked back at his daughter.

"I think it's time we get some sleep," he said, placing the globe back down on his desk.

After Zhira had tucked her in, Mara laid wide awake in bed. Her imagination ran wild with animals made of stars leaping across the sky. Horses made of the brightest stars chased rabbits composed of many smaller ones against the black background of the night. She smiled as she looked out her window and saw the stars poking through the trees, which were shifting back and forth in the breeze. Eventually Mara drifted off to sleep, comforted by the connection she felt with the night sky.

Chapter Five
The Last Wizard

Gjanion took the bronze key from his pocket and unlocked the door to his study. He made sure it locked behind him as he snapped and lit the candles in the room. With the red book tucked under his arm, he strode over to a large armchair and took a seat.

The king opened the cover of the book; on the first page was an inscription:

The Book of the Line of Radion

I know that when I awaken again, I will no longer remember who I am. Cursed by the goddesses, it is by their hands I suffer this fate. I hope to find enlightenment in my next life.

Gjanion stared at the notation. Who had written this? Surely not his grandfather; the writing looked nothing like the notes and decrees he had penned in his lifetime. Gjanion flipped to the next page and found a family tree; there at the top was the name Radion, but not the grandfather he knew. According to the tree, Radion was a name used several times over the centuries preceding him, starting with the first recorded patriarch of the family line.

Gjanion read for some time, looking for any mention of special powers his grandfather had wielded in his reclaiming of Kyros. The stars traced their paths across the velvety black sky outside the windows as he scoured page after page of long dead family members: Elenti the Wild, who imprisoned the chef for bringing him things like mushrooms for dinner, King Vex who hypnotized people to make animal sounds for fun, and Tyran the Reclusive, who never left the castle and gave the duty of ruling Kyros to his wife. A few pages were missing here and there, which Gjanion figured was due to how old the book seemed to be.

Eventually, Gjanion came to a blank page. He had just finished reading his grandfather's entry, which served as nothing more than a refresher of the things he already knew about him. It seemed that the book had not been updated since then; frustrated, he thumbed through the last few pages until he came to the back cover. There, written on the inside in small gold lettering were the words:

This Book is The Property of Knorr, God of Power

Gjanion stared at the line for what seemed like hours. This book belonged to a god? How is that possible? Knorr was an all-powerful being; he didn't need a book. Pondering this for a while, he suddenly remembered something his father had taught him; he went over to a table covered with roots and berries, picked up a bloodwood root, and snapped it in half. He rubbed it on his hands and thumbed through the blank pages again. On the last page was writing that had been previously hidden:

This book contains the lives of Knorr, the forsaken god. He shall be reincarnated every other generation, always as a son. This is willed by the goddesses Eres and Dazel, who banished Knorr to an eternity of life without magic.

Gjanion nearly dropped the book. None of this made sense. *How could I be the descendant of a god? How did Lord Geralith know?*

He thumbed back through the book to the blank page immediately following the section documenting his grandfather. There was a note written in the old king's handwriting that had not been there before:

The time has come to take back what is rightfully mine. No longer will I be subject to the reign of these well-fed pigs. They are not gods. I will find my way to the top of the mountain. I will be one of them. I will show them what it is like to be ruled by their own hand. I will find my true power and regain my throne above men.

The king read the note over and over again until it started to fade. He knew what happened next, how his grandfather had overthrown the wizards and taken the throne with magic. How did he find his powers? Could he, Gjanion, copy the feat? He made his way back down to Geralith's chambers and let himself in.

Shutting the door behind him, Gjanion asked, "Are we alone?"

"Yes," Lord Geralith replied. The old Lord had apparently been awake, sitting at his desk, "Seeing as how it is well past midnight, we are quite alone."

"How did you know?" Gjanion demanded as he placed the book in front of Geralith.

"Your grandfather entrusted me with the secret before he died. He wanted to be sure the knowledge was not lost. It is why your father was so adamant you learn alchemy. Knowing he would be skipped, he put all of his efforts into teaching you so that you could rediscover the powers your grandfather had."

"Why didn't my grandfather pass on how to obtain the powers?" Gjanion asked.

"There is another book. One that not even I was entrusted with learning the location of. Your grandfather claimed that only his soul would know. He trusted that when he was reborn as you, the knowledge of who you are would lead you back to where it was hidden."

"And nobody else knows this?"

"Nobody outside of this room," the old man confirmed as he replaced the book in the chest and slid it back under his bed. "The world believes you to be the last true wizard, the descendant of an outcast who exacted his revenge upon the greedy upper class of magical users."

"And Long remains unaware that you know I am not a wizard?" Gjanion clarified.

"The general still believes he is the only one who keeps your secret. Though I am unsure why it is important he thinks so," Geralith responded.

"Because if the secret gets out, I'll know who to behead," Gjanion said threateningly.

"A smart ploy, Your Majesty."

The king stood there silent; how was he going to discover this godly gift? Where did he need to go to unlock this potentially world-changing power?

"I am returning to the library. I believe that if my grandfather…I…hid the secret to the power of the gods, it would be there." He swept out the door without another word.

~~~

Gant sat with his mother in the shop. Rats had started to find their way in as the weather got brisker, so
~~~

they decided to clean the place and patch some of the stone work along the walls.

"I think Zhira is giving her too much free reign. She is going to slip up," Gant complained as they sorted through a box of gortroot.

"I think you're too wound up," his mother replied.

"I care about her! I want her to be safe! How can I do that when she is…magicking everything in sight?" he asked, tossing another bad root into a box with others like it.

"You think it was easy keeping you and your brother safe? What you were doing was forbidden by the king himself, yet you two were blowing up half of my storeroom every time you put two new ingredients together. I didn't want to suppress your interest and obvious aptitude for the craft, but I knew that if we were discovered, I would be taken away for allowing you to hone it. I taught you both control, and you need to do the same for Mara. If you continue to suppress it, bad things will happen; her lashing out will get worse. Help her, don't hinder her."

"She's only eight; she is too young to start learning," Gant said defiantly.

"Do you remember what you were doing at eight?" she asked knowingly.

"Potions are different," he said weakly, knowing he had already lost this argument but too proud to admit it.

"You think making potions was safer? You almost floated out of the house! It was my fault; you two were just trying to be like me, mixing things to help people. The difference was that you tried things I'd never done."

"But then you made a deal with the town to protect us. We were and are safe here," he reminded her.

"Did you not do the same for her eight years ago?"

"I'm not saying we shouldn't tell them, but once the word is out, it's out. Right now, nobody but us knows that she is a wizard. The king is supposed to be the last one."

"This town has proven twice that it can keep a secret: first with you and your brother's alchemy, then a child found in the woods. They can keep one more," she said as she moved on to a box of small green bulbs.

Gant considered this. She was well-liked amongst the residents of Saros; he didn't see a reason why anyone would give her up. There was just one problem:

"I don't know how to do magic. Nobody does. How would I train her?" he questioned his mother, but she was ready.

"You don't. Let her figure it out on her own. Your job is to teach her to control her emotions and her thoughts. Mara already knows more magic than you two can do with potions. Let her test it and figure it out."

They sat quietly for a few moments sorting the rotted bulbs. Gant cut his hand on the side of the box and pulled out a bandage from his bag. Wrapping his hand, he looked at his mother; he knew she was right. Mara might very well be the only wizard. Who was he to stop her from learning all she could about herself?

"I'll talk to Rezzik in the morning, let him in on the secret and come up with a plan to inform the town."

"I think that's a great idea," Fiona replied. She smiled softly at her boy; a man now, a father.

The next morning, Gant and Zhira dropped Mara off with their mother and walked up to a big wooden building overlooking the town square. Constructed five years ago, the town hall housed the governor, which was elected by the town's people every three years. Saros was hardly a town, and most people in it were apathetic towards having a governor. Eventually Rezzik, a pushy, excitable, yet somewhat useless man, decided that his calling was leadership. He had gone around town pestering people to agree to have a governor, and enough people agreed if only to shut him up. Immediately after he was 'elected', Rezzik converted his home into the town hall, adding rooms on both floors and expanding it using the help of the alchemists.

Gant did not like Rezzik much. He found him overbearing but not maliciously so; Gant figured Rezzik was so intent on making himself look good and giving himself a purpose that he gave no thought to actively taking advantage of people. He was unaware of how annoying he could be, but there was a naiveté that Gant found reassuring. He knew that Rezzik would never betray the secret he was about to share.

Zhira pushed open the double doors that led into a large receiving hall. Tall windows above the doors let in copious amounts of light, eliminating the need for any torches or candles during the day. They turned and walked down the hallway to their right, making their way towards Rezzik's study. When they entered, he was sitting at an overly large desk, scribbling away on a piece of parchment as if it was the last words he would ever write. His head popped up suddenly.

"Gant! Zhira! What a charming surprise! Do come sit down." He motioned towards the two polished wooden chairs that sat opposite him. Rezzik looked quite similar to his older brother Litik, except for that he had no mustache. His bald head gleamed in the light from the wide windows behind him and his feet barely skimmed the floor while he sat in his chair.

"Hi Rezzik," Gant started as he took a seat.

"Ah, ah, that's Governor to you!" Rezzik interrupted. Gant and Zhira just stared at him. "…but of course Rezzik is fine too." He tried to play off his little power move as a joke. "What can I do for you gentlemen on this fine day?"

"Do you remember the deal our mother made for us to practice alchemy here?" Zhira asked.

Rezzik regarded them a little more seriously now, "Yes I do. It's been marvelous for the town. Never a bad season thanks to you two! We are so grateful for your help, especially in down years!" Gant thought Rezzik was laying on the flattery a little too thick.

"Yeah, well anyways," continued Zhira, "we need to expand on it. You see our daughter…"

"Ah! Mara, yes, what a sweet child! So she has taken to following in her fathers' footsteps?"

"Not exactly," Gant replied, "Mara has a different predisposition than we do. She can do actual magic."

Rezzik looked at Gant, then to Zhira, and back to Gant. "She can do…actual magic? I thought only the king…"

"We thought so too, Rezzik. We didn't believe it, but even the day we found her she was showing signs."

As the brothers recounted the details of her discovery, Rezzik hardly moved and did not speak; he was riveted, his hands folded under his chin as he leaned on the desk. Gant explained that they wanted somewhere for her to learn to control herself and explore her powers safely.

"Of course, of course!" Rezzik said after the alchemists had finished their tale and request. "Mara could be even more helpful than you two, if everything you say is true!" he laughed. Zhira gave a small chuckle. Gant did not react.

"So how shall we inform the town? This will be big news and we don't want it leaving here. With Mara being a true wizard and King Gjanion claiming to be the last wizard himself, it would definitely draw the wrong crowd to our doorsteps," Gant said, wanting to be sure his little girl, as well as the town, was safe.

"Leave that to me. I will get the word around using great discretion," Rezzik said with an air of importance. "I thank you for trusting your governor with this important information."

"Thanks, Rez," Zhira said as he slapped him on the back. He and Gant made to leave the room.

"Gentlemen, just one question," Rezzik said as Gant opened the door; "How can you be sure she won't destroy the whole town if she hardly knows what powers she has?"

"I guess if she does, it won't be your problem anymore, Governor." Zhira gave him a smile and the two departed.

~~~

The town gathered in the square the next morning; autumn was creeping in, and the mornings had gotten chillier. Litik could see his breath as he stood next to Fiona amongst the crowd.

"Do you have any idea why my eccentric brother asked us to show up this early?" he asked her, arms wrapped around himself as he shook a little in the dawn air.

"Eccentric? Coming from you?" She pointed out the formal leather outfit he had donned. "Not such a formal occasion, this," she jested. Fiona and Litik had
~~~

grown up together with Rezzik being the annoying little brother wanting to be included in any game they were playing. She found it fitting and mildly amusing, that the townspeople had gone along with his governor idea just to give him something to do.

"One must always look his best! Never know when you'll need to impress!" he said, pulling down his vest to remove the wrinkles. Litik had never married, but not for lack of trying. He had attempted to woo almost every woman in town, including Fiona multiple times, to no avail; Litik was an acquired taste. Fiona admired his never-ending optimism.

The crowd got thicker as Keylon joined them, her brown hair in a tight bun and her apron patterned with different foods.

"Sari can't leave the forge unattended. Kei isn't old enough to watch it on his own yet," she said as she took up a place to the right of Fiona. "Where are your boys?"

"They're coming," Fiona replied, looking at the little stage Rezzik had set up overnight.

Over the next few minutes, the crowd grew until the square was full. Everyone looked confused as to what Rezzik had called this meeting for with almost no notice. Fiona looked around and saw Bess, the innkeeper, gossiping with another older lady with long white hair drawn up like hers, no doubt predicting the worst from this meeting.

Seemingly out of nowhere, Rezzik's voice suddenly cut over the chatty crowd,

"Ladies and gentlemen, welcome! You're probably wondering why I called you all here today." People nodded and a few murmurs of agreement rose up from the sea of heads.

"Well, wonder no longer!" Rezzik said as he hopped up onto the stage, revealing himself in an overly bright purple tunic.

"He always did have a flair for the dramatic," Litik leaned over and whispered to Fiona.

Rezzik continued, "Today, we have a new secret for this town to keep. I confirmed with Bess that she had no visitors last night, so I decided that this was the opportune time to share with all of you."

The sun peeked over the trees, as if curious about what Rezzik had to say to the people of Saros. The self-serving governor had the town's full attention, and he couldn't be happier. He tried to milk the moment all eyes were on him for as long as possible.

"Today, the stories come true. When I was a child, my mother would tell me tales of amazing things that seemed impossible: people who could perform magic."

The crowd mumbled and whispered amongst themselves.

"I must ask you, before we go further, to keep what I am about to tell you in the same confidence that you keep our dear alchemists. If the wrong people were to learn of this secret, the quiet life we enjoy here in the woods would be forever shattered."

Every person standing in the morning light either nodded or voiced agreement.

"Alright, then." He paused for dramatic effect. "The king is *not* the last wizard!"

With a flourish of his arms, he motioned to a spot on stage where Gant walked up, Mara shyly holding his hand and standing behind his leg. The crowd noise began to rise.

"Hello everyone," Gant said, raising his voice above the din, "I want to thank you for the last minute meeting. We know this is rather shocking, but we appreciate your secrecy and confidence on the matter."

One of the villagers shouted, "Why didn't you tell us you were a wizard?"

"I'm not." Gant stepped to the side to reveal Mara completely to the crowd. "She is."

The crowd fell silent. Not a single person made a sound as they stared at the little black haired girl.

A woman's voice broke the tense silence. "Prove it," she demanded.

Gant turned to Mara, "You ready?" he asked, and she nodded.

Zhira passed a pot with a flowerless stalk growing in it to Gant. He took it and held it out in clear view of everyone; Mara stared at it, blue eyes unblinking. Suddenly, a yellow flower appeared at the top of the stalk, then another just below it, then another. The crowd began to cheer.

Mara smiled as the stalk grew dozens of flowers; the cheering got louder and her excitement grew with the noise. She had worried that people would be scared; instead they were exuberant. Turning to Gant, Mara smiled larger than he thought possible, and he smiled back, handing her the plant.

Gant watched Zhira come up behind Mara and give her a hug, then start laughing.

"What's so funny, Daddy?" she asked.

Zhira pointed to Rezzik; in her excitement, she had turned his purple tunic the same vibrant yellow as the flowers.

Chapter Six
The First Snow

Mara woke up early the next morning, eager to begin the unfettered exploration of her powers. Gant and Zhira were still asleep; once Mara was old enough to warrant her own space, Zhira had moved into the tower room so that she could have his. She crept out and made her way across the kitchen. Grabbing an apple, she climbed out the kitchen window, aware that the front door groaned quite loudly every time it was forced to do its job.

Once outside, Mara walked to where a tree lay freshly fallen from a recent storm. She placed the apple on the stump and took a few steps back. There was no plan; she figured she would just try different things: thoughts, motions, and feelings. First, Mara tried raising her hand, palm facing up. She didn't know why she chose this motion, it just felt natural. The apple rose from the stump. When she stopped raising her hand, the apple stopped, suspended in midair. It slowly returned to its original resting place as she lowered her hand.

She grinned. That was an easy start. She turned and looked at the wheelbarrow next to the house. Raising her hand again, the wheelbarrow mimicked the apple. Mara's grin morphed into a fully-fledged smile. She turned back to face the fallen tree; it was about fifteen feet long and a foot thick. Her eyebrows narrowed as she concentrated.

The tree began to move slightly on the ground. Mara felt like she was trying to lift a ton of bricks with one hand. She tried harder and harder, and eventually the tree levitated a few inches off the ground. She put it back down and squealed with delight, clapping her hands, and a lightning bolt struck the tree.

After the massive crack filled the air, the tree caught fire and Mara began to panic. Zhira and Gant came running out of the house, Gant in his orange nightgown and Zhira still in his robes from the day before, evidence that he had been up late stargazing.

"What happened?!" Zhira asked as he filled up a pail from the well next to the house.

"I don't know!" Mara began to cry, "I just clapped my hands. I made it fly. I was excited!"

The fire on the tree started spreading; Zhira went to put it out but Gant held him back.

"No, she needs to learn control," he said calmly, heeding what his mother had said. "Mara, this is a great first lesson: your actions have consequences. You have amazing powers at your fingertips and if you don't exercise caution with them, this won't be the last fire you'll need to put out."

She looked worriedly at him but nodded, tears still making their way down her cheeks.

"Now, focus," he said as he stood next to her facing the fire.

Mara had no clue how to put out a fire, but she figured that like making the apple fly, her body would just know.

"Keep yourself together, don't panic," Zhira added reassuringly.

The fire had not yet spread to the grass so there was still time to contain it. With a few deep breaths she calmed herself down and concentrated on the fire. She had no idea how to control water, but something inside her told her to reach out towards the bucket that Zhira was holding, so she did. Instinctively, she drew her hand up, pointing her fingers down, and the water flowed upwards out of the bucket. The water followed the path her hand traced in front of her until it hovered over the fire; Mara relaxed, dropping her hand, and the water fell directly onto the burning tree.

"Good job!" Gant said with a smile.

Mara beamed, she had simply followed her instincts again.

"I don't know what I did, Dad…" her smile fading as confusion set in. "I just…did it."

"Slow down, Mara, and you'll figure it out," Gant said as he rounded up some kindling to make another fire. "You got excited and your powers got away from you. Control yourself. You don't know what you are capable of, so be careful."

Mara nodded. "Patience and practice."

"Patience and practice," Gant repeated back to her with an approving nod.

Mara practiced the rest of the day as Gant set up fires for her to put out. In between each fire being made, Zhira would have her practice making different objects levitate. She quickly realized that if she didn't focus on how large whatever she was trying to lift was, she could get it off the ground with considerably less effort.

The day went by and then another, and soon the days turned into weeks, which turned into months. Winter was mild until one day, without warning, several inches of snow were dumped on the town overnight. The blanket of snow muffled horses' feet on the main road, voices got swallowed up in the drifts, and the air was still and cold. The world was silent.

Mara opened the door and ran headfirst into the snow, excited to see what she could do with her newfound abilities. Within minutes she had made a snowman, launched some snowballs at Gant without touching them, and managed to turn the snow to ice sturdy enough to stand on without falling through it to her hips. Zhira walked out in a heavy brown coat made of deerskin and joined the other two as they began to trudge towards the town.

"I think today might be a great day to show off your progress," Gant said.

"What do you mean?" Mara responded as she traced a winding and whimsical path between the trees, leaving a rut in the snow behind her.

"Well, this is a lot of snow at once. The townspeople are going to have a lot of trouble clearing it. We should help them out!"

"Oh, okay! I can do that!" Mara extended both of her hands, and in front of her a wide swath of grass was uncovered.

"Think you can do a whole street?" Zhira asked as his daughter traipsed around.

Mara loved the snow. Even before she had learned to walk, bringing her inside was a battle that often ended in tears. Mara seemed to have a sixth sense about when it would snow and was nearly always right, getting her fathers up as soon as she awoke to go play in it.

The three of them approached the street to find it largely empty; most of the storefronts were closed, their doors and windows adorned with decorations to match the winter season. Sari was working hard as ever despite the snow. The heat from his forge turned the falling white flakes to rain and made his shop an island, the snow eventually finding a place to stick some feet away and gradually growing as it got further out.

Mara stood between Gant and Zhira, eyeing the street. Her eyes appeared to be glowing as they reflected the white world around her. As she put her hands out, she slowly pushed outwards and the snow covering the street was moved by an invisible plow. Sari put down his hammer to watch the small miracle occur. Mara walked up the street, her black hair poking out of her fur cap slightly.

"Nice goin', wee lass." Sari gave her a thumbs up. "Saves us old folk a right bit o' trouble." He added a friendly wink before picking up his hammer and continuing on with his work.

She beamed back at him and cleared the rest of the street. Zhira took her hand, praised her work, and walked up to their mother's storefront.

"Grandma, look what I did!" Mara pointed out the window excitedly.

"Wow…" Fiona looked genuinely impressed. "I am so proud of you! That is fine work, my rose." Mara giggled with delight.

"We're just here to pick up a few things," Gant said as he and Zhira made for the back room.

Gant and Zhira had run low on supplies for making fire potions, and until Mara was more comfortable with her powers, they made sure to have control over the notoriously dangerous element. A few minutes later, arms laden with bags of roots, seeds, and small leafy plants, they left the shop. A guest from Bess's inn was saddling his horse and looking around rather confused at the cleared street. Zhira turned to Mara and gave her a knowing look, smiled, then put a finger to his lips.

~~~
~~~

Rylan watched the snow fall past her window. She sat propped up by her elbows in her bed, too excited from today's lesson with her father; he had given her a potion that allowed her to levitate objects, but it took a lot of concentration.

Staring out beyond the glass, Rylan wondered what it would be like to fly in the snow, twirling and twisting between the flakes as they floated down around her to the ground. And then, she realized that she didn't have to wonder. There were bound to be more potions somewhere in the castle! All she had to do was find them.

Her brain churning, Rylan thought about where her father might keep his potions. She had asked him incessantly at each lesson but he refused to tell her, citing boring reasons like patience and control. "You are my only daughter," he had said, "I never want anything bad to happen to you."

Rylan decided that her best course of action was to find her father. She was small enough to hide behind the tapestries and suits of armor that lined the halls of the castle, but she had to be quiet enough as well. First though, she would have to get past the guard at her door. Her small head poked out of her room just enough to see where the guard was sitting off to the left.

The guard was sound asleep. *Some guarding,* she thought. Rylan crept out the door and made her way across the hallway to the stairs that led down into the great hall, taking care to listen for anyone coming up. At the bottom, she slipped behind a tapestry of a wolf prowling through trees; it wiggled slightly as she shimmied behind it.

She waited for the nearest guard to turn his back before bolting to the next hiding spot behind a suit of armor with a large shield. Repeating this method, she patiently made her way around the great hall until she came to the other side. Rylan slipped out from behind the banner she was using for cover and took off down the hall.

As she passed Lord Geralith's chambers, the door opened; Rylan took refuge by grabbing a ledge that supported two statues of gargoyles next to the doorframe and pulling herself up. As long as he did not look left, she would be fine. She held her breath and watched Geralith close the door to his study behind him, lock it, and turn his back to her. As he walked down the hall, Rylan let out a sigh of relief.

She was safe.

Rylan hopped down from her little ledge and crept along the hallway a good distance behind the elderly lord, keeping an eye on his lantern. Eventually she came to a set of stairs she knew led up to her father's study. Rylan peeled off from behind the hunched man and let her eyes adjust to the darkness; no torches lit the stairwell, only a small window every dozen or so stairs. The hallway turned out of sight in front of her as the spiral stairs wound up the tower.

Rylan took the first step and nearly fell. As her eyes focused in the dim lighting she saw that each stair was a different size, and some were angled either up or down. She remembered her father explaining that this was to make it much more difficult for any invaders to make it up quickly, should they ever get this far into the castle. Carefully, Rylan restarted her climb up the spiral staircase. If anyone came up or down now, she'd be discovered and her adventure would be fruitless.

As she crept over the top stair, Rylan came face to face with a massive wooden door. She pulled on the handle, which squeaked a little in its hinge, but the door didn't budge. Rylan decided she would wait for someone to open it and then sneak in as it closed. She waited as ten minutes went by, then ten more, then another ten…

"Rylan?" King Gjanion's voice scared her, and she hit her head on the stone wall she had been leaning against. "What are you doing here?"

Rylan looked out the nearest window, rubbing her head where a bump was already forming. The sun was rising, shining extremely bright on the fresh reflective snow. She had fallen asleep waiting for her chance, and now she was about to give it up.

"I…I was…sleepwalking?" she said with such little confidence that she was sure her father would not buy it.

"Sleepwalking, you say?" Gjanion's face gave away that he knew she was lying, but he went on. "You know, I think I have a potion for that…" he trailed off, watching his daughter's face grow in anticipation.

"Really?" She felt she had regained a fighting chance. "Where…" she slowed herself down to seem less excited about what she was going to ask, "Where would it be? Do you need help finding it?"

"You know, I think I do." Her father took the bronze key from somewhere underneath his robes and let himself and his daughter into his tower-room study. She gawked at the ingredients in the cabinets. On display were multitudes of vibrant green roots, a rainbow of flowers scattered between many dark colored pods, and containers of seeds spanning from pale to black. The vast quantity of prepared potions was overwhelming. Tall, thin bottles stood amongst squattier ones while wooden stands were full of vials of liquid, some of which glowed. There were even a few with contents that moved about like captured smoke.

"We are going to keep this our little secret, okay? Nobody else knows what is in this room except you, me, and General Long. Promise you will keep it safe?"

"I promise, Daddy."

"Good."

"Daddy, why do you make potions if you are a wizard?" Rylan asked.

~~~

The question blindsided Gjanion. In his eagerness to share something special with his daughter,
~~~

he had not considered what she would think when she saw the study and its contents. *She is all I have left. I cannot ruin her dream,* he thought. *She'll hate me.*

"Potions are very important. They can enhance one's abilities or even mimic magic." *That much is true, but how do I explain why I need them?* Gjanion struggled to find a way to keep up the ruse but, at the same time, explain his store of potions. He decided that his best course of action was to lie. *Rylan is only eight, she does not need to know everything. Not yet.*

"I use them for the former—I enhance my powers with them," Gjanion said, hoping Rylan would accept his explanation.

"Oh," she said, her attention not so much on him as it was the shelves and their colorful ingredients.

He rolled his eyes. Of course she would ask such a hard question then not listen to the answer. Children had a way of doing that: asking tough questions without meaning to. Her unbridled curiosity was endearing.

"When am I going to be a wizard like you?" Rylan asked suddenly, turning her big golden eyes on him.

"I don't know," he said. *Another lie.*

"Why not?"

"Because…" Gjanion faltered again. "Because being the last wizard, I only know what happened when I got my powers. I don't know if it's the same for all."

"What happened when you got your powers?"

"That's enough questions for now, Ry," Gjanion said sternly, tired of lying to his daughter. "Just promise me you'll keep these potions a secret, okay?"

"Okay," she replied, smiling up at him.

Damn those golden eyes, Gjanion thought. *They'll be the death of me one day.*

Chapter Seven
Control

King Gjanion once again found himself poring over stacks of books, convinced he could unlock the powers his grandfather had written about. He had been scouring the library for anything that referenced Knorr and his grandfather's line of descent.

The king walked down the aisle, scanning the spines for any titles that were even remotely related to his cause. He passed over titles such as the *Complete Guide to Farming, Castles of Kyros,* and *How to Train a Dragon.* As he paced along the shelves, his robe dragged behind him kicking up the thin layer of dust that coated the floor. And then it snagged.

Gjanion choked and turned to unhinge his robe from the loose floorboard. As he bent down, he noticed that the dust was not hanging in the air but instead was filtering down underneath the board that had caught him. A draft. Placing his lantern on the ground, he ran his fingers around the edges of the wood until he found a lip.

Unhinging the floorboard, he looked down and saw that sitting underneath the wood was a tattered green leather book. Judging by the miniscule scraps of paper that lay strewn about around the book, there had been additional scrolls stored with it. Now they were nothing but memories thanks to bugs and other vermin that had eaten them over time.

The king reached his ring-laden hand down into the gap and gently pulled out the book. It was covered in cobwebs and a few bug shells and the leather was chapped and dry. He blew the debris away and replaced the board in the floor. Gjanion took the book over to the table he had been using, where fresh candles stood tall next to the depleted nubs of their predecessors.

The chair scraped across the floor as he pulled it close to the makeshift desk, the echo drawing out in the empty library tower: a cavernous, lifeless section of the castle that only a select few ever visited. Gjanion gently opened the book to the first page; it creaked a little and crinkled as he pulled the cover away from the pages for the first time in what was obviously a long time. Staring up at him was his grandfather's handwriting. Heart pounding, he lit more candles and began to read:

My only need for this diary is for when I am reborn. Having no memory, I must teach myself what I learned so that I may better myself with each attempt. I have entrusted the record of my line to Lord Geralith, but even he does not know of this book.

Gjanion skipped ahead, the first few pages reiterating most of what he had learned when he was younger about the uprising Radion had planned and led against the wizards.

I have discovered a way to amplify my powers. The ancient people who worshipped the gods created relics to offer to them. Over time the weaker and lesser known relics were destroyed or lost to the ages, but the ones that survived, ones built strong and cared for well, remain. These ancient artifacts are imbued with magical ability. I intend to find them and use them to conquer in the name of the downtrodden and claim my place.

The king stared at the page. *So that's how he did it, that's how he unlocked his god-like powers. But if he had reached those powers, how had he died?* Gjanion questioned as he absorbed what he was reading like a starving plant. As he continued to turn the tattered pages, the tower could have fallen down around him and he would not have noticed. He was engrossed, obsessed even. Here finally were the answers he was looking for: ways to protect himself, his family, and his kingdom from future threats.

After extensive research and chasing loose threads, I have determined that there are three remaining relics. I obtained the sapphire crown with ease and have tracked the ruby sword to the town of Chir in the western mountains, no more than three days' ride from the capital, where we currently hide in plain sight from the monsters who run this kingdom. There is no word of the emerald staff, but I will find it before long.

Gjanion nearly fell out of his chair. *All I have to do is find some relics?* Further into the book King Gjanion went, hoping that his grandfather had done the task for him and found all three of these supposedly powerful artifacts. The candles that once stood tall were now barely more than puddles of wax, the only indication of the hours that passed in the silent and still library.

I managed to acquire the relics and have dealt with the pigs who thought they had the right to rule. Those fools, so drunk on their power they believed they could never be overthrown. How blind they were, with Geralith working right under their noses to steal the emerald staff. Once he obtained it, we were prepared to lead our assault on the castle. It was a quick affair. Their defenses were minimal and our resolve was strong. The people sided with us the moment we entered the gates, and despite their power, the wizards were horribly outmatched.

These relics are miraculous—there is no better word. The staff gives control over natural elements, the crown imbues focus, and the sword grants strength the likes of which I have never felt.

Gjanion's desire for this power reached a boiling point as he read his grandfather's words with fervor. After reading about the unification of the kingdom under Radion's rule, Gjanion came to the entry he had long been looking for: the fate of the relics.

I regret that in my confidence I was blind. The staff was stolen in the dead of night. Not a trace was found. None of the guards heard a single noise, and there were no witnesses outside the castle…no reports of seeing anyone with a silver staff. I now guard the crown and sword closely. I was fortunate enough to have the foresight to keep the gems separate from the relics. Without the gems, the magic of the relics is nothing. The crown will hold the power I wielded until such time that the staff resurfaces.

Gjanion leaned back in his chair, exhausted from his journey through Radion's notes. He had been in a state of excitement for so long that when he closed the back cover of the book and finally looked up from its pages, he got dizzy. Gjanion touched his hand to the crown that adorned his head. He removed it and looked it over, shocked that the power he had been searching for was on his head the whole time. There, on the front of the silver headpiece along with the sapphire was the ruby and emerald his grandfather had removed from the other relics.

Gjanion started laughing. *I already have one!* He spun the crown around in his hands, looking at every edge and cut as if memorizing it would do anything. He didn't care. In his hands was a powerful relic that would help him obtain god-like powers. Gjanion came down from his elation and continued to look at the crown. Wondering how his grandfather had lost his relics and eventually his life, he closed the back cover of the book. Gjanion's plan of revenge was falling into place. *Never again will my family be threatened.* He stowed the book back in the floorboard and set off to find General Long.

<div align="center">~~~</div>

Long was gearing up his men for a raid against a nearby village that had decided to go into open rebellion. He was preparing a full cavalry unit armed to the teeth with spears, swords, full armor, and a handful of archers to keep the perimeter closed. When the king strode into the stables, the men who noticed turned and knelt while others were oblivious, finishing up preparations for their raid. Gjanion didn't notice either way.

"General, can I have a moment?" The sound of the king's voice startled the knights who hadn't noticed his entrance. They quickly dropped to their knees. Noticing the sudden scramble, Gjanion waved half-heartedly, motioning for the knights to go back to their duties.

"Of course, my liege." General Long finished strapping his saddle to his large black horse, who was also outfitted with recently polished armor along its head, flank, and front legs.

"I need to ask a favor of you. In my studies, I have gained new knowledge that our family had two artifacts taken from them during the rebellion years."

"And what does that have to do with me?" Long asked.

"A sword and a staff, both made of silver, were taken from my grandfather during his reign. These relics are magical in nature and will…help me accomplish my goals."

"And what might those goals be, sir?" Long raised an eyebrow.

"To expel any threat to my family and this kingdom from our borders. We will purge Kyros of those who wish to do us harm. I need these relics in order to access the same great powers that my grandfather did."

"By 'we', you mean…" Long trailed off, gesturing towards the knights in the stable.

"No, general, I will be helping you personally this time. Have your men search the villages as you bring them back to order, and imprison whomever was found to be in ownership of the treasures. I want to be able to question them."

It took a lot to surprise Long, but at Gjanion's insistence on assisting with the grand scheme of unifying Kyros, the king had accomplished just that. Long had suspected Gjanion would hoard power in the castle, building his legacy and legend to dissuade others from trying to take the throne from him while Long and the army he commanded did the dirty work.

"It will be done," Long said with a newfound respect for Gjanion.

Without a word, the king left the General and his men to their duties.

~~~

The logs toppled and Mara huffed in frustration. She had been working for an hour on stacking up firewood, practicing object levitation and other skills using smaller, more precise movements. She could lift the fallen tree, set anything on fire, and even grow plants at will, but she wanted more control, more specificity to her actions. To practice, Mara stacked the logs up into a delicate pyramid and as she was placing the final one on top, they fell.

As Mara sat in annoyance and glared at the heap, a thought came over her. Could she move them all at once into the stack she wanted? For weeks she had been working with one or two objects at a time, but how many could she actually move? She refocused her efforts and tried to lift almost one hundred logs.

About thirty of them floated and started colliding in midair; Mara lost control quickly as she became overwhelmed trying to maneuver each log. Mara sat momentarily frustrated until she remembered what her father had told her.
~~~

"Practice and patience," she said to herself. She stared at the logs and an idea occurred to her: maybe instead of treating the logs like many individual pieces, she should try working with them as one large mass.

She tried again. Slowly, more than half of the logs rose up and worked their way into the stack she had envisioned. Once they all settled, she attempted the same thing again with the rest of the logs. They made their way to the stack, but a few got loose and knocked everything over. Nevertheless, she was pleased. It was a start! Treating many objects like one fluid thing was much easier than thinking about moving several individual pieces at once. As the sun set and the world went from white to grey, Mara's skills improved. Through her patience, she managed to get all the logs stacked into the stack she had envisioned earlier that day. Happy with her results, she waltzed back into the cabin, humming happily to herself.

After dinner, Mara stared at the stars with Zhira. The two of them laid flat on their backs and looked up into the velvet tapestry above them. The Bright One hung almost perfectly centered in the view they had from the tower. It dipped lower in the summer months, but in winter it was on full display. Gant opened the door carrying a tray of two teas for him and Zhira and a hot chocolate for Mara.

She leapt up and grabbed her mug, then settled on the stool that Zhira normally occupied at his desk when he was making notations about the stars.

"Guess what I did today!" Mara bounced on her seat as she spoke. Before either of them could guess, she blurted out, "I stacked all the logs at once! I picked them all up and stacked them! Look!" She pointed out the window.

The brothers peeked out of the tower window and saw the logs stacked neatly in a sturdy pyramid under one of the trees.

"Well done!" Zhira exclaimed, impressed by her fast-growing abilities.

"Indeed, that must have taken a great deal of patience and practice. You're learning fast," Gant added.

"It works because I can see what I want them to do in my head, then I make it happen," she explained.

"Visualization is a great tool, good for you for figuring it out," Zhira said, continuing to praise his daughter.

"Want to see them move?" she asked, clearly excited to show off her skill.

"It's pretty cold out. Why don't we do it tomorrow?" Gant recommended.

"I can do it from here, it's ok." And with that she pulled the stool up to the window, stood on it for a good view of the log pile below, and held out her hands. Zhira and Gant watched as she moved her hands and fingers in ways they had not seen her do before. As if controlled by a puppet master, the pile lifted off the ground as a unit and then split into its smaller parts. The logs spun around but never hit each other and reformed as a stack surrounding the tree that they had been resting under. Mara continued to flick her hands this way and that, and again the logs danced around in the cold night air, restacking themselves as a square pile where the original pyramid had been.

Mara put her hands down and turned to her fathers.

"Ta-da!" she grinned.

Gant was speechless and Zhira's mouth was agape as they regarded their little wizard. This morning she was moving logs one by one, but tonight she had manipulated them like a flock of birds in perfect sync.

"That was AMAZING! I've never seen anything like it!" Zhira exclaimed.

"I'm impressed!" Gant added, not even trying to match Zhira's level of enthusiasm. There was no point; he would never get close.

"You're going to be one strong wizard when you grow up!" Zhira smiled at their daughter.

"Thanks, Dad!" she beamed up at him and gave him and Gant each a big waist-level hug.

Gant looked down at his daughter and smiled. His mother had been right: guiding her emotions and teaching her patience was paying off. Zhira was right, if tonight was any indication, Mara's abilities were going to blossom into something truly spectacular. Gant was happy that he had heeded their mother's advice.

"You should show your skills to Grandma tomorrow. I think she'd love to watch you make all sorts of stacks and towers out of her ingredients at the shop!" Gant suggested.

"Oh yeah!" Mara replied, excited.

Gant got a look from his brother. "What? Mom *will* be excited to see her powers at work."

"At the cost of her ingredients?" Zhira cracked a grin.

"It's been a little while since we caused some chaos in that back room." Gant grinned back.

Gant turned back to the wide open roof and its brilliant view of the winter night sky. Mara laid down next to him and snuggled up, a smile on her face, and soon fell asleep beneath the stars.

Chapter Eight
Twelve Years Later

General Long looked down on the burning village, the last of the western territories.

"Make sure there are no survivors," Long said coldly to the cavalryman beside him. "The king wanted this place burned to the ground."

"Did he say why?" The mounted knight asked.

"He is the king, he does not need to explain himself."

"Very well, but…"

"I said no survivors." Long glared at the knight, who had gone white underneath his grated helmet.

The man simply nodded and rode towards the front lines to give the command. General Long watched him go, silhouetted against the many fires burning the village down. The buildings were made mostly of wood, given the few rock quarries in the west, which made it easier to burn them down. The fires jumped from building to building, consuming the timbered constructions with ease. People ran screaming as royal guards chased them down mercilessly. The smell of acrid smoke filled Long's nostrils even from the top of the hill on which he had set up his camp. It was a proud sight for him, a marvelous execution of duty by his troops at the end of a long and grueling campaign.

The last to fall, this town had once been a pathetic excuse for civilization, but in its final days it had played host to the rebellion's main outfit in the west. It was also the place Long used to call home. Long had been a child when King Radion had gone on his victory tour, claiming territories and boasting about how he, the outcast wizard had conquered the elite ruling class for the people of Kyros. The general had been young when the king had completed his conquest and didn't remember much, only that Radion hadn't spent much time here; there was little to admire about this pathetic village. Long had realized as he grew up that there was nowhere for him to go in this town. He needed a way to rise up above it all, but had not been not graced with magic or any other special abilities.

Long before his hair had gone grey like the ashes that flew up into the air around him, Long decided to make a name for himself by joining the Royal Guard of the king. When he was old enough, he packed up and left, to his mother's dismay, and never returned. It wasn't a hard choice. He hated this town and its apathetic people, content with their miserable lives out in the rocky plains in the shadow of the mountains.

Long worked harder than anyone else in the guard to get to where he currently sat upon his horse, casting his shadow over the fiery remains of his old home. Endless days of grueling grunt work did little to phase him. During his time as a lowly patrolman, he went on many lengthy shifts that often weeded out lesser men. Long made sure that nobody ever questioned his resolve. If he was tired, he never showed it. He took every opportunity to show his devotion to being part of the Royal Guard, never disobeying a rule, or talking out of turn.

After a few years, his dedication started to pay off. Long was promoted to the scouting parties: the patrols that left the capital to survey the surrounding regions to make sure there was peace and prosperity. On one excursion, the town in which they were making a routine stop was attacked by a raiding party of trolls from beyond the Northern border of Kyros. The knight he had been accompanying was gruesomely injured during the raid, so Long had to single-handedly defend the town from the invaders. The knight watched in awe as Long masterfully wielded his sword, slaying several of the trolls and driving the rest away. Upon their eventual return to the castle, the story of Long's incredible skill and heroism spread all the way up to General Geralith. Long quickly earned a reputation as an unflappable, dependable, and loyal knight.

Not long after, General Geralith selected Long to be a part of his personal squadron. Long was always in peak physical condition, even now, and trained more each day with a sword than any other knight. Geralith took a liking to him and groomed him to take over as general when he became too old to continue on. When Geralith retired, Long assumed control.

Throughout all of his time rising through the ranks, Long was worried that his past, specifically where he was from, would undermine his ascent. Coming from this little nothing town had him in fear that his peers, who were all born into military families, would see him as nothing but a lowly slum kid who had nothing to offer. As a result, he could not afford the luxury of making mistakes.

Now with grey stubble sprouting from his chiseled features, Long looked upon the burning cesspool that he managed to crawl out of. Upon their arrival the day before, Long had felt some small semblance of conflict over destroying his home. It was a deplorable town, but it had given him the motivation he needed to reach the heights he had obtained. Harboring the rebellion had been the thing that put his mind at ease enough to burn it to nothing. He also took a slight comfort in the fact that his parents were not suffering; he never held any of this against them, but he also never felt bad for leaving them. His life was his own, and he had made it a respectful and noteworthy one.

The night before the raid, Long had gone into the village under cover of night and returned to the house he had grown up in. Nobody was home, and it was clear they had not been for some time. He casually asked about his parents to a local tailor who was closing up his shop late, and the merchant informed him that the elderly couple who lived there had passed on a few years back. Knowing his parents had nothing to do with the rebellion had given him some small relief he did not know he needed. Coming from a town that had been grossly unimportant and ended up a makeshift rebel base was not an origin Long wanted. He was almost pleased that Gjanion had ordered such a pitiful place burned to the ground.

The remains of the village smoldered and smoked into the afternoon sky, blocking out the sun and making it seem later in the day than it was. General Long sat at a small table with his group of squadron leaders pouring over a map.

"This is the last village west of the mountains. We are low on supplies, so we shall make our way back to the capital. We will rest, resupply, and then begin the coastal campaign to the East," Long said definitively.

"I suggest we leave at first light tomorrow," a gentleman whose gut made it clear he hadn't seen much action in recent years said, "the men have had their hands full demolishing this town and chasing down survivors. Give them the night's respite for a job well done."

"I agree," said a woman taller than everyone else around the table. Her long brown hair was tied in tight twin rows on the back of her head to fit the helmet under her arm. "They'll be rested and ready for the ride through the mountains tomorrow."

General Long nodded in agreement. "Very well. Deliver the news and get some rest yourselves. Well done, commanders. This rebellion is all but finished."

The three commanders saluted the general and made their exit.

The next morning, squadrons saddled up and fell into line behind the burly general. It was an impressive sight: over two hundred mounted knights all in silver armor with most of the horses outfitted to match. A few of the knights worked as banner men, carrying the seal of King Gjanion: a white moon with a lightning bolt cutting across its face on purple tapestries.

The ride to the mountain pass was routine. The battalion rode efficiently and before long they arrived at the base of the path. General Long signaled for the group to stop for a brief rest and to water the horses before the arduous climb. He walked his horse to the river that flowed from the base of a waterfall cascading from a high cliff on the mountain's face and let him have his fill. Scanning the many heads, some still sporting helmets, he found Commander Mai, the tallest of his squadron leaders, her hair no longer tied back as it had been the day before as they were not geared for battle.

"Commander Mai, can I speak with you?" He beckoned the knight over to where he was standing, away from the groups of soldiers eating their rations.

"What is it, sir?" she asked as she walked her palomino over with her and let him mingle with the general's horse by the river.

"I'm beginning to worry about the other mission," he said quietly.

Mai looked down at General Long; she stood a head above him and in an effort never to compromise his command of the battalion, often tried to keep a step or two distance so as not to highlight the height difference.

"We still have the entire eastern territories to search. There are many places to hide it," she responded.

"Yes, but I fear we will not be able to take the eastern port cities without it. They play host to the remainder of the rebellion and its leadership. They know we are coming, and they know they are the last defense of their cause. They'll be ready," Long said with grim conviction, knowing it was going to be all out war to take back the largest cities in their kingdom. With the rebellion backed up against the Eastern Seas, there was no doubt in his mind that they would pull out all the stops.

"True sir, but there are ways of uncovering the secret we seek without ramming down the door," she said pointedly.

The grizzled general looked at her and considered her unspoken proposition. "I assume you want to lead the team?" he asked.

"As your second in command, I think I would be most qualified for the task."

"Very well," he said without hesitation, "Pick your team, no more than three others, to accompany you. You get one day's respite when we return to the castle and then you will leave under the cloak of darkness. We don't want any possible spies knowing this plan."

"Yes sir." The commander turned and went to fetch her horse.

As the outfit passed through the mountains, a pack of hungry Lunawolves, large and white with silvery grey markings on their fur, attempted to attack them and steal some food. A small group of knights broke from formation, drove them off, and rejoined the march with machine-like discipline. Not a single order needed to be given and hardly anyone else even turned to look. General Long had the battalion drilled to perfection, an example of his dedication to the cause.

The rebellion had gotten worse in the year that followed the assassination of the queen and prince. Soldiers were openly mocked and harassed in the towns and villages that immediately surrounded the castle. Further out, it was worse. Villages that felt they were far enough away that they wouldn't face retribution tried to drive out whatever military presence was there. Not every town had soldiers; only the towns with notable populations or importance to the kingdom for a particular resource had a military post.

In a passionate speech, King Gjanion had declared total war on the rebellion, claiming that any village that did not bow down would be burned to the ground. He had set General Long to taking the important northern territories first, as those held the bulk of the resources needed to support a war effort: mining metal ores for weapons and armor and mills for mass quantities of food. The campaign was short and swift. Most of the towns didn't have the assets needed to put up a fight and didn't care to. They mined and farmed regardless of who was in charge.

After two years, and with the northern territories secured, the bulk of the military made its way south. General Long strategized that by creating a united strip in the middle of the kingdom, the rebellion would fracture as their communications and supply routes to each side were cut off. He was nearly right, though somehow information flow didn't seem to halt as quickly as he had anticipated. This led to the suspicion that there were spies on the inside and as a result their tactics had to become more clandestine.

With the king's blessing, Long had chosen three commanders he knew could be trusted without question to lead on a small council with him. Mai was his second in command, a stand out recruit and not just for height. She reminded Long of himself; she was hungry to get to the top and to prove herself. Mai was a skilled and tenacious fighter as well, training hours a day in many different fighting styles. Commander Hearth, the large man who required a massive black horse as a mount due to his weight, came from a suggestion by Lord Geralith. Not so much a fighter as a strategist, Hearth managed the logical and practical side of war: resources. He kept his eye on things like food and weaponry as well as the energy being spent by the soldiers. He was well liked by the knights, as he never sought to overwork them.

Commander Tren rounded out the three. Tren was one of the knights that had fought alongside the king and General Long in the great hall the night of the assassination. He had proven his loyalty as well as his ability with a sword that night, and was a worthy choice in Long's eyes. Tren was the youngest but his lack of experience never showed at any point in the campaign.

Together, these three commanders provided the war effort with a stable, classified channel by which to pass information when it was necessary. The knights and their battalions had taken the southern territory with precision, but not without resistance. Tren bore a scar on his right cheek as a reminder that even a scared villager with a spear is not to be underestimated.

Thanks in large part to General Long's disciplined and methodical approach, the southern territories had been taken three years after the north. The rebel presence wasn't strong, but the extremely dangerous southern deserts made travel a slow-going endeavor. Now, seven years after their Southern conquest, the West had been won, the mountains regained, and it was time to shift their eyes to the final prize: the East.

General Long's stallion whinnied as its eyes recognized the castle gate. They had made it home. The train of knights filed through the main gate and paraded themselves to the stables. The people of the castle city had seen them approaching and crowded the street in anticipation. Now as their heroes returned home, the people cheered them through the streets.

Long ignored this display and broke from the group, setting off to the castle. King Gjanion was waiting for him just past the drawbridge, which was lowered at the sight of Long's steed coming up the cobblestone road. As he dismounted, he bowed to the king, whose hair was now peppered with grey.

"Oh come now!" the king said jubilantly as he held out his hand, "Congratulations, general! The western territories are once again ours!"

"It was a hard fought campaign, but one that I think will remind the remaining rebels that they should be scared of what we can do." Long gave a rare smirk.

"Let us discuss the victory. Tonight we feast!" the king declared as he and the general walked into the main hall, his golden staff tapping on the stone as they walked.

The king lowered his voice. "Any sign of it?"

"I'm afraid not, my liege." Long conveyed his disappointment clearly.

"A shame, but not entirely surprising. There was always a chance it could be somewhere in the eastern territories."

"I do believe we will need it before we attempt to take the eastern port cities. They know we are coming, they know they're the last..." the general began to repeat what he had stated to Commander Mai earlier, but the king cut him off.

"Not now, Long! Didn't you hear me? Tonight we are celebrating! Strategy can wait until morning."

"Yes, sire."

~~~

Books and vials and jars floated everywhere; gravity seemed to have lost its effect on this particular space as items drifted slowly or spun in place. Mara remained perfectly still, eyes closed and cross-legged on the floor meditating, her long black hair tied in a ponytail so as to keep it from floating too wildly around her head.

Zhira made his way quietly up the stairs, taking care to skip the creaky second step. He didn't want to scare her as he made for the door. He opened it as silently as he could, hoping he wouldn't hit any of the flying objects with it and make a sound. Carefully he crept to his desk, retrieved a book of notes he had been working on and made his way back to the door.

And then he sneezed. Mara jumped up from her position on the floor faster than the eye could follow, and threw every object in the air at him simultaneously in a defensive reflex. Scrolls, roots, heavy jars, and much more flew straight at the source of the noise. Zhira cried out as the objects overwhelmed him and he tumbled backwards down the stairs of the tower. Mara gasped and ran down after him.

"Dad, are you ok?!" she yelled as she leapt down the stairs two at a time.

Zhira groaned and held his right leg, writhing on the ground. Mara didn't know much about the human body and its bones, but she was sure that legs shouldn't bend the way her father's currently was.
~~~

"Oh no…Dad I'm so sorry!"

"It's…ah…it's all right, I surprised you. It's my…ah…fault." He was grimacing in pain as he tried to converse with her.

"I…I can fix it," Mara said as she cracked her knuckles and looked down at the leg.

Mara snapped her fingers and moved her fingers in a way that made it look like they were weaving thread. As she did, Zhira's leg magically regained its natural straight form. He stopped moaning and looked up. Mara's eyes were glowing blue as she focused on his leg and her fingers finished their short interwoven dance.

"How does it feel?" she asked as her eyes returned to normal.

"Much better," he replied as he tried to stand up, wincing a little as the leg bore his weight. "It's sore, but not agonizing. Thanks, Mar." Mara smiled an apologetic smile, still sorry for hurting her father so badly. "Did you know you could do that?"

Mara's smile turned to a look of confusion. "I think so? I mean…I've healed little cuts and stuff before. I guess it was just sort of the same idea with more effort."

"Hm…and your eyes?" Zhira asked her.

"What about them?"

"They glowed."

"They…what?" Mara stared at Zhira, but before he could respond, Gant came in, rain and wind howling behind him.

"You're twenty years old and you're telling me your eyes have never glowed?" Zhira asked suspiciously.

"No. I mean, I wouldn't see them if they did, and I'm usually alone when I'm practicing…" Mara trailed off, the confusion settling in.

"Hi, all," Gant said as he forced the door closed against the wind, "I have news on the rebellion."

Saros had eluded the clash between the rebellion and the crown for most of the last twelve years, mostly because not many people cared that they were there. The occasional squadron would pass through, but the town was well protected by its small size and the unimportant demeanor of its citizens; most of the time the knights didn't stop for more than some food.

Gant ran his hand along his cloak and it dried instantly, the water forming a blob around his hand as he removed it. "I believe the king's forces have finished conquering the west and are now finally going to shift their focus eastward."

"Oh no…" Zhira frowned. "I want to meditate on this, hopefully the sky is clear tonight."

"I think we can expect a steadier flow of his royal highness's bodyguards coming through," Gant said, a grim look on his face.

"So we need to be really careful not to reveal ourselves, don't we?" Mara asked.

"We do. I've also been experimenting with memory loss. We can see memories if they're fresh, so I thought it would be possible to actually extract them.

Using food as a method for delivery of a potion, Bess might be able to cover any loose ends."

"That's dangerous, what if they forget too much?" Zhira questioned.

"They'll probably write it off as one too many blows to the head or something," Gant replied nonchalantly.

Zhira made his way to the table, limping, and Gant noticed. "Z, are you alright?"

"Yeah, yeah, I'm good. I just…hit my shin against the table." He didn't look at Mara, whose eyes were locked on him. She was confused as to why he didn't tell Gant.

"I have other news," Gant said, dismissing Zhira's supposed clumsiness, "I think Kei might be spying on us."

Mara's jaw dropped. "Kei?!" she exclaimed, "You think Kei, who works the forge all day, is somehow also spying on us? For who, the king? His forces have been so infrequent here that I forget they exist until they show up! What could possibly be so interesting about our dinky little town?"

"You, Mara. He was asking me a lot of questions about you specifically! It was odd."

"It's not odd, we are friends!"

Zhira gave a snort, and both Gant and Mara turned on him. "What?" Zhira asked, "Isn't it obvious?"

"No," they replied in unison.

"Kei has a crush on Mara!"

Mara went blood red and Gant turned a ghostly white. Zhira just laughed. "You two are so oblivious."

Later that afternoon, the rain stopped and Mara decided to walk into town to visit her grandmother. She enjoyed the shop; it was small, quiet, and her talks with Fiona were always interesting. Mara knew more about Gant and Zhira than they were aware, thanks to her grandmother. Mara weaved through the trees towards Saros, the fresh rain already evaporating in the afternoon sun.

As she walked towards the main street, Mara heard voices and the rattling of saddle bags. She ducked behind a tree just before a group of knights came up the trail towards town. There were four of them, clearly not worried about an ambush as they had hardly any armor on. Mara decided to go after them, intending to have a little fun at their expense, when a hand clamped over her mouth and eyes.

Instinctively, she rolled her hands and the grass around the assailant grew and covered their feet so they couldn't move. She threw an elbow behind her into the person's ribs and peeled away from her attacker's hands; her own hands sporting blue flame, she turned to face them. Laying on the ground rubbing where she had just jabbed him, was Kei.

"Kei!" Her flames went out and she rushed to his side, "I'm so sorry! I didn't know it was you!"

"S'all right," he groaned as he wheezed air back into his lungs, "I scared you, it's my fault."

Kei slowly got to his feet. He was roughly the same height as Mara, the sides of his head shaved with a thick strip of hair down the center of his head that went on into dreadlocks falling to his shoulder blades. His green piercing eyes stood out against his dark skin, and the muscles he had developed from working the forge with his father were well defined and on full display in his sleeveless tunic. Patches of soot from a hard day's work checkered his skin and clothes.

"What are you doing out here?" Mara asked him.

"I was coming to look for you; remember that stone you wanted me to look at?"

"Yeah, the purple one?"

"Yes, it's an amethyst. It's beautiful! I managed to get it out of the rock it was lodged in." Kei held up a stone that looked like a shiny purple berry. Perfectly symmetrical, it glimmered in the light that shone down through the canopy above them.

"It's stunning!" she exclaimed, taking it from him.

"It's a nice find. I wonder if there are any others like it where you found it."

"Well, I found it in the quarry while practicing. It can't hurt to go look for more. Besides, I'm not very comfortable moving rock and dirt yet. It's not like water. Water is consistent and flows easily, while rock is disjointed, clumpy and never the same twice. It takes so much more effort."

"Sounds good. I can study your movements more for my project too!" Kei said, then realized he had let slip something he had not intended her to know.

"Your project?" Mara questioned him.

"Yeah, just something I've been working on…a little…surprise if you will!" He smiled slyly.

"Tell me!" She shoved him playfully.

"That would ruin the surprise!" Kei snatched the stone from her hand and ran off towards the quarry.

Chapter Nine
Murderer

"Rylan, for the last time, the answer is no," Commander Mai said as she stood up from packing her saddle bag.

"Why not? I'm a great rider, and you're just going on a scavenger hunt!" Rylan snapped back. "None of your knights can beat me around the training course. I can easily keep up."

Mai regarded the princess, who stood with her arms crossed in front of her, and said, "Ry, I know you are a phenomenal rider, you don't have to remind me! But this is a dangerous mission, and your father can't lose another member of his family. You're all he's got left."

"Psh, not anymore. He hasn't ridden with me once since *she* showed up." Rylan said in reference to her stepmother, Stella. The princess turned her head up, though her façade of harshness was weakening. She knew Mai was right. She couldn't hurt her father like that. Despite the fact that he had his new wife, Rylan was his true family.

"Rylan, please." Mai stared her down with a kind but firm look. They had always gotten along; Mai was almost like a mother to her. She had given Rylan lessons with a spear, despite her father's hesitation. She had convinced the king that his daughter needed to know how to defend herself, and promised that they wouldn't use actual spears, just staffs. She had also taught the young princess how to stand her ground, speak her mind, and be extremely sarcastic when necessary.

"Fine." Rylan gave in. Seeing the look on the commander's face broke her down just enough for her to surrender. "I just want to get out of here. I'm cooped up in this castle with his new floozy and all I want to do is go out and ride!" Rylan walked over to Neela's stall and fed her a carrot from the bucket beside the door.

"I know you don't like her, but she isn't a horrible person. Your father cares about her, and you care about your father. Try to get to know her instead of cold shouldering her every chance you get. Maybe you'll actually like her!" Mai said in mock surprise.

Rylan appreciated Mai always looking out for her. She cringed at the thought of spending any more time with her stepmother than she already had to, but Mai was right. This woman was not going anywhere, so she may as well make the most of it.

Rylan sighed. "All right, I will try. But I'm desperate to ride."

"I won't tell. Be back before I leave in an hour." Mai whispered.

Rylan's face lit up. Without a word, she opened Neela's stall and mounted her in one swift motion. She kicked once, and they bolted out of the stable. Her blonde curls whipped behind her as she rode Neela through fields of long grass that were bathed in the fiery orange glow of the setting sun.

~~~

The stars began escorting the Bright One across the deep purple sky as Rylan made her way back to the castle to freshen up from her brief ride of freedom. She flopped down on the bed and called the chambermaid to draw her a bath.

Rylan gave herself a good scrubbing, donned a fresh set of red robes, and went down to the kitchens to see what the cook had whipped up for dinner. In the dining room, she found her stepmother sitting by the hearth in a large armchair. Rylan put on the least fake smile she could muster and walked over.

"Evening!" she said a little too cheerily; she dialed it back a bit.

"Rylan, how wonderful to see you!" Her stepmother, Stella, had a high, clear voice that came from a face with a very pointed nose that reminded Rylan of a bird's beak. She was a tall and slender woman with green eyes that looked like two gems set in marble against her pale face.
~~~

"And you, my queen." Rylan gave a little bow.

"Have you eaten yet? The chefs put together a marvelous beef stew," Stella said as she folded her skinny hands on her lap.

"No, not yet. I was just on my way to…"

"Oh! I just can't keep a straight face!" she cut Rylan off excitedly. "I have wonderful news!"

Rylan kept her cool. She was trying her best to give this woman a chance, like she had promised Mai.

"What is it?" Rylan feigned interest as best she could.

"You're going to be a sister!" the bony woman squealed with delight.

Rylan was speechless. Her eyes glazed over as it hit her that she was about to be bound by blood to this woman.

"You're going to have a baby brother!" she said a little more calmly, trying to get through to Rylan.

Inside Rylan's head, there was the loudest buzz that she had ever heard, and it was the only thing she could process. *This woman had been in my life barely a year. The wedding was last month, and she is already expecting a child? What was dad doing? Why would he do this to me? Why was he moving so fast?* Rylan wondered if she had enough strength to pop her stepmother's head off.

"That's…amazing!" She grinned and tried her absolute hardest to look happy for Stella as the woman rambled on about baby names and how great of a sister she thought Rylan was going to be. At the first chance she could get, Rylan made her exit and fled into the kitchen to finally get some food. After dinner, she went to find her father in his study.

"What. The. Hell?" she asked, storming in after her father opened the door.

"Rylan!" Gjanion said startled. "What happened?" He tucked a book he had been reading under his robes.

"*You* happened! Stella told me about the baby!"

Gjanion relaxed a little. "I figured you wouldn't take the news well. I had hoped to be there when she told you."

"Well you weren't, and now I'm bound to this wench by a brother?!"

"Watch your tongue, young lady. She is my wife, I love her, and we are extremely excited to bring new life into this world together," the king said sternly.

Rylan did not back off. "She is like…TEN years younger than you! Why are you rushing into this?"

"I'm not going to live forever! I'm enjoying my life, and I don't need you telling me how to live it."

"You might be enjoying yourself, but you're being a really lousy father. I'm doing my best to be there for you but it's like I don't even exist anymore!" She instantly regretted saying that, she knew it stung him.

"Rylan…I've tried to be the father you deserve. Once your mother died, you became all I had in the world. I did everything I could to raise you as best I could on my own." Gjanion's voice conveyed the hurt he felt from his daughter's attack.

"Dad, I know, I'm sorry. I didn't mean it," Rylan said, feeling guilty for storming in and immediately berating her father.

"I know."

There was an awkward silence between them as they stood in the study looking at each other, both trying to think of how to move on from the fracas.

"What was that book you hid when I barged in?" she asked, pointing to the book protruding slightly from his robe in an effort to change the subject.

"I'll tell you when it's time," he replied.

~~~

Mai and her team rode at breakneck pace, and only at night. They didn't want to be seen. As General Long's second in command, Mai carried with her a reputation that put a large target on her back. Away from the main army, she was much more vulnerable to assaults from the rebellion. She had destroyed too many lives, burned down too many buildings, and fought too many battles for people not to want to take her out of the picture.

At dawn after the fifth night, they came upon a town. They knew that to travel fast they needed to pack light. As a result, they had to constantly resupply as inconspicuously as they could. This town was perfect:
~~~

off the main roads and hidden in the woods. Mai and her three companions rode in on a small path that wound through the trees and up to the town's main drag. A little wooden sign that read *Saros* stood near where the cobblestone road began.

The sun peeked over the tops of the buildings that lined the road, as if stealing a look at who these new guests were. A bald, bearded man working his forge didn't look up as they rode by, the horses' shoes clopping on the stone road. Further along, Mai spotted an inn and made her way up the street. Mai took in the town, and it didn't take her long. Barely big enough to be called a town, she found Saros completely uninteresting. Just another stop as they avoided main roads and routes. As they reached the inn, she and her men tied up their horses and went inside.

The entry hall had two long tables with benches on either side of them; one bench supported a man who seemed to have fallen asleep while enjoying whatever was still in his mug. Two chandeliers that sported various lengths of candle hung from the wooden rafters and a bar with three barrels on their sides behind it completed the scene. It was a humble inn, perfect for them to lay low, gather their supplies, and be on their way.

The innkeeper, a hefty old woman with stark white hair, walked over to them.

"What can I do for you folk so early in the mornin'?" she asked rather grouchily.

"We have ridden through the night and require a couple of rooms for the day to rest. Some supplies to help us on our way to Varyn would also be appreciated," Mai replied.

"Alrigh' then, two golds apiece for ye." Bess held out her hand.

"Steep price for a small…inn," one of the knights said judgingly. Mai shot him a dirty look over her shoulder.

"Sorry, m'boy. Visitors don't come often. Gotta make the money when I can." Bess continued to hold her hand out for the gold pieces.

"Eyy, Bess. You don't gotta take that. 'Tis a fiiine establishment!" The man that had been asleep on the table groggily lifted his head as he defended the old woman. He stood up and squinted; the light coming in from the windows seemed to cause him pain.

"Heyyyy…don't I know you?" he slurred as he pointed to Mai. She made no moves as the man peered at her, recognition slowly dawning on him.

"I'm sure you are mistaken sir. We are from just east of the mountains," she responded as she rummaged through her bag for her coin purse, annoyed at the drunkard.

"I'm from far away too." He continued pointing, though his aim needed improvement. The man attempted to move towards them, stumbled on the bench, and leaned on the long wooden table he had just been sleeping on. "You burned my hoooouse,

Commander Mai. Or should I call youuuu…Murderer Mai."

Mai's eye twitched, but she gave no other indication that this man had figured out who she was, or that he had gotten under her skin. "Sir, I'm afraid you are probably too drunk to…"

"I KNOW WHO YOU ARE," he yelled suddenly, spit flying everywhere. One of the knights drew his sword, Bess gave him the dirtiest look he had ever seen.

"I ran from you…ran for daaaays with nothing! You took everything from me! My home, my…my family, friends…I ran with the clothes on my back! I'd NEVER forget your face." The man had found a sobering new energy in his boiling hatred.

"What's this now, Reg?" Bess looked skeptically at Mai.

"I've been stayin' here awhile now 'cuz I thought she wouldn' find me here!" He started to weep. "Go on, you murderous wench, finish what you started." He sank back down onto the bench with a hiccup.

"Who are you?" Bess turned to Mai, who stood perfectly still, rooted to the spot she had occupied since she had entered the inn.

"Just a traveler in need of some respite," she responded cordially.

"Where did ye say ye were from?"

"I didn't." Mai was irked. Who was that man? Why had he chosen this exact moment to wake up?

"I'm gonna need more information than that, miss." Bess stood her ground between Mai and Reg.

"Ma'am, we just need a day's rest and we will be on our way. We don't want to cause any trouble."

"You've caused enough already," Reg said from the table.

"That man is drunk and doesn't know what he is saying!" Mai retorted.

"I know you murdered people who did nothing to wrong you!" Reg yelled back at her from behind Bess.

Mai stepped around the old lady and faced him. "And what do you plan to do about it?" she asked him, her face darkening as she stared him down.

The broken man stared back, "I'll avenge them." He pulled a knife from his belt and held it threateningly.

"I have the bigger knife, I'm afraid." She motioned to her sword.

"No honor, just hiding behind shiny weapons. No wonder the rebellion would rather fight to the last man than give in. It's 'knights' like you who support the power hungry ways of 'his royal highness'," Reg said with hate and a few burps as the standoff escalated.

"Fine then," Mai said coolly; she removed her sheath and handed it to one of her knights, "Let's take this outside." She turned and exited.

He followed her out, still brandishing the knife. A small crowd gathered quickly as Reg and Mai began circling each other.

"You disgraceful excuse for a woman. I'll teach you to mess with the likes of me," Reg yelled as he made a pitiful jab at her throat. The confrontation had sobered him up some, but Mai easily parried the drunk man's attack and awaited his next move, perched on the balls of her feet.

"You should have died with the rest of them instead of running, you coward," Mai taunted him, and it worked.

"Murderer!" Reg threw his whole body behind his next lunge, and Mai used it to her advantage. She blocked the knife hand and grabbed the back of his shirt, tugging him to the ground and pinning him by the throat with her foot. Squatting over him, she drew her own knife from its concealed sheath in her waistband.

"You foolish man," she said before she slashed at his throat.

Except his throat didn't cut. Her arm didn't move. It remained where she had raised it; she willed it to slice the disgusting man open but no matter how hard she tried, it felt like she had been glued in place. Mai turned and saw a girl with black hair and piercing blue eyes holding her hand out in front of her. Mai's eyes widened in shock. This wasn't possible; only the king could perform such feats. She released the knife and Mara let go of her arm. Mai stood up and faced her.

"Who in the name of Eres are you?" she asked, stunned.

"Someone you shouldn't mess with." Mara stepped forward. The circle of people morphed to surround the two women.

"How did you do that?" Mai asked more confusedly than accusingly. "Only the king has magic…"

"The king is wrong," Mara replied, and then lifted her hands, palms facing the sky; Commander Mai and her three knights lifted into the air. Mara released her hands and they all fell back onto the stone, groaning.

"You get out and stay out. This is my town and you will not bring death here. We will not be part of your conquest." Mara surprised herself with how confidently the words flowed from her mouth.

Disheveled, Mai stood up, her eyes wild, "How *dare* you!" She charged Mara, who simply tilted her head to one side. Mai's foot sunk into the stone to just above the ankle. Not expecting the sudden change, she fell and the crowd around her gave a few chuckles. This girl was embarrassing her!

"Who are you?" Mai asked again, hair wildly out of its bun and foot still magically sunk.

"I am a wizard. Now leave. My. Town." Mara said defiantly. Her eyes flashed blue as she levitated them up over their horses and dropped them down on their saddles. Mai and her knights sat up and turned to go.

"This isn't over!" Her horse whinnied and took off down the street.

Gant came up beside her. "Can I speak with you for a moment?"

They walked away from the crowd. Gant's face conveyed no emotions; Mara was nervous. Fiona stood there with him.

"I am really proud of you for saving that man, but that was just about the stupidest thing I've ever seen you do," Gant said to Mara.

"I'm not going to let some punk woman we don't know kill a man in our town!" she fired back, feeling misled.

"That wasn't just some punk woman." Reg had emerged from the throng of people, still off balance but speaking much more soberly now after his ordeal. "That was Commander Mai of the Royal Guard. She is a monster who kills first and doesn't even ask questions later," he said with no attempt to hide his hate.

"What did she do to you?" Fiona asked.

"Let's talk later," Reg said, suddenly dropping to his knees as the adrenaline wore off.

Gant lifted him under the arm and supported him as they walked back to the inn, where Reg promptly fell asleep. Later that afternoon, Reg, Gant, Mara, and Fiona sat at a table in the inn.

"Her squadron came to my little village with more men than I had ever seen all dressed in shiny silver; they outnumbered us five to one. Mai claimed that we had been harassing soldiers and stealing their supplies. Most of us denied it, but there were a few that stood their ground. We didn't even know they had done it! Most of us were completely innocent, but it didn't matter to her," Reg said.

"She decided that because we had shown defiance, we were to be the example for all the other towns and villages in the region. They…" he began to tear up, "they burned everything. Our homes, our stores, our farms…they destroyed our village. Before I knew what was happening, it was gone. We never stood a chance. Commander Mai condemned us and her exterminators did their jobs. They chased down survivors, torched buildings full of food, and tore up our roads so that if anyone did survive there would be no way for them to live.

"I hid myself in our cellar. Our house collapsed and buried it, so nobody found me. I waited three days in that dark, damp space before I forced my way out through the charred logs. When I emerged, I was standing amongst nothing but ash and soot. I ran as fast as I could, worried she would leave behind scouts to take care of anyone that had not been in town. I lived off the land for a few months, foraging and catching all of my food, taking shelter in any form of cave, overhang, or dense canopy until I stumbled my way here a few days ago," he finished. Fiona's eyes were laced with tears, and Gant sat there silently, his eyebrows raised in shock.

"I didn't realize it was that bad. I thought they were just after the rebellion," Mara responded after a moment.

"The king is a tyrant. He wants complete obedience or complete destruction. I've seen first-hand that there is no alternative," Reg said dejectedly.

"We have to help." Mara turned to Gant. "Those monsters will be back. We need to prepare." She was hot with rage; Gant could see it in her eyes.

"Why did your eyes glow when you sent them onto their horses?" Gant asked her.

"I…don't know. That's the second time it's happened," she replied, her rage diffusing as she tried to explain it to him. "It's almost like the energy is overflowing, and that's where it goes. It's hard to contain."

"What was the first time?" Gant asked in response.

"Ask Dad." Mara gave him a guilty look.

Chapter Ten
Preparations

Commander Mai brought her palomino to the river and sat down on the bank. Her companions did the same, sitting in silence until their leader spoke.

"What the hell was that?" she asked nobody in particular.

One of the knights spoke up. "Perhaps it was a trick, a clever stunt to fool us into thinking she has magical powers."

"No," Mai replied sharply. "I felt it. That was no trick."

They sat there as their horses mused around in the grass. With little food and five days of hard riding ahead, Mai started to think about how they were going to get back to the castle to tell the king of this development. After an hour, Mai decided it was time to get moving again.

"We have barely any supplies. We are going to need to forage and hunt our way home. It'll be tough, but it's what we train for. Are you ready?"

The three men nodded, gathered their things, and mounted their horses. The next three days were hard on them; food was scarce in the somewhat barren landscape of the east. The moors and grasslands that stood between the forests they'd left and the one surrounding the capital provided little cover for game; only small animals occupied the fields. Being the dry season, foraging too was poor.

During the third night of their trek, one of the knights fell ill due to bad fruit they had found that day. His body quickly went into shock from dehydration and lack of nutrients, and eventually Mai realized there was nothing more they could do for him. The man was in no state to ride, and Mai didn't have time to waste. He died honorably, asking that the commander put him out of his misery. They gave him a brief burial and set on their way, one horse free of its rider's weight.

The following two days went better. As they made their way closer to the castle, the woods they were familiar with providing more abundant resources to get them home safely. Mai gave her horse's reins to the stable hand and made her way to the castle. She didn't think that King Gjanion would be pleased to see her and she was right. The king fumed at the sight of her without the sword they had set out to find until she told her story about encountering Reg.

"A girl stopped me from killing him, but didn't touch me. She performed magic—even called herself a wizard. She restrained me with nothing but her mind…or the air…or something. We stood no chance, not even being able to get close, and were caught incredibly off guard."

The king's face was scarily calm. "That's not possible. I am the last wizard, there are none but me."

"My king I assure you…"

"Get out. Unless you want to join your dead comrade." His quiet anger was unnerving.

Commander Mai knew how to pick her battles; seething with frustration under her black tunic, she left the throne room.

<center>~~~</center>

"How?" Gjanion asked Long with a calm voice, though Long could see the king's face began to betray his true feelings. Long was sure he was going to die.

"Sire, she was killed. I confirmed it myself." The burly general held his ground, hyper aware of the king's every move.

"And she had no children?" Gjanion did not blink as he stared down his right-hand man.

"We disposed of them."

"So there is absolutely no way this girl is at all related to Heron?" Gjanion's face was so close, Long could count the individual hairs in his beard.

The general paused, which was all the king needed to go into a rage the likes of which Long had never witnessed.

"YOU WERE SUPPOSED TO KILL THEM ALL!" the king bellowed.

"Sire…"

"We are on the verge of finally defeating this wretched rebellion…so close to our goal of a peaceful kingdom I rule over…and NOW we have to deal with YOUR failure, which could undermine EVERYTHING we have accomplished in the last twelve years!" The king roared as he tossed his goblet across the room and started conjuring blasts of wind with every flail of his arms.

"Sire if I can explain…" the general said, remaining calm in the face of the king's rampage. "There was no sign of the baby, and the rest of the family was confirmed dead. I knew that even if it did survive, nobody would know who she was."

"You…*knew*? You *knew* she was never going to survive? You *knew* that she would never discover her powers? What else do you know, General? That the rebellion is in Varyn? That despite our best efforts, they still have a firm grasp of our plans? There is a traitor who walks these halls and I think I *know* who it is." He stared with wide accusing eyes at Long, who held his spot so well, most would have mistaken him for a statue.

"Sire if there is one thing that I am not, it is a traitor. I have dedicated my life to this force, to protecting you, and I regret that I made an error. I will fix this at once."

"No." The king turned and was suddenly nose to nose with General Long. Neither man blinked. The only sounds were the fires crackling in their grates. "I will do it myself."

At that moment the door opened and Rylan walked in. The king quickly removed himself from the general's personal space and turned to greet his daughter.

"Rylan, what are you doing up so late?" the king asked with a soft, caring voice. His anger and threatening tone had disappeared.

"I just walked past Commander Mai. I thought she was on a mission?" Rylan asked.

"Her mission was…interrupted. They suffered some setbacks, including the loss of one of their riders. They came back to regroup," Gjanion explained to his daughter without revealing any important details.

"That's unfortunate! Maybe you should let me go with her next time. I'm a better rider than most of your knights!" Rylan said confidently.

"That you are, my princess," Gjanion replied affectionately.

~~~

Commander Mai was walking back to her chambers and bumped into Commander Hearth.

"Oh! Good evening, Mai! Glad to see you up and about!" Mai and Long had decided to keep her
~~~

mission a secret even from the other commanders, giving the excuse that she had gotten sick upon their return from the campaign in the west and was isolated for recovery. Mai wasn't sure the ruse would work, especially after Rylan had discovered her in the stables, but the princess had agreed to keep quiet and now here she was with Hearth, who believed the lie.

"Ah, yes, I was quite unwell…I have finally been permitted to walk about and be around others again," she lied.

"Well it seems due! You look ghastly, like someone drained you." Hearth looked concerned for his companion, Mai gave a half-hearted smile.

"I'm okay, really. Happy to be back on my feet."

"Good. I do believe the general will have us depart for the eastern campaign within the fortnight!"

"I hope to have regained my health by then. I would hate to miss any part of our victory," she stated, the latter of which was not a lie.

A squire politely interrupted them with scrolls bearing the king's seal, one for each of them. He gave a short bow, and hurried on his way. The two commanders opened the scrolls, and Hearth read his aloud.

"Due to a recent development, an emergency council meeting will be held at midnight tonight." Hearth looked up from his scroll. "I wonder what happened."

"I think I have some idea…" Mai sighed.

She filled in Hearth on the way to the council chambers, explaining the sickness lie and what had happened to her and her team in Saros.

"A shame about your man, bad way to go," Hearth remarked when she had finished. Mai nodded in agreement. They said nothing more until they had reached the room already occupied by General Long, hands behind his back staring into the fire blazing in the fireplace. Commander Tren sat at the table patiently, his eyes greeting theirs in a friendly but cautioning way.

"General, what is this about?" the young commander asked, trying to get a read on the situation before the king arrived.

Long turned to face them. "I have unfortunately made an error," he said flatly. The general never made a mistake, and his admission of one made the room suddenly very cold. None of the commanders asked any further questions, as King Gjanion strode into the room, scepter in hand. His hair was tied back in a tight bun, supporting the silver crown. Streaks of grey adorned his temples and faint lines were beginning to form around his eyes; nevertheless he looked as fierce and commanding as ever. He shut the door behind him with a wave of the staff-laden hand, and motioned for everyone to take a seat.

"Thank you for joining me on such short notice." The king took the high-backed chair at the head of the table and addressed the four military leaders in front of him. "We have a new obstacle that I had not foreseen in our quest to reunite the kingdom."

He paused as his eyes shifted around the table.

"My grandfather was an outcast, a wizard who was thrown out by the elite. He sought revenge and destroyed them all...or so he thought. I have recently learned that one of those bloodlines has survived. I am not the last wizard."

Tren's jaw dropped, Mai and Hearth exchanged worried looks, and Long simply sat where he was, not looking at anyone.

Gjanion continued, "Twenty years ago, we discovered a family of them living in the woods outside of a small unmapped town. The cowards knew they had lost and secreted themselves away. Now, their offspring has challenged us. Commander Mai encountered her on a secret mission to locate the whereabouts of the sword relic."

Tren's head whipped around to Mai, who did not meet his eyes but instead remained focused on General Long. "I thought you were sick?"

Before Mai could explain, Long interrupted, "We provided a false narrative to everyone who was not directly involved with the covert mission. We didn't want the rebellion to know who was doing what and why. They still don't know about the relics, and the longer we keep it that way, the better chance we have at finding the sword."

The king nodded. "We know there are spies amongst us and we know they infiltrate high into our chain of command. We couldn't take the risk. I apologize for keeping you two in the dark." He regarded Hearth and Tren.

"The good of the kingdom comes first, my liege," Hearth replied.

Again, Gjanion nodded. "Now, onto the matter at hand. I am going to personally see to the removal of this new threat, before the rebellion catches wind of her existence and rallies to her."

All three commanders stared at the king; it was an unnecessary risk for him to go out in the open this close to total victory, let alone face another wizard whose powers he had no bearing on. Tren spoke up first.

"Sir, I don't believe the risk is worth it. If the rebellion ambushes us…or the wizard…" he trailed off, not wanting to complete the thought, though they were all thinking it.

"It is indeed a dangerous move, but I believe it would be more dangerous to leave this problem unattended. She could provide the rebellion a spark to help push back against the work we have done to unite our people."

"I think you are more than capable of taking on this threat, sire. What would you have us do? Protect you? Scout a safe route?" Hearth chimed in.

"I appreciate your enthusiasm, Commander, but I have already formed a plan with General Long. I am going to take him and Commander Mai with me to confront the wizard. You and Tren will stay here, as Rylan is not yet old enough to rule, and we lost our dear

Lord Geralith last year. I need your trusted leadership while I am away."

Tren straightened up and looked at Hearth, a sense of importance and pride visible across his clean shaven face. As the youngest commander, he was always trying to prove himself to the king and was eager for this opportunity. Hearth returned the look with an overly enthusiastic thumbs up.

"You can count on us, my king," Hearth said for the both of them.

"Excellent. Commander Mai, I know you have been through an ordeal over the last week, but I need you to rally your forces and prepare to leave again. Take tomorrow to gather all that you'll need, we will leave as soon as your squadron is prepared."

"Yes, sir." She got up from the table and exited with General Long.

"Perhaps some of our best fighters should accompany you?" Hearth suggested, Tren nodding in agreement.

King Gjanion nodded. "Long and I have already laid out the plan. We don't know what we are up against—we will be prepared."

"I will send word to my troops to stand down for the time being. What shall we tell them about the delay in riding out to finish off the rebellion?" Hearth asked the king.

"Tell them they've earned the break or something. It'll keep morale high," Gjanion responded dismissively, his mind fully focused on the matter at hand.

Hearth nodded and walked out with Tren, leaving the king to himself at the polished wooden table.

~~~

"I think it's time you see my project," Kei said as he watched Mara from atop the boulder she was lifting.

"Oh, you mean your surprise you've been 'studying me' for?" She dropped the boulder out from under him but caught him with her other hand, cushioning his fall; she gave a sly smile.

"Yeah, that one." He straightened his dark red tunic and brushed off his pants. "I think it might help you when the soldiers come back."

Mara had been working herself to the bone every day for the last week trying to get a handle on the finer points of her abilities. She had no problem producing all sorts of fire or lifting and moving objects; she could manipulate water, make things grow, and even get brief glimpses of thoughts from people if she concentrated. She still struggled with handling rocks and soil, since there were vast differences between every kind of material that made up the ground. Different densities and compositions made every attempt unique.

She also struggled with control; for as patient as she was, it was a lot easier to move objects over large
~~~

distances than it was to do precise and finer actions. Often her more minuscule targets would move too fast or go flying out of sight because she put too much effort into her actions. Working out here in the quarry, she didn't have to worry too much about messing things up, but back in town she was much more cautious. Windows, carts, and more had been unfortunate victims of her practice over the years.

Everything Mara knew about magic she had learned on her own. Unsure of why she had her powers, and knowing that King Gjanion would never be a source of training or education about herself, Mara had taken it upon herself to discover all she could. She didn't know if there were other wizards out there, but she hoped that the knowledge she obtained would be helpful to someone in the future, maybe even her own children.

Mara picked up two rocks and spun them in orbit around each other slightly above her palm. "Where is this surprise? Is it a weapon?" she asked him.

"You think I made you, the only person who can move things without touching them, set things on fire just by snapping her fingers, and grow plants at will, a weapon?" Kei asked her.

"I don't know, I've always felt my hands were rather…naked while I do all the things I do!" she shrugged.

"Well we will have to remedy that issue at a later date. For now, you'll have to make do. Meet me at the shop after dinner! I'm going to go get it ready." He scrambled up the hill that overlooked the earthy patch of rock and dust and waved goodbye from the top.

Mara turned back to her work, spinning the rocks in her hand rapidly and launching them at a dummy she had set up on the far end of the rock field one hundred feet away. One hit home, tearing through the torso made of hay, while other flew over the melon head she had stuck on top; she groaned.

The sun traced its path until it was dipping into the tree line. Mara, sweating, made her way back to the cabin to wash up and help prepare dinner. Gant was stirring a pot on the stove.

"Good session?" he asked.

"I guess. I don't know what to expect though…the king is the only other person that can do magic, so unless he shows up himself, I have a pretty big advantage already…"

"That's true. I doubt he will come, but it never hurts to be ready," Gant said as Mara lifted the soup out of the pot and separated it into three balls in midair before landing them into the bowls sitting on the table.

"Kei says he has something he thinks could help me," said Mara, testing the waters on her dad's feelings towards the boy.

"Does he now? You know, I'm sorry I thought he was a royalist. I've always liked Keylon and Sari…and he's pretty cute," he added with a wink.

"Dad!" Mara yelled, suddenly very red.

"Yes?" Zhira stepped out of the door leading up to the tower.

"No…not you." Mara rolled her eyes.

Zhira joined them at the table for dinner, after which Mara made up an excuse to go to her grandmother's shop and sprinted out the door. Zhira gave his brother a knowing look.

Mara walked up to the forge, heat waves wiggling in the cool evening air. Sari greeted her with his usual grunt as he heaved his hammer over to an anvil and beat a blazing hot piece of metal.

"Mara, over here!" Kei beckoned through a door that led to the room behind the forge.

Kei opened two windows, providing a view of the boring alley running behind the shops. Mara had never been in the back room before; there were piles of ore that seemed to have been organized in some way, though Mara couldn't figure out what way that was. It all looked the same to her. There was a pile of poorly forged metal items: cracked blades that had splintered during quenching, dented helmets from being struck too hard, and several shields that were either too big or too small. In one of the corners, something stood about her height covered in a blanket.

Kei lit three torches mounted in the walls, helping to illuminate the room as the sun set. "I know you have no idea what you're in for when those soldiers get here, but I figured some extra protection wouldn't hurt." With a flourish, he removed the blanket to reveal a set of armor.

Mara hadn't seen much armor in her life, but she could tell this was unique. It was made of leather that was as black as night, but around the edges of each piece she saw the material was different: it was a metal that was slightly lighter in color than the leather and had small red and blue stones inlaid. The minuscule pieces shimmered in the torchlight. On the back of the right hand, almost like a signature, was the amethyst stone she had found. There was no helmet, but it looked like it would protect the rest of her body well.

"After watching you practice for so long, I realized you needed mobility and flexibility," Kei explained as Mara took it in, "I made the armor out of hardened leather. It's durable but also very light and more flexible than steel. The edges are reinforced with carbon steel and inlaid with small gemstones I found, which is why it sparkles.

"Where did you find so many gems?" Mara asked.

"After you found your first one, I knew where to look. There's a small deposit nearby that gave me what I needed," he said.

"Kei… it's…" Mara couldn't find the words; she ran her fingers along the ridges of the overlapping leather. It was beautiful, it was fierce. She wanted to put it on immediately and see how good she looked in it, and how badass she would seem.

"Don't mention it! It's…" Kei was interrupted as Mara kissed him.

After a moment, they separated. Kei stood there sporting a stunned look.

"Don't mention it." Mara winked as a smile spread wide across her face. "Now help me get it on!"

~~~

"No, we're staying!" Rezzik said defiantly.

"Rez, I just don't see why you should endanger yourselves. None of us have any idea what we are in for."

"Gant, I appreciate your concern, but this is our home too. We have every right to defend ourselves as you do."

"Yes but we don't know when Mai will be back, or how many knights she brings. We can't assume we have time to train everyone," Gant replied.

"You don't have to train us, we can fight for ourselves."

"Yeah, but..." Gant stammered

"But what? We don't have magic powers? Neither does the royal guard and they seem to manage." Rezzik stood with his arms crossed. He, Gant, and a few others had gathered to decide the best course of action for protecting the people of Saros when the king's forces arrived.

"I don't know, Rezzik," Litik said. "It might be best for us to let them handle it, and avoid unnecessary losses."
~~~

"Litik, you'd really run instead of fight?" Fiona challenged him.

"If it means a longer life, then absolutely. I don't pretend to be a sword-swinging hero! I want to live."

"Let's leave it to choice then," Zhira said from his seat next to Gant. "Someone will take those who wish to leave to a safe place while the rest stay and fight."

"Who would protect those that go into hiding?" Fiona asked.

"I will," Zhira responded.

All eyes turned on him. As one of the three people in town capable of any sort of magic, everyone had assumed he would stay and fight.

"Zhira, wouldn't you be more needed here?" Keylon asked.

"No. If there are people from this town going out into the wilderness alone, one of us should bring our abilities and protect them until this is over," Zhira said with conviction. "We promised to protect you in exchange for keeping our alchemy a secret. That means ALL of you."

"Where will we go?" Litik asked the group.

"What if you hid out down the cliffs?" Gant suggested.

"That could work, but we are going to need time to get everyone out and we don't know when Mai is coming," Fiona said.

"It's likely a week's ride from the castle, depending on how many knights they travel with. The larger the outfit, the longer it will take. We are a small town, and they'll only see Mara as the threat, so likely they'll be here sooner than that" Keylon responded. "Why don't we aim to have everyone out in five days' time, just to be sure?"

The group concurred and the small assembly dispersed. Litik walked back to his shop and Zhira walked with his mother. Sari and Keylon were halfway out the door when Gant called out to Sari.

"Sari, a moment please?" Gant beckoned him over. "We need weapons for those who are staying to fight. I hate to ask you to make so many weapons in so little time, but…"

"I have enough," Sari replied in his gruff voice, cutting Gant off.

"Great, I will send people your way."

Not one for talking much, Sari simply nodded and walked out with his wife. Gant stood with Rezzik, torches casting their shadows in several directions along the stone walls of the town hall.

"Do you think this is going to work?" Rezzik asked him as they watched everyone depart.

"It has to, or we die," Gant responded grimly.

Chapter Eleven
The Battle of Saros

Over the next few days, Sari saw too many people for his liking. The reserved blacksmith preferred working hard in his forge, beating metals into submission and not talking to anyone unless he had to. The only exception was his wife; Sari loved Keylon more than anything in the world and would do anything she asked of him without question.

Keylon had agreed to help Sari hand out weapons and provide basic handling training for whatever weapon a person chose. She had not been born in Saros like most of the residents, instead Keylon had come to town as a teenager from the capital with no family to speak of. Kind-hearted and caring, she was instantly taken in by Fiona until she got on her feet. She had fallen for Sari fairly quickly and, not being shy, wasted no time in letting him know it. The two of them had hit it off well, got married soon after, and settled into their home above Sari's forge. Nobody understood how two completely different people were such a good match, but they had as happy a marriage as anyone in town.

Keylon didn't talk much of her past, but her proficiency with multiple kinds of weapons, on full display now as she trained the town, led some to believe that she had been a recruit in the royal guard before she ran away. She never answered any questions about her history, preferring to focus on the now: her husband, her shop, and their son Kei.

Rezzik was watching intently as Keylon showed him how to wield a mace Sari had made; it was a simple design: a wooden handle about two feet long with a rounded metal head that tapered into spikes.

"Being top heavy, you need to use its weight to your advantage. Don't work against it, let it work for you," she said as she gave it a couple of looping swings. "The more you go with its flow, the more useful it will be in return."

Keylon handed the mace to Rezzik, who took some clumsy swings with it. After a few minutes he appeared to have a non-self-threatening handle on it.

"I'll practice some more. Thank you, ma'am." Rezzik gave a small polite bow one would give to a master, and headed off towards the town hall, still taking a swing here and there.

"That's the last of them," Keylon said to Sari as she walked into the forge.

"Thank goodness, I don' think I could handle one more blabberin' monkey," Sari responded, hunched over with a small hammer, detailing a helmet.

"They're not that bad. You should be more patient with them!" she replied.

"But then they would talk to me, and when would I get work done?" Sari still did not look up.

"Work for whom? How many customers do we get that require so much from you?" she challenged him.

Sari finally put down the hammer and turned to face his wife. "It's for them. It's always been for them." He pointed out towards the street. "I knew somethin' like this would happen someday. I knew they would be in danger. The world grows smaller and smaller around us, Keylon. Don' tell me ya ain't noticed the increased traffic at Bess's. More people are on the run from the king. Hidin' in the woods was only gonna work for so long. When it came time to defend ourselves, how would it go without weapons? Or worse, bad weapons that broke on the first swing?"

Keylon looked at her husband through new eyes. "I didn't realize you cared about them so much. You are a noble man, and I am a lucky woman." She hugged him and sat with him, chatting while he worked until after the sun went down.

"I've noticed Mara has been around a lot lately. Funny what ya notice when ya keep to yerself." Sari gave a rare grin.

"Yes, I think her and Kei are rather fond of each other...I wonder if Gant and Zhira know," Keylon mused.

"I am sure they are well aware. If we know, they do."

~~~

The sun sank into the night and the stars were out in full force, surrounding the Bright One. Mara crept through the woods towards the cabin.

"Please be asleep..." she whispered to herself as she snuck towards the window in the kitchen. Her armor glinted in the starlight, the ruby and sapphire flecks along the edge almost glowing.

Mara lifted the window without touching it, making no sound as she leapt through and rolled to avoid the chair that stuck out from the table. The house was dark and she could hear Gant's snoring coming from his room. She tiptoed through towards her bedroom door when a light suddenly came on behind her; sitting at the table with one hand cradling a flame was Zhira.

"You're up late," he said as he got up to shut the window Mara had left open. "Care to explain where you were?"

"I was training." She had rehearsed her lie before she climbed into the house. The truth was she had been with Kei, but her father didn't need to know that.

"Training...I see...and what are you wearing?" Zhira acknowledged her armor.
~~~

"It's armor. Kei made it for me."

"He made you armor?" Zhira came over and inspected it. He noticed the glinting flecks of gems in the trim under his firelight and how sleek it was. "This is incredible craftsmanship. The boy has real skill."

"Yeah, he is really good."

"I bet he is." Zhira grinned. Mara could tell he knew exactly where she had been.

"He's…" Mara didn't know how to share how she felt about Kei with her dad. She felt awkward and stood there until Zhira took mercy on her.

"He's a great boy, and anyone who would put this much thought and time into protecting you clearly cares about you. You have good taste."

Mara gave him a hug, thanking him.

"Now go get some sleep; tomorrow we begin the evacuation. We are going to need your help."

~~~

Zhira reached the top of the tower and sat down in the middle of the floor, stars twinkling above him. Zhira breathed slowly and methodically until he reached a meditative state. His mind focused on the events of the last few days: Rezzik organizing the townsfolk that wished to leave, Sari and Gant putting together a defense plan of Saros, Mara sneaking off to see Kei. Bess had even closed her inn earlier that day in order to remove any innocent people from the impending fight.
~~~

The stars were bright in the new moon, and Zhira could almost feel their presence as he sat perfectly still. Without any warning, Zhira's mind raced and swirled, his visions running together and coming so frequently he couldn't get a grip on one before it was replaced by another. He grabbed his head and pulled his hair as he fell over. Vision after vision flashed before his mind's eye. Zhira tried to get a handle on it and eventually, after an excruciating effort, his mind settled on one vision of the town.

His view was that of a bird's, high above the main street. The cobblestone had turned red, though Zhira couldn't identify why. His sight followed up past the town hall and looked off into the forest, in the direction of the castle. There he saw a trail of smoke coming off the horizon, a grey streak against a suddenly starry sky. The Bright One soared past him like a comet before coming crashing down on their cabin.

Zhira opened his eyes and pulled himself up to a sitting position on the floor, sweating.

"What the hell was that?" he wondered.

~~~

The next morning, Mara donned her armor and met Rezzik and Sari in the town square with Gant. Zhira began organizing those who were planning to leave. He was to take them down the cliffs and set up camp in the woods until someone came and got them. Most of the children were going, along with the elderly.
~~~

A smattering of adults had agreed to accompany Zhira to help him take care of those who couldn't take care of themselves.

"Please be careful," Gant said to his brother.

"You too, Mom will kill me if you die and I wasn't here to help," he replied with a halfhearted smile.

Zhira used a few potions to enhance his voice, his stamina, and his patience. The last one was just coffee, but it still helped. Using his amplified voice, he began to instruct the group of hideaways; Rezzik, in his bright blue tunic covered with mismatched pieces of armor, pointed at the tree line.

Three mounted knights, one of whom was obviously King Gjanion judging by the crown he was wearing in lieu of a helmet, rode into view surrounded by two dozen soldiers on foot. Mara recognized Commander Mai as one of the other riders, and the third was a likely General Long, who she had heard about through stories Bess relayed from her guests over the years. Zhira's group started to panic, but he quickly corralled them with some influential gusts of wind. They began to follow him down the main street quickly as Gant, Fiona, Sari, Keylon, Rezzik, Kei, and Mara, along with several of their neighbors, stood between the invaders and their kin. Sari was a particularly impressive sight, having spent years working on a perfectly fitted suit of metal armor, polished to a mirror-like shine.

King Gjanion rode ahead, followed quickly by his companions and ground troops behind them. They came into the square and Gjanion dismounted. Mai and

Long stayed where they were on their horses. Long was holding a silver staff with an emerald in the head. King Gjanion's full plate armor creaked and clanged as he stepped down from his horse, whose armor matched its rider's.

"Which one of you is the wizard?" he asked commandingly.

Mara stepped forward without hesitation. "I am."

"So you're the one who claims to be a wizard. Well allow me to introduce myself, I am King Gjanion, ruler of Kyros and protector of all its people."

"Not all of them," Mara said to him while looking at Commander Mai.

"I protect the people from those who wish to destroy everything my family has worked so hard to build! My grandfather, King Radion, was a hero. He took control of this kingdom for the people. I simply defend it, following his lead." Gjanion was a polished speaker; Mara had to give him credit.

"You are a tyrant, keen on controlling all that you can see and touch," Gant stated from behind Mara, his right hand engulfed in flames while his left sported a sword.

"Are you a wizard too then?" The king acknowledged Gant with a slight furrow in his brow.

"I wish, but I still have more than enough in my arsenal to take you down."

"Men," Gjanion said, motioning to his soldiers. They reacted instantly, fanning out and surrounding the square.

"This fight is not theirs," Mara said motioning to the people standing behind her. "You came for me. They have no part in this, this isn't their fight. This is about you." She took a stance indicating that she would happily take him on.

The king laughed. "You are quite naïve, but I admire your spirit." And without warning he launched a bolt of lightning directly at her.

Gjanion thought he caught Mara by surprise, but to his astonishment his bolt didn't even make it across the thirty feet between them. It was suspended in midair; Mara's eyes glowed and her hand was outstretched as if pushing the bolt back to where it came from. The lightning crackled and fizzed as it hung in the air between them. Mara's eyes stopped glowing.

Her armor was doing something she had not expected. The edges began to glow, the flecks of ruby and sapphire channeling her efforts in a way that felt almost like the armor was doing the work. She marveled as she pushed back, invigorated by this new realization that she had a medium to help her control her power. Gjanion let go of the bolt, diverting it to one side. It hit one of his soldiers, instantly frying him in his metal suit; the soldiers cried out and charged Mara. Gant yelled and the band of townsfolk that had stayed to defend Saros ran at the soldiers.

"You're stronger than I thought!" the king yelled at Mara over the clash of steel and cries of battle. He adjusted his crown and turned to Long, who remained on his horse, holding the staff. Gjanion held out his hand and the general tossed it to him.

"You're not the only one with fancy toys!" The king whirled around and thrust the staff forward, sending shards of rock at Mara from the ground around him.

The rocks reached her, but she jumped, aiding herself with wind, landing closer to the king. Her hands lit up and she began throwing blue fireballs at him, which he countered with his own. Several fireballs glanced off each other and shot through other battles being waged around them.

Mara caught a glimpse of Kei, who was swinging an axe with one hand and wielding a dagger with the other. He easily bested a soldier whose spear broke as soon as Kei's axe made contact. A wave of emotion washed over Mara; knowing Kei could handle himself was a relief but she didn't realize how much she cared until now. Kei swung his dagger, narrowly missing another man's throat. He used the momentum to quickly follow through and land a kick squarely on the man's chest. The soldier fell, and Kei knocked him out with the axe. Kei's yell of fury rose above the noise of battle.

To Mara's right, Gant and Keylon had engaged three soldiers. Gant threw fire like his daughter, but the fireballs barely left a mark on the soldiers' metal armor.

Keylon brandished a sword in each hand and overwhelmed one of the soldiers with surprising speed. Working as an efficient team, Gant ditched the fire in favor of ice, and managed to freeze the two soldiers' feet in place while Keylon came up behind them and disarmed them, leaving them frozen where they stood.

"Gant! Heads up!" Keylon yelled as she turned to face three more soldiers.

Keen on keeping them away from his daughter and reaching his brother, Gant left the frozen soldiers where they were and turned on the newcomers, engaging them with furious swings of his sword. As he fought, his mind briefly wandered to Zhira, wondering if they were safe or if there were other soldiers they had not seen. Gant surveyed the crowd for his mother, who seemed to be holding her own in tandem with Sari. Suddenly, Keylon rushed past him and brought his attention back to the matter at hand: the soldiers they could see. He charged after her.

Sari and Fiona had taken on yet more faceless invaders and were leveling them with ease. Sari swung his two handed sword like a madman, crying out in rage and taking multiple soldiers down with each swing. Fiona cleaned up behind him, going toe to toe with a soldier whose shield had been cracked by Sari's sword. Gant watched out of the corner of his eye and was stunned by his mother's agility.

Some of the other villagers were not so lucky. The highly-trained knights made their way through the square and felled several of the less experienced villagers. Those that were skilled with the weapons Sari had given them did what they could to defend those who were clearly outmatched, but numbers were not on their side. Most of the people of Saros were not fighters and had gone with Zhira to stay safe in the forest beyond.

Mai and Long remained atop their horses, observing the brawl going on before them. Gjanion had instructed them to remain at the ready as the fight began, acting as a reserve should the fight go poorly. As more cries and clashes came from the conflict around them; Mai and Long got off their horses, deciding it was time to intervene.

As the battle raged on, Mara wore the king down. She sent wave after wave of fire and managed to get him on his heels. She reached for the knife she had hidden under her back plate, the same one Mai had used in her quarrel with Reg, and launched it at the king.

Gjanion flicked his wrist and deflected the dagger off to the side, "You think a mere knife could take me down?" he laughed as he swung his staff, pulling up a slab of stone beneath Mara's feet and tripping her.

Mara took the fall and sunk into the ground, disappearing below his feet. The sapphire in the king's crown began to glow as he manifested a sphere of energy around himself, glowing a light purple, as he anticipated Mara's next move. She came up underneath him, hands covered in water to freeze his feet, but was staggered by the shield. She put her hands on the shield and channeled pure energy through her fingers, destroying the shield and retreating to a safe distance to prepare for his retaliation.

Gjanion turned and fired another bolt of lightning. Mara dodged the crackling bolt and grew thorn bushes up around the king, tripping him and ensnaring him. Acting fast, she charged him shoulder-first, and knocked the staff from his hand, which rolled away on the cobblestone to where Gant knelt.

Mara turned to see why her father was down, hoping he wasn't hurt. The king took this opportunity to get free and take a shot at Mara. He threw both hands out and hit her in the back with a large hunk of earth; part of the armor on her right arm broke off as she went tumbling.

Getting up on her knees, Mara spun around to see a purple hilt sticking out of her grandmother's side. The dagger she had thrown at the king had kept flying, hitting home between Fiona's ribs after Gjanion deflected it.

Mara screamed. A shockwave of energy exploded from her in all directions, knocking over everyone in the square. The world seemed to stop. Nothing felt real. Mara's insides burned and her mind was blank. She stared at Gant kneeling over her grandmother, his mother, with the knife Mara had thrown protruding vividly from her side. She wanted to rush over and help but knew it was too late by the look on her father's face. *If I had been paying more attention, maybe she could have saved her,* she thought. Anger welled up inside of her. She had challenged Mai, she had saved Reg, and now her grandmother was paying the price. One life for another. *I was wrong to use my powers. I am no hero.* The anger boiled over.

"It's over!" she cried out to Gjanion, tears falling from her eyes.

"What do you mean, it's over?" the king questioned her as he got to his feet, pointing his staff right at her.

"This is not their fight. Look around, you've lost soldiers, I've lost innocent people. They don't need to be subjected to this." Mara tried in vain to fight back the tears as she said everything she could to end this conflict and keep anyone else from suffering the same fate as her grandmother. She looked around and saw bodies scattered around the square; her heart broke for those families on both sides.

"What would you have me do? Leave you alone? Let you build an army to take me down? I think not," the king replied.

"No, take me with you," she said impulsively.

"What?!" Gjanion, Kei, and Gant all exclaimed simultaneously.

"Take me prisoner. You'll have me under your watch, and I can't usurp you from jail."

The king considered her proposal for a moment, then replied, "And what do you get out of this?"

"You leave my people alone. They aren't rebels, hardly anyone comes through this town. They were living a quiet life until I came along." The guilt was starting to hit her hard. Mara didn't realize she had felt so strongly. "Leave them be, and I'll go with you."

"What about your alchemist friend there?" The king pointed at Gant. "Alchemy is forbidden."

Gant spoke up from his kneeling position next to his mother. "I only do what is necessary for these people to live."

"That is no concern of mine," the king said, dismissing Gant's words with a wave.

"I go if you leave *all* of them alone," Mara said. "My father included."

As Gjanion seemed to ponder this, Mara held her breath. She could not lose her father too. "Fine," the king finally responded, "I will leave a garrison here to watch you. If as much as a whiff of alchemy is detected, your head rolls."

Gant nodded and turned back to caring for Fiona, whose gray tunic was turning dark with blood around where the knife protruded. Mara locked eyes with Kei and tried to communicate with him wordlessly, begging him to follow her. He was looking back at her like a lost puppy.

"Commander Mai, you and your men will remain here in Saros to keep watch over the alchemist," Gjanion commanded.

"Sir, I…"

"That's an order, Commander." Long said, cutting her off.

"Yes, sir. Will you have enough men to bring her back safely?"

"Yes, because if she tries anything, you'll kill the alchemist," the king replied, confident in his plan.

"And what if he tries anything?" She nodded towards Gant.

"If I don't get a weekly report from you, I'll kill the wizard. If you don't get a report from me, kill him," he replied matter-of-factly.

Gjanion tied Mara's hands behind her back and led her off to a couple of soldiers who began to escort her to the woods.

Mara turned back to see Gant shaking over his mother, weeping. She looked white as a ghost and Mara's heart broke. She would never get the chance to say a proper goodbye to the woman who helped raise her. Never again would she be her rose, and it was all her fault. Her dagger, her fight with the king, all trying to defend the people who had given her a safe home.

Kei stood dumbstruck as he watched her get led away. In a final act of solidarity, Mara tilted her head and the broken piece of armor that still lay on the ground rolled towards him.

Chapter Twelve
The Funeral

Time seemed to warp as Gant knelt beside his mother's body. He couldn't tell if hours or minutes passed, but at some point, Zhira had appeared next to him. Gant could not bring himself to look at his big brother; he wasn't sure he could handle watching Zhira's heart break.

Zhira put an arm around him; he didn't cry, which Gant found unusual.

"Are you okay?" Zhira asked him.

"Physically, yes, I'm fine. I wasn't hurt…but I'll never be okay." His eyes did not waver from their mother's lifeless body. He was afraid to look away, worried that somehow if he stopped looking at her, she would disappear forever.

Apart from the knife and blood, Fiona could have been sleeping. Keylon and Sari came up behind Gant and Zhira, placing a hand on each of their shoulders. Kei followed, then Rezzik, and eventually Litik as he returned from the cliffs where Zhira had taken most of the town to hide. Echoing the emotions of others who were discovering they had lost loved ones, Litik added his tears to the rest and put a comforting hand on Gant's shoulder. The moment seemed to last a lifetime. Eventually, Litik broke the silence.

"Fiona was a dear friend, and an all-around wonderful woman."

"I wouldn't have become the woman I am today without her," Keylon added.

"There was no purer heart in our town than hers. She was always helping others," Rezzik said.

Even Sari offered a few words. "Her legacy will live on forever."

Zhira looked up at their friends and smiled in appreciation. He stood up, looking around at them all. Struggling to come up with any words without breaking down completely, Keylon stepped forward and embraced him.

"We will help with whatever you need," Keylon said.

"We should move her," Gant finally said, still kneeling.

"I'll start digging her grave," Kei said.

"I'll join you." Litik followed the boy to get supplies from the town hall.

"We will have the burial at sunset. Please let the others know," Zhira said to Rezzik. "She'd want us to move on and take care of the town, so we will not wait. We will see to this now."

Rezzik nodded and set off to inform the residents of the tragedy, a part of his job as governor he would have loved to do without.

Mai stood at the edge of the square, unsure of how to proceed. She did not wish to be here any more than the people of Saros did; she was aware that her presence was looming over this great sadness, and wanted to be away from it all. The king had marched into Saros and attacked, almost entirely on impulse, before leaving her here alone to bear the brunt of the town's anger. She was now the face of the crown in this place, and Gant let her know it.

The alchemist got up from his knees, which were numb from kneeling for so long. He wobbled slightly, grabbing onto Sari's metal-clad shoulder until he gained his balance, and turned to face the commander.

"You," he said, eyebrows low.

"Gant…" The burly bearded blacksmith tried to stop him but Gant shrugged his hand away.

"YOU!" Gant shouted as he took powerful strides towards Mai; the soldiers who had remained behind with her started to close in and protect her.

Mai waved them off. "If you're going to blame me for your mother's death, I suggest you reconsider," she said.

Gant stopped marching towards her, standing about ten feet away. Two of her soldiers still had their spears pointed at him.

"You may as well have killed her. It's your presence here that led to all of this! Now my daughter is gone, my mother is DEAD, and I'm stuck with YOU to babysit me!" Tears welled in his eyes as he shouted.

"Gant, I really think…"

"SHUT IT, Zhira!" Gant yelled over his shoulder.

"Gant, is it? Do you think I wanted to return after your daughter bested me? I want to leave more than you want me to. I can assure you of that. But if I leave now, I will be killed," Mai explained.

"Sounds like a fair trade to me. Reg was right. You are a murderer, and you deserve to pay for the death you brought to our village," Gant snapped.

Mai's eye twitched, but she kept her composure. "I did not kill your mother. It may have been my knife, but your daughter was the one who wielded it."

That was enough for Gant, who launched himself at her. He moved so suddenly that the knights did not react in time, as he tackled Mai to the ground. They scuffled for a moment, trying to pin each other down and take swings to knock the other out until Sari came over and lifted them both off the ground by the scruffs of their tunic and armor respectively.

"ENOUGH!" he bellowed. They stopped struggling against his grip and looked at him, anger swapped for fear on their faces. "She didn' kill her,

Gant. Let it go. And as fer you…" Sari turned to Mai. "We don' want ya here, ya don' wanna be here, but yer here. If yer not, lots o' bad things happen to both sides. Get over it." Mai's face reddened with frustration as he spoke.

"Best we stop tryn' to kill each other or there won' be anyone left to protect."

It was Mai's turn to shrug off Sari. She gathered herself and set off without another word to find Rezzik and discuss housing for her and her soldiers.

"Come on, Gant. We need to prep fer yer mum's funeral." Sari put his arm around the exhausted alchemist and led him to his shop.

~~~

That evening, as the sun set in a dazzling array of colors, the people of Saros gathered at the small cemetery on the edge of town. Sari had engraved a headstone for Fiona that read:

Fiona

Pure of Heart and Mind

Mother, Friend, Angel

954-1021
~~~

Gant stood with Zhira in matching black tunics as Rezzik said a few words about their mother.

"Many of us were touched by Fiona's selflessness, her friendship, and her caring smile. Those that knew Fiona knew love, and it is our hope that the rest of us carry that on in her memory."

Zhira thanked Rezzik as they lowered her coffin into the grave that Kei and Litik had dug throughout the day. Gant placed a rose on the wooden lid as it was lowered into the earth. The brothers thanked everyone for coming and began shoveling dirt back into the ground. They insisted on doing this alone, so their friends and neighbors dispersed. As they refilled the grave, Zhira and Gant remembered their mother together, swapping memories and reminiscing about their fondest moments growing up. It was cathartic, and Zhira could see the anger lift from his brother for the first time that day. They worked well into the night, finishing their shoveling under the many twinkling stars that peppered the sky above. Gant finished packing the soil down around the headstone, and then began walking back home with his brother.

"What are we going to do about this commander?" Zhira asked, shifting the focus from their mother for the first time that day.

"I don't know. We need to do something to save Mara. Who knows how long that will last before he just decides to kill her," Gant replied.

"She does have more power than we do. Maybe she will figure it out on her own. If we try anything, Mai will just report it to the king and he'll kill her."

"Yes, but if Mara tries anything, Mai will kill us."

"Do you really think that woman can take both of us on?" Zhira asked his brother confidently as they turned off the main street and headed towards their cabin.

"No, but the last thing we want is more fighting here in Saros. If she knows she can't take us on, she will use our concern for our friends and neighbors to keep us in check," Gant said.

Zhira nodded. "Okay, so we need to come up with a plan that keeps the king from being alerted by Mai. What do we do?"

"Well, thanks to some talkative guards at Bess's, we know that Gjanion's forces finally defeated the rebellion in the west and are soon going to move east."

"And?"

"If they've taken the rest of the kingdom, and are headed east, where would the rest of the rebellion be?"

Zhira caught on to his brother's idea. "East, but if Gjanion's forces keep winning, what makes you think the rebellion is going to be strong enough to help?"

"Can you think of a better plan?"

Zhira shook his head. "No. You're right, we need help and they're the only ones who *might* have enough information to do so."

Gant nodded in agreement. "Then I think it's time we found the rebellion."

~~~

Mara sat staring into the fire while the soldiers sat and ate their rations and Gjanion discussed plans with his general over a map. The image of her grandmother lying motionless on the ground burned into her mind. Grief and pain washed over her in waves as she sat wishing she was back home, where she could be alone. Mixed in with the sadness she felt was a feeling of guilt that stung; it was her fault Fiona was dead. If she hadn't challenged Mai that day, and if she hadn't saved Reg, the king wouldn't have brought his troops back to challenge her. Additionally, it was the dagger she had thrown that had killed her grandmother. Her courage had saved a life but cost another.

Mara was distracted from her sorrow momentarily when she heard an unfamiliar noise in the trees off to their left. None of the others around her seemed to have noticed the sound, so she made no indication that she had either, choosing to sit still and listen for it again. Growing up in the woods, she was familiar with how the animals moved, how they called to each other, and the sounds that they made; what she had just heard was foreign to her ears.

For a second time, she heard it: a noise like a large animal moving from tree to tree in the canopy, but with a call that sounded like a bird, but wrong
~~~

somehow. Suddenly, from the opposite direction of the sounds, several brown and black striped tigerdeer burst from the trees, startled by a sudden *crack*. Running at full speed, they took the knights sitting around the campfire by complete surprise.

In the confusion, several men came tearing from the trees on all sides, using the frantic deer as cover from any retaliation the king and his protectors might put up. General Long was on his feet before the rest of the soldiers, thought they were not far behind the grey-haired general. The king grabbed his staff and ran straight for Mara.

"You'd better help protect us! If Mai doesn't hear from me, it's your father's head." He undid her binds without giving Mara time to consider, and turned to face the assailants.

Mara's head was spinning. Everything was happening around her so fast; her grieving mind could not process it. The king had just released her, and already the rebels had used bows to pick off some of the panicked soldiers. Several knights fell, giving the assailants a more manageable fight. Adrenaline was not enough to help her keep up with the attack; Mara could feel the exhaustion from earlier that day finally setting in. The first rebel to reach them took on the nearest two soldiers, utilizing his speed and taking advantage of the blind spots of their helmets. Before Mara knew what was happening, the knights fell to the ground, one without a head, and the man charged the king. Mara realized that she needed to do something or Gant and the rest of Saros were in trouble.

Acting mostly on reflex, she lifted her right hand and sent the man flying. The king turned and smiled a horrible smile that was distorted in the firelight; it made Mara sick. She hated helping him, but she had no other choice. She had saved the rebel man's life for the time being and had to figure out a way to save the others. She turned to face the ambush with Long and the remaining soldiers, intending to help them to dissipate the attack. Before her dazed mind could formulate a plan however, she saw firsthand the devastating abilities of the grizzled general.

Mercilessly, Long cut down three men on his own with a flurry of attacks and parries that she could barely follow, while the remaining six soldiers took care of another two ambushers without help from Mara. The king finished off the last man with a bolt of lightning from his staff, which Mara was beginning to recognize as his go-to choice of attack. The fight was over as quickly as it had started.

Mara looked around and located the man she had blown over earlier. He was staring right at her. He had fallen into the shadows beyond their campsite and gone unnoticed by the knights. *Run*, Mara mouthed at him. The man nodded and melted into the shadows between the trees, as silent as a ghost.

Turning back to their campsite, she watched as the knights began disposing of the bodies. Mara understood that these men she was traveling with were not to be messed with, which dashed any remaining hopes of overpowering them or escaping. Without help, taking on Gjanion and his entourage was a fool's errand; simply thinking about it was exhausting.

Gjanion turned to Mara. "Thank you for your assistance. Mara, was it?"

"Yes," she replied shortly.

"Well, Mara, I hope you know how much I appreciate you keeping me safe! I will make sure you get the comfiest cell in the dungeon."

Long gave an amused snort from behind him.

~~~

The sun had long set and Kei was exhausted: first fighting the King's Guard, then mourning Fiona, and now circling back to the realization that Mara was gone. He paced around the square and his shadow followed, weaving in and out amongst the torchlight.

As he traced his path around the square, his eyes caught something glinting under the remains of a bush that had been burned by a stray fireball. He bent down and found the right hand of Mara's armor, the purple amethyst catching the light of the torches.

Kei stared at it for a moment until suddenly he realized what Mara had been trying to communicate to him after the battle with the king. He rushed back to the forge, ran up to his family's living space, and hastily wrote a note. After he pinned it to the table with a knife, Kei packed his knapsack and set out into the woods in the same direction that the king had taken Mara.
~~~

Chapter Thirteen
New Alliances

The presence of Mai and her small garrison of knights had everyone in Saros on edge. In the days that followed the funeral, the atmosphere was subdued; nobody knew what to expect from the commander and her force. People kept to themselves, ducked into the nearest shop at the first sign of a knight, and did not speak of Mara. Mai sent her first report off to the king by raven, and received one from him as well stating he had reached the castle and that they had been assaulted by rebels along the way. Knowing there was no way the people of Saros could have organized the attack so quickly—their return route had been a secret—and quoting Mara's 'eagerness' to help keep him safe, King Gjanion ordered Mai not to take action.

Frustrated and bored, Mai decided to bring this information to Gant. She was eager to pick a fight, frustration at being left behind starting to boil over. She needed to blow off steam.

"So your daughter seems to have warmed up to the king rather quickly."

The ruthless commander sat down next to Gant in Bess's inn, who appeared to have been there a while, judging by his disheveled appearance and slumped posture.

"She'd never join your side," Gant said with a hiccup.

"It appears she has." Mai slid the letter over to him and watched as his eyes traced the lines of smooth slanted handwriting she knew so well.

"He's lying. Mara would never help him unless her life depended on it. He forced her to act," Gant said, unfazed by her attempt to egg him on. He shoved the paper back at Mai and beckoned Bess over to ask for another beer. The stocky, white-haired innkeeper topped off the mug and Mai watched Gant open his flask and add something to it.

"What's in there?" she asked him, suspecting a potion of some kind.

"The beer isn't strong enough," Gant sighed. "Here, want some?" He held out the flask.

Mai waved it away and returned to their conversation. "Maybe Mara has realized that the winning side is the right side to be on. Maybe she wants to *live*." Mai made sure that last word hit him hard, and she saw in his eyes that it did.

"I won't let you provoke me," Gant said, taking a rather large drink from his mug.

"You know Gant, I feel bad for you. You've been through so much. Losing your mother is such a dreadful reality. You're handling it…quite well, considering." She watched his face for any sign of retaliation.

"All I had left was Zhira, and he disappeared," Gant said dejectedly, surprising Mai with such a tame response.

"Zhira?" Mai was unfamiliar with the name. She couldn't match a face to it, but she vaguely remembered Gant yelling at someone during their scuffle the first day. It was all a blur.

"My brother," Gant replied. "Don't worry, he isn't an alchemist. He just likes to stare at the stars. Thinks they mean things or some nonsense like that." Gant took another swig.

What a boring little town. Do they really have nothing better to do here than look at the sky? Mai thought. The last week had been rough. Everyone was tense around her and her knights; nobody even glanced at them when they walked by. Mai didn't care that the people who lived here disliked her and her knights, but her knights were not as cold. Most of them were recruits from the dungeons, or youths who had no other aspirations, dropped off by their guardians when they came of age to be trained. During their campaign in the west, Mai had learned that decent living conditions went a long way towards troop morale, and that included getting along with the locals when they were stationed somewhere for an extended period of time. As Gant finished speaking, an idea popped into Mai's head: a way to make living in Saros slightly more agreeable for her team and as a result, herself.

"Perhaps as a show of good will between us, I can send out a scouting party to go look for him?" Mai offered, her desire to pick a fight fading as she saw an opportunity.

Gant looked at her suspiciously. "You'd do that?"

"It's the least I can do. I realize my presence here is nothing short of uncomfortable for the citizens of this town…it certainly is for my knights. Maybe a show of good faith could help?"

"Good faith? You brought your king here to kill my daughter. I don't want to hear about 'good faith' from you."

Mai sighed. "I told you before, I don't want to be here. Neither do my men. But we can't leave. I'm trying to do what I can in order to make this situation…tolerable."

"That's not my problem, and I won't risk my brother's life so you can be marginally more comfortable here. I know what will happen. You'll send your men to 'look for him', then some 'accident' will happen, and you'll bring me back another body to bury." Gant lifted the mug to his mouth and drained the remainder of its contents. He waved Bess over again.

Mai stared at him, frustrated. *He's right to think that way. I don't have a leg to stand on.*

"Have it your way, then. Let your brother be lost." Mai stood up and stormed toward the door of the inn. When she reached it, she paused and looked back at Gant. "You know, I am stuck here with you as much as you're stuck with me. When you're ready to coexist, let me know."

Gant looked up at Mai. "When you're ready to not murder the rest of my family, you let me know."

"Thaaaat'll never happen," Reg slurred from the table behind them, punctuating his statement with a burp.

Mai stood with her hand on the doorknob, ready to walk out of the inn. *He won't come around. I have to earn this, just like I earned everything else.* She turned the handle and stepped out into the afternoon light.

~~~

"That was too close," Gant said as soon as Mai left the inn.

"What was, dear?" Bess asked, topping his mug off yet again.

"I was just trying to get Mai to leave me alone. I figured a drunk man, grieving the loss of his entire family, would come off as no threat to her. Getting Mai to back off would allow me to do some alchemy again. She's been watching me like a hawk, even at the cabin. She has knights stationed there constantly."
~~~

"You didn't expect her to offer to help, did you?" Bess asked him.

"No, I most certainly did not," Gant replied, pouring more of his sobering potion into the mug. Normally reserved for particularly bad hangovers, the potion mitigated the effects of alcohol on the body. Gant had decided to use the potion in a slightly different way. By adding it to his ale, he could drink as much as he wanted without getting drunk. That way, there was nothing to tip Mai off to the fact that he was faking it; the ale smelled and tasted like ale, should she ever want to check.

"Well lucky for you, the issue seems resolved," Bess said, as she went to clean up Reg's mess. Reg himself was passed out on the table.

"Let's hope," said Gant. Only he knew where Zhira really went, and it was imperative that Mai did not follow.

~~~

Rain ran down Kei's face as he trudged through the mud, tracking a trail of hoof marks and footprints mixed together that could only belong to King Gjanion's entourage escorting Mara back to the castle. The tracks had become easy to follow since it started raining; Kei had picked up the trail at a campsite that had not been far from Saros. It had appeared to be the site of a gruesome fight, though he couldn't find any bodies, only blood.
~~~

Kei's foot got stuck in a deep patch of mud and as he bent down to free himself, someone ran into him at full speed. Kei fell over, his boot remaining stuck in the mud pit as he went flying; the body that hit him fell the opposite way.

"Zhira?" Kei sat up to find the alchemist lying next to him under the canopy of trees.

"Kei?" Zhira asked, surprised.

"What are you doing out here?" Kei asked him.

"You didn't think Gant and I would just sit idly by while Gjanion took Mara to the castle, did you?" Zhira smiled slyly. "I am looking for the rebellion. What are you doing out here? Why are you not back in Saros?"

"Same as you, I guess. I couldn't do nothing!" Kei exclaimed as he got up and tried to wipe the mud off of his pants and tunic.

Zhira assisted by drawing some of the moisture out of Kei's clothes. "Your parents raised you well to be so loyal and caring. Won't they be worried about you, by the way?"

"I left them a note so they know where I've gone and don't draw attention to my being away. My father will burn it as soon as he reads it. No paper trail."

"Smart. Gant knows where I am and what I'm doing. It was his idea actually."

The two unlikely companions resumed tracking the king's trail. Zhira took the lead for a bit while Kei kept an eye on their surroundings and covered their tracks as they went. Travelling as a pair, they made much better time with Kei tracking and Zhira providing alchemical awareness and speed. Before long, they managed to find a camp that looked to be fairly fresh.

"We aren't far off. They can't be making much better time than we are. Most of their men are on foot."

"Wait…this is still warm," Kei said as he touched a small pile of cinders. He instinctively ducked down into the ferns and looked along the relatively open horizon. The rain impeded their ability to see clearly in the distance, but Kei could feel the presence of someone else close-by.

"What happens when we find them?" Zhira asked in a much lower voice as they crept cautiously along the tree-spotted moor.

"I…don't know. Hopefully Mara will be able to help us…" Kei replied.

"Shh! I hear something." Zhira put a finger to his lips and he and Kei stood back to back underneath a tree, surveying the land around them.

"Hey, up here!" A voice came from above them. They both looked up to find a wiry disheveled man hiding amongst the leaves.

"What the…" Kei trailed off as he realized what he was seeing.

"Who are you? What are you doing up there?" Zhira asked.

"Please, don't hurt me!" The man looked at Kei, who held his axe menacingly.

"Who are you?" Zhira repeated his question.

"I'm a friend. I assume you're tracking the king as well?" the man asked as he began to climb down from his perch above them.

Kei put down his axe. "Yeah, what's it to you?"

"I'm Forbin. I couldn't help but overhear that you're seeking out the rebellion. Well, I'm with the rebellion! My team was charged with ambushing the king. We took out a good number of his knights, but we were no match for them."

Zhira and Kei regarded the man as he stood up between them. He was scrawny but seemed strong for his size. He was shorter than Zhira and Kei and wore brown clothes that blended well with the trees.

"Where did you come from?" Zhira asked.

"Our base is not too far from here. It's not much, just an outpost we use to relay information to other groups further east."

"Can you take me there?" Zhira asked Forbin.

"What?!" Kei stared at Zhira in disbelief. "Your daughter was taken by the king, who we are currently tracking, and you just want to jump ship and go fight with the resistance?"

"Kei, please."

"Your daughter? Why would they take a hostage…" Something clicked in Forbin's head. "It was her!" he exclaimed, confusing both Kei and Zhira.

"What are you talking about?" Kei asked.

"They had a woman with them I hadn't seen before. At first I thought it was the princess, but I couldn't be sure; there were lots of shadows, see. She saved me. The rest of my men were slaughtered but she pushed me out of the way…without touching me."

"This is good. Kei, you need to go and locate Mara if you can. At the very least, you'll get us a man on the inside so we know where to go when the time is right," Zhira said, before turning to Forbin. "I'm assuming you all have contacts in the capital?"

Forbin nodded. "We can find you, don't worry," he said to Kei.

"And you're going to…?" Kei asked Zhira, a disapproving expression on his face.

"Help. The rebellion may be our only shot. The king took her to the castle, which we know nothing about. Its defenses, its layout, nothing. We need information, and in exchange we can provide hope. We can give them Mara to rally around," said Zhira.

"Who's Mara?" Forbin asked.

"My daughter, the wizard," Zhira replied.

"A wizard?! A real wizard?! I thought only the royal…"

"Yeah, the royal family are supposed to be the last wizards, we got it," Kei said, taking his annoyance at Zhira out on the innocent man. "Sorry." Kei added after a moment.

"Ah, it's all right. Quite a stressful situation you've got here!"

"Kei, go. I'll find you," Zhira said.

"How?"

"Presumably, this man here has a way of getting information from the capital. I'll follow those channels. You'll know when it's me. Oh, and Kei?" Zhira asked him, a sudden change in his tone catching him off guard.

"Yeah?"

"If things don't go as we hope, give this to Mara." Zhira pulled a red book out of his bag.

"What is it?" Kei asked as he took the book from him.

"Her notes from stargazing with me, but I wrote her something in case…" Zhira trailed off, Kei understanding what he meant.

Zhira turned to Forbin. "Now, about this outpost of yours."

~~~

General Long sat at a table with commanders Tren and Hearth, going over their report from watching over the castle during the king's excursion to Saros.

"All was quiet, no signs of resistance, and the princess was safe the whole time. We had guards watching her constantly," Tren summed up confidently.

"We managed to step up security without anyone really noticing…or if they did, they didn't say anything," Hearth added from his seat beside Tren.
~~~

"Good. I'm glad all went smoothly here." Long had already briefed them on the events of Saros and their eventful return trip. "I just don't understand how they knew we were coming. Nobody saw us leave, we met nobody on the road, yet they had an ambush in place in a matter of days!" The general brought the conversation back to their stressful ride home.

"Sir, perhaps one of the knights that went with you was a spy," Hearth suggested.

"They wouldn't have had time to give a signal to the rebels…unless they have a hideout nearby that our scouts haven't discovered," Long considered.

"Sir, I think in order to get an ambush in the proper place, they would have needed to tail you for a while. They couldn't have known which way you were going back, we chose a route that was different from the one you took to get there specifically to add another layer of protection in keeping the king safe. If they knew where you were going to be, then that comes from much higher up," Tren said.

Long looked across at both of them. "What you are suggesting is that the rebellion was tipped off before we even left for Saros, and found us before we reached that dismal little town?"

Tren nodded, seemingly afraid to put his thoughts into words. Hearth, however, was not as fearful.

"Commander Mai did have the advantage of scouting the area on her way back the first time. It is possible she influenced the plans to better accommodate an attack."

Long stared at the heavyset man. What he had said made sense, and Long hated it. First his failure surrounding Mara's survival had been revealed, and now here they were, discussing the possibility of his hand-picked second in command being the main rebel informant in their ranks. Panic began to creep in, but he held it at bay, quickly drumming up a plan to keep this under wraps from Gjanion.

"You have a valid point. I shall put our spies to the task of discovering hard evidence. If we can disrupt the rebellion's chain of communication, it may be possible to expedite our impending victory. Though I must say, I truly hope you are wrong. No part of me wants to believe that Mai is the spy, but this possibility cannot be dismissed. I myself will report this to the king. Speak nothing of this to anyone, including Gjanion. You are dismissed," Long said, giving them no time to cut in.

The commanders stood, bowed, and left the room, leaving Long to consider his next move. The wizard girl's existence alone constituted one too many mistakes on his part, and now this? He couldn't bear to think of what the king's reaction would be if he found out that Long's top commander was the one who was feeding information to the rebellion. On the other hand, it would clear his name to the king. Outing Mai as the spy would eliminate the doubt that surely still existed in the king's mind that he himself was the rebel informant.

On two pieces of parchment, he wrote the same note, stamped them with his seal, and called in a squire to chase down the two commanders he had just dismissed.

~~~

"Hello?"

Mara stirred at the sound of the voice, which was unexpectedly calm and comforting in contrast to the small and gloomy cell she currently occupied. "Who's there?" Mara asked.

"I'm Princess Rylan," a girl stated formally, stepping into view. Mara noticed she was cradling a flame in her left hand. "I am the daughter of King Gjanion, the last wizard."

"Well that's some nonsense," Mara said sharply.

"I beg your pardon?" Rylan gasped, taken aback by Mara's attitude.

"Oh, sorry, I'm just sitting in a pitch black cell with no windows and only rats to keep me company. Where are my manners! I'm Mara, welcome to my beautiful home…" Mara waved her arm sarcastically around at the cell while giving Rylan a blank stare.

"There's no need to be rude."

"There's no need to be wrong," Mara shot back.

"Wrong?" Rylan asked, confused.

"He isn't the last wizard, otherwise I wouldn't be here." Mara was already tired of this girl.
~~~

"Oh…well, yes I suppose that's true," Rylan responded.

"Uh huh." Mara stared at the girl. She was quite pretty, her long pink dress and cloak went well with her golden eyes and hair that fell down her shoulders in curls. Mara could tell that this girl was taller than she was, even from her seated position on the stone floor.

"Anyways, I was wondering if I could ask you something. When did you get your powers?" Rylan asked nervously.

"I…what?" Mara was confused by the question. As long as she had been alive, she had known magic.

"Oh, well, see my powers haven't exactly…shown up yet."

"They haven't…wait. So you think you're a wizard too, but you can't do magic?" Mara's curiosity overpowered her annoyance. Apart from the king, she had never met another wizard. Nobody had ever taught her about who she was, and the king didn't seem a likely teacher. The sudden possibility of having another source of information was overwhelmingly enticing. Mara had the urge to befriend the girl that stood before her, if only to learn more about herself.

"Yes, I guess I'm a late bloomer." The princess gave a half-hearted smile.

"I'm sorry, I can't be of help. I was orphaned so I don't know anything about myself other than what I've figured out on my own."

"That's so sad! Did anyone raise you?" Rylan showed genuine concern for Mara, which confused her.

She was the daughter of the king, why wasn't she like him?

"My dads," Mara replied. She was fine revealing things about herself, but was hesitant to give away anything about her family. She still wanted to protect them at all costs.

"Dads?" Rylan tilted her head slightly, like a puppy. Mara found it surprisingly endearing.

"They're brothers actually…"

"Isn't that forbidden?!" Rylan was shocked.

"No, no, no!" Mara laughed; it felt good to laugh after everything she had been through in the last week. "They found me in the woods and decided to raise me together! That's all. They're not married or anything."

"Oh, okay." Rylan's shoulders relaxed.

"So, what do you know about wizards?" Mara asked the princess as she stood there, features outlined in the firelight.

She doesn't seem harmful, just curious and a little desperate. Mara thought, observing Rylan's body language. This girl seemed honest, genuine, and not at all like the man she had dueled a week prior in Saros's town square.

"Not much. I know my grandfather was one, and he got rid of the rest, fought the bad ones. That's why we thought we were the only ones left. My father told me that before his powers had appeared, he used potions to compensate, which is what I do now!"

Mara recognized alchemy when she saw it. *At least I know she isn't a liar.* Having grown up around two alchemists, the differences between real magic and alchemy were obvious to her. Everything an alchemist did was an attempted mirror of some kind of magic. It technically worked, but something seemed off and slightly fake once one knew what the real thing looked like. Mara stared at Rylan. Maybe alchemy was a common temporary solution; maybe not all wizards were like her from birth and their powers took time to develop. *How would I know?* Mara thought, keen to hear what Rylan had to say.

"He also told me that my powers should come in by my twenty-first birthday, which is tomorrow!"

"Let me guess, there is going to be a big party?" Mara rolled her eyes.

"Yes, but I don't care about that at all. I'll finally be old enough to make my own decisions… go where I please when I want to, it will be wonderful. I don't have to spend another minute cooped up in this…" Rylan went silent as she stared at Mara.

"What? What is it?" Mara shifted uncomfortably as the princess's golden eyes locked with her own.

"Your eyes…they're blue!" Rylan exclaimed.

"So?" Mara did not understand her excitement.

"My father told me that only animals can have blue eyes! I've never met someone with blue eyes before. Mine are golden brown." The princess turned the firelight so that Mara could confirm, but Mara had already noticed.

"Oh…well congratulations, now you have!" Mara replied, realizing that she never really paid attention to other peoples' eyes before.

Rylan looked puzzled. "I had better get going, plenty to do before tomorrow's festivities! It was nice to meet you!"

"You too," Mara said reflexively. She watched the firelight fade along the stone walls, reducing her cell back to its natural state of darkness.

Chapter Fourteen
The God of Power

"Isn't it all so exciting?" Stella clapped her hands together in delight as the seamstress finished hemming Rylan's dress.

Rylan was indeed excited, but it was for every reason her stepmother was not. She couldn't wait to see the library, available only to the of-age royal family and senior advisors. Rylan's conversation with Mara the previous night had left her itching to do more research on wizards, and the library was the perfect place. Her father knew so much, and she wanted to be just as smart; finding a way to unlock her powers wouldn't be a bad thing either. Additionally, she could hardly contain her excitement at being able to ride whenever she wanted; Neela would be so happy.

"Yes, it's such a special day. I look forward to everything it has to offer," Rylan responded formally.

"Now now, you could stand to show a bit more excitement! It's a grand day! There will be loads of presents, an amazing party, and on top of that, you'll get to make your first official decree!"

Rylan thought her stepmother's enthusiasm was a bit much, but smiled to herself at the thought of her first official pronouncement. Most of the time, a royal family member's first act was ceremonial, ordaining some small change that makes no real impact. Rylan hoped that her decree of a new training pasture outside the castle walls for the royal mounted knights would go over well, even though it was entirely self-serving. She just wanted a space to ride whenever she pleased.

Rylan looked up at the full-length mirror and smiled. She thought she looked quite pretty in her flowing blue gown, her silver tiara sat nestled amongst her blonde curls. With the help of the seamstress, he stepped down from the dais, hemming done. The elderly woman bowed and exited, leaving Rylan alone with her stepmother.

"Your father wanted to see you before the festivities began. Apparently he has something special for you." Stella's dress was cut cleverly to hide her growing belly, which began to show quickly on her wiry frame.

"Where can I find him?" Rylan asked.

"I believe he said to meet him in his study," she said.

Rylan thanked her and left, traversing many hallways and flights of stairs until she arrived at the study, the contents of which she had helped keep secret all these years. She buzzed with excitement as she knocked; her father's deep voice came through the door, telling her to enter. The curtains were pulled back to allow the bright sunlight free passage between the windows. Small dust particles floated in and out of the beams and the king's table remained covered with the same tapestry that covered it from the first day she had walked in twelve years ago.

"Happy birthday, my princess!" Gjanion exclaimed as he embraced his daughter. "Your dress looks absolutely stunning."

Rylan grinned and gave a twirl to show it off.

"I have something for you," her father said as he handed her a tattered green book.

She examined the old tattered cover. "What is it?"

"This is the entire history of our family. One of our ancestors started it long ago. Now that you are of age, it is time you knew the whole truth." Gjanion looked down at his daughter. He was taking a risk by telling her, but if anything happened to him, there would be nobody left who knew the secret. After Geralith died, Gjanion had decided that it should stay in the family.

"What do you mean?" Rylan looked at him inquisitively.

"I mean…that I am not a wizard, Ry."

Rylan was stunned, her mouth agape as she struggled to find the words she was looking for. Her conversation with Mara the previous night lingered in the back of her mind.

"Not a…you're…how could…" Rylan faltered until finally she formed a question. "Does that mean I'm not one either?"

"Unfortunately," Gjanion said, sympathetically.

"I…I don't understand." Rylan looked at the book.

"Our family is actually much more than wizards, Ry. So much more." His chest puffed up a little as he heralded this revelation to his daughter.

"What?" she asked, her sadness held at bay by the promise of something better.

"Our family is blessed with the lineage of a god. That book contains proof that we belong to a very noble family…descendants of Knorr, the god of power!" Gjanion said triumphantly.

"How is that possible?"

"Well, long ago, the goddesses Dazel and Eres banished Knorr for abusing his powers. You may recall the "Broken Planet" fable from your youth; that fable is based on this story. Knorr drove the humans to desire his power and in the process, they began killing each other and destroying the world that the three gods had created for them. Dazel and Eres enslaved him to a life of no magic, doomed to be reincarnated forever in a mundane, magicless existence."

Rylan stared at him, then at the book. How could this be possible? She was a god with no powers? Her father seemed to be reading her mind.

"There are ways of tapping into our former power as a god. My grandfather found three magical relics which helped him take back the throne all those years ago. He drew power from them, and they granted special control over certain kinds of magic. The staff controls elemental magic and the crown imbues magical strength. There is also a sword, but it has eluded me. According to Radion's notes, when I combine the sword with the staff and crown, they will allow me to control all forms of magic."

Rylan took in everything her father had said, hardly blinking as she watched her father animatedly tell what he knew. His enthusiasm was palpable, and she was excited to learn about what she could do.

"Wow…so how do I unlock my powers? Use the relics?" she asked eagerly.

"Actually…" the king's voice dropped its excited tone in favor of a more somber one. "I am reincarnated from my grandfather, Radion. Once I die, I will be reincarnated…as your son. The cycle skips a generation every time, and we are always reincarnated as men. I do not know why. You are not a god."

Rylan felt a numbness creep over her. Today was supposed to be the day she became what she always wanted to be: a wizard. Now, she would never be more than what she was now. A powerless princess of a warring kingdom. Rylan tried her best to keep her face from betraying her true emotions, but it was a pointless attempt.

"So Stella…" Rylan started to say as she began to comprehend this life-changing information.

"Is an insurance policy. If something were to happen to you, I have no more children to carry on this cycle," Gjanion said, finishing his daughter's thought for her.

Rylan felt an odd sense of satisfaction amidst the heartbreak of losing out on her dream *At least Stella has a purpose besides replacing mom.* She began to process all of the new information her father had shared. The silence that followed lasted for several minutes as she contemplated each piece of this revelation. She wasn't a wizard and never would be, and her father would reincarnate as her son: a banished god with no powers.

Finally, her father broke the silence. "Ry, I need you. When I die, I won't remember any of this. I'm entrusting you to reteach me everything so that this legacy can live on, so that we can find a way to return me to the power of the gods. Starting from the beginning each time will ensure we never make progress."

Rylan understood what he was asking, but it didn't make the blow of her biggest hope being crushed any less painful. Still, at least he was at least being honest with her.

No he wasn't. He lied to me for my entire life.

Rylan turned away from him and ran out of the study, making straight for the stables.

<div align="center">~~~</div>

Kei stared at the large iron gate that led into the castle. *How am I going to get in?* He had been milling around the town outside the castle for the entire day. The day before, Kei had watched as the king had marched Mara through the gates and up into the castle, which he assumed housed the dungeons below its magnificent towers.

From his hidden spot in an alley behind a cart laden with cabbage, he observed the comings and goings of those with access to the castle. He watched as several shipments of supplies were brought in through the course of the day. Guard patrols came in and their replacements went out. On one occasion, a man that looked like a doctor arrived at the gate and flashed a large piece of parchment that Kei assumed could only be a summons. *Not going to get my hands on one of those,* he thought.

As the sun began to set, Kei turned back into the alley and began to look for a place to hunker down for the night. The stars began to dot the sky above the castle looming over the town. There were plenty of townsfolk who spent their nights in the back alleys and streets, nobody would notice one more street urchin. As he passed a tannery, he tripped on a gap in the stone that paved the road and his knapsack fell to his side dumping its contents. Among them was the book he was to give to Mara as well as the piece of her armor he had picked up back in Saros before chasing after her. The amethyst sparkled in the setting sun's light and gave Kei an idea.

It was probable, he thought, that she no longer had her armor. It would likely be taken from her and either destroyed or fashioned into armor for the king himself. Kei had no idea that her magic would have an effect on the armor he had made; but he was sure the king had taken notice of that as well.

Kei had watched the edges glow as she performed stronger and stronger magical feats, and realized that it was probably the flecks of ruby and sapphire that were reacting. Maybe she was drawing power from the precious gems. *Maybe they were a catalyst for stronger magic,* he thought. He could tell they were useful, so he decided to have another go at it.

Scanning the markets, he searched for a forge. All he had was the amethyst, which was far more common than the tiny gems he had used for the armor to make it look so dazzling. He rolled the stone between his fingers as he walked down another street, and saw a blacksmith's forge that had been boarded up for the night.

Kei snuck into the alley behind it and broke in through a window that led to a storage room. He shut the window behind him, closing off the last bit of sunlight that was still streaking the purple sky with orange. His eyes adjusted to the small amount of light coming from the smoldering coals still glowing a soft red in the forge. Waiting until he was sure that the blacksmith who likely took residence above was either asleep or gone, Kei scanned the room looking for something he could make a new weapon with. There were half-beaten shields, boots far too big for him or Mara, and loads of scrap metal.

Suddenly, Kei had a stroke of inspiration, based on something Mara had said to him about his first surprise.

"Is it a weapon?" she had asked. "My hands feel rather…naked when I do the things that I do."

He scoured the place looking for something that he didn't have to forge or hammer, nothing that could wake a sleeping blacksmith. Carefully, he rummaged through the scrap metal until he found the perfect thing: an unfinished dagger with no guard and a polished wooden handle with a metal loop on the end of it, presumably to tie to a belt or saddle. He removed the unsharpened weapon and held it up to the amethyst. It was a perfect fit.

~~~

"You want us to do what?" Casby, one of the knights under Mai's command, asked incredulously.

"I want you to find the alchemist's brother. The longer you stand here, the longer it is going to take you. Now move!" Mai said with authority.

Casby nodded and hurriedly left for the stable where Mai had arranged for their horses to be kept. As Casby left, followed by two other knights, Mai sat down in the closest chair. Rezzik, the governor of this small town, had offered them the east wing of his home,
~~~

which had been converted into a town hall. The wing had four rooms, three of which were sleeping quarters and one of which Mai had designated as the soldiers' common area. Mai had one of the rooms to herself and split her knights up between the other two.

Now, sitting alone in her quarters, Mai sat and pondered her decision. Her time here was becoming increasingly miserable. *I am the second in command of an army, how did I get relegated to babysitting?* Mai's anger flared as she thought about how Long had done nothing to convince Gjanion that this assignment was a waste of her talents. *Get a grip,* she thought to herself. *Long would never question the king, and neither would you.*

Loyalty and devotion to the king had gotten her to where she was, and she knew the same went for the general. Mai relaxed and turned to look out the window. She watched Casby and his team march down the street. *Hopefully they'll bring back Zhira and things here will get a little bit easier,* she thought as Casby rounded the corner and disappeared.

Chapter Fifteen
The Rebellion

Commander Hearth handed a scroll to General Long. "Sir, I think I may have some idea as to how Mai was able to set an ambush so quickly. Saros may not be the innocent little town we all thought it was."

Long opened the scroll, unfurling a map that had Saros clearly marked. To the west and slightly north was another marked location in the middle of the moors.

"What is this?" Long asked.

"It's a hidden outpost, or a base of some kind. An easy location for Mai to set up support from." Commander Hearth watched Long's eyes trace over the map again, then added, "After the attack, I had some of my scouts search the surrounding area. This is what they found."

"Excellent work, Commander. Should this all prove true, Mai's position as second in command will need filling," Long said.

"It would be an honor, sir." Hearth gave a slight bow over his barrel of a stomach.

"I need fast riders. We need to act on this immediately. The longer we wait the less chance we have of catching them."

"I'll get Commander Tren." Hearth slapped his stomach with both hands and laughed. He knew he wasn't built for such a mission.

Not an hour later, General Long led Commander Tren and two other knights out of the stable in the direction of the location on Hearth's map. They rode fast, wearing light armor made from leather to help ease the load on the horses.

When the small squad arrived at the location marked on their map, they tied up their horses and began to search for the hidden entrance that Commander Hearth's spy had reported. The moors were fairly empty, with boulders of various sizes strewn about and the occasional unimpressive tree broke up the otherwise flat terrain. The grass waved lightly in the breeze, giving the illusion of a green sea rolling beneath their feet. Long paired up with one of the knights while Tren took the other, each team beginning their search in opposite directions.

It didn't take much time before General Long's partner signaled for him near two large boulders. Long walked over and the knight put his finger to his lips; ever so lightly, he tapped his finger on one boulder, then the other. By the sound the second boulder made, Long knew it was no rock, but instead a fake made of wood and parchment; the general could hear a faint echo when the knight tapped it.

Long waved Tren and the other knight over and the four men surrounded the boulder. On Long's silent count, the knight who had discovered the fake boulder threw it back and jumped into the exposed hole, sword drawn. Long jumped in after him, followed by Tren and the last knight. It was nothing but a small room with a table, some provisions, and a cage that contained two messenger pigeons. *An outpost. Hearth was right.*

Long took one of the two pigeons from the cage, turned to Tren, and gave him a simple command.

"Follow it."

Tren nodded and took the bird from the general. His leather armor made climbing out of the hole one handed fairly easy, and he made his way back to the horses where he released the pigeon and took off after it. The other two knights remained with Long in the outpost.

"We are going to wait for the rebels to return, and I want you to kill all but one," he said to the men, who sat down in two of the three chairs that surrounded the lone table.

Time to see which side our dear Commander Mai is loyal to, Long thought as he absentmindedly fiddled with the visor on his leather helmet.

~~~
~~~

Forbin had promised that the outpost was close, but after two days, Zhira was questioning what the word 'close' meant to the man. Zhira wasn't sure about Forbin yet; annoying, naive, and energetic, he had a curiosity that never seemed to be satisfied. All that aside, Zhira appreciated what the rebel was doing for him, so he tolerated it.

Most of their first day together had been spent quietly traversing the thinning trees. The next morning however, Forbin had begun inundating Zhira with question after question.

"How did Mara get her powers?"

"I don't know. My brother and I adopted her."

"Is she related to the king? He *is* supposed to be the last wizard…"

"I don't know. We found her abandoned in the woods."

"Do you think the king is worried that another wizard exists? Do you think there are more?"

"I imagine he is quite worried, seeing as he took my daughter. As for other wizards, I have no idea."

This went on for some time. Zhira wished he hadn't sent Kei to the capital; at least he would have had some company to suffer through this interrogation with.

"So I have to ask, how did you plan on finding us if we hadn't run into each other?" Forbin asked.

"Honestly, I was hoping to get to the capital and find some leads. I have a couple of potions that would help me, but mostly I was going to-"

"You're an alchemist?!" Forbin interrupted.

"Yes," Zhira replied warily.

"That's amazing, I've only met one other alchemist, but he doesn't tolerate my questioning quite like you do," Forbin said, somewhat sheepishly.

"I can't imagine why," Zhira said, chuckling slightly.

"Could you…make me fly?" Forbin asked with a look of genuine wonder on his face.

"Technically, yes I can," Zhira said. "It's pretty simple, I just need some Selaroot and a few kinds of berries."

Forbin's face lit up. "Oh that's exciting! I'll keep my eye out for some! What else can you do? Can you make me a sword?"

"What? You mean from thin air?" Zhira asked.

"Yeah!" Forbin exclaimed.

"No, I can't. There are rules to science. We can't just make a thing that doesn't exist, it has to come from somewhere. We also can't do the opposite. No making anything disappear from existence. No breaking the physical laws," Zhira explained.

"So I can't run super-fast?" Forbin looked slightly dejected.

"Yes, well…let me explain. I can make you run faster than you can now, but only to the absolute maximum your muscles can work. A simple strength potion unlocks all of the potential in your muscles, which your brain otherwise limits to protect your body. It's dangerous but useful.

"Alchemy is not unlike being an herbalist. You mix ingredients to encourage the body to do certain things: heal a cut faster, calm nerves, increase energy, and so on. As an alchemist, I do the same, but on a more extreme scale. Most potions push our bodies to their ultimate limit, but that limit is different for everyone. A very fat person who can barely run anyways would still have trouble running fast even with the help of alchemy. Potions are no substitute for skill.

"The exceptions to this explanation are the potions that let us mimic magic. We don't know why those work, but they do." Zhira hoped this explanation would make Forbin feel a bit better and stop him asking so many questions.

"Oh, okay, that makes sense," Forbin said, digesting this new information. "So does your daughter's magic abide by the same rules?"

"That's a complicated answer. As far as we can tell, the answer is 'mostly yes'. But Mara can do things we couldn't dream of, and she doesn't need the resources that we do. For example, I can produce a potion that will give you the ability to create and throw fire, but that ability runs out when the potion wears off. Mara, however, can conjure up fire at will. I can pour a potion on crops to enhance their growth, but Mara will simply point at a stalk and a flower will grow."

"Wow...that's incredible!"

"It really is." Zhira felt pride talking about his daughter; she worked hard to master the skills she was blessed with. "Her magic is not bound by resources like our potions are, and she has helped us realize that there are things we haven't even considered trying yet."

"That's fantastic, I'll have to try my hand at alchemy sometime." Forbin grinned at Zhira. "Oh, we're getting close to the outpost," he said as they rounded another boulder.

Suddenly Zhira pulled Forbin down behind some shrubs. They watched in silence as three knights, clad in full metal armor, poked around where Zhira assumed the entrance of the outpost was.

"It looks like the jig is up on this place; we had better move before they find us," Forbin whispered to him. "I'll take you to another base, one I know they haven't found yet."

"How did they find this place?" Zhira wondered.

"Beats me, but we need to move," Forbin replied, more concerned about their well-being than the knights' methods.

Forbin and Zhira crept slowly from behind the shrubs so as not to alert the knights. Luckily, a dense fog had fallen on the moors to make their departure much easier; once they were out of sight, they took off as fast as they could.

"Where are you taking me?" Zhira asked Forbin as they ran.

"To our main base. We have some forces on the eastern coast but our head of operations is hidden much closer to the capital; it lets us get the information we need in a more timely fashion," the scrawny rebel replied.

Zhira was impressed with the organization the rebellion still had after a steady string of defeats over the last decade. Hiding their leadership this close to the castle was a risky tactic, knowing that the king was out for blood. Keeping their leaders alive kept the rebellion alive.

~~~

Casby crouched down by the fake boulder one of his men had discovered. On his count, they threw back the false rock and Casby led the descent into the outpost. When they reached the bottom of the ladder, Casby and his team discovered three more men sitting at a single table in the small room, clad head to toe in familiar leather armor.

"You thieves," Casby said menacingly, thinking the men they had discovered were rebels using stolen armor. Mai had instructed them not to kill anyone and to find someone named Zhira, but their blood boiled at the sight of rebel insurgents using armor that had clearly been taken from other knights loyal to the king.

"Thieves? We're no thieves," said one of the men seated in front of him; the voice was familiar.
~~~

"Where is Zhira?" one of Casby's men asked aggressively.

"Zhira? Who is that? A rebel friend of yours?" The man stood up, taking off his helmet. Revealing his face to the newcomers, General Long sported a look of displeasure.

"General, I—" the knight stammered, realizing his mistake. A sword through his neck put a quick end to his fumbling for words. Casby watched as one of the knights that accompanied Long skewered his other companion. Being the only one left, Casby dropped to his knees and begged for his life.

"Please, I'm no rebel. Mai sent us to find some man named Zhira. I don't know why."

"You may not, but she does," Long said, sensing the honesty in the man's desperation. "Men, I believe we have uncovered our spy. Tie this one up. I have a message to send."

Long sat at the table, wrote out a short note, and climbed out of the hole.

~~~

Mai dislodged the note from the pigeon. *The report from the king is supposed to come in two days. Did something happen?* As she removed the scroll, Mai noticed that the seal wasn't the king's but was in fact General Long's. Even more confused now, she opened the note:
~~~

Commander Mai,

I found your knights at the rebel outpost looking for your companion. They told me everything. You know where to find me. Don't make me hunt you down.

General Long

Mai's heart started beating out of her chest. She read the note over a dozen times; what the hell was she going to do? *What did he mean, 'they told him everything'?* She stuffed the note into her pack and started to panic. She had tried to do something to better her situation, and now it was far worse. Without thinking, she marched towards Gant's cabin. People scurried out of her way as she huffed all the way down the main street and off into the woods. She banged on his door without pause until he opened it.

"What do you want?" Gant asked, annoyed by her absurd knocking.

Mai simply held the note out to him and stared worriedly as he read it over.

"What's this?" Gant handed it back to her confused.

"I sent men to look for your brother, as a peace offering, and—"

"You did *what?*" Gant asked incredulously.

"You said Zhira was missing, and I wanted to earn some semblance of trust from you and this pathetic town, so I sent a party out to look for him," Mai said, frustrated with Gant's lack of appreciation for what she had done.

"Shit," Gant said as she stormed into the house and started pacing.

"General Long now thinks I helped the rebels ambush them. He and Gjanion have suspected that there is a rebel spy in our ranks for some time and now they're going to think that it's me!" Mai yelled.

"…you're not, right?" Gant questioned carefully.

"OF COURSE NOT!" If it had been possible, fire would have shot from her ears.

"Okay, okay! Calm down. We'll think of something." Gant tried to neutralize the commander.

"Calm down? I've worked my entire life to get to where I am, and now it's all about to be taken away from me because of a misunderstanding. General Long thinks I'm a traitor!"

"But you're not."

"No, I'm not, which makes this worse. I'm being set up! Someone is working against me," Mai said, lamenting her position.

"So why did you come to me?" Gant asked her.

"Because…" Mai trailed off. *Why* did *I go to him?* She had marched over without a second thought. Why?

Mai thought about it for a moment, then answered him. "Because it was your brother my men were after."

"I didn't ask you to send them!" Gant exclaimed.

Mai nodded. "I know. Look, this isn't a great situation. Long thinks I am a traitor, he has my men, and for all we know, Zhira as well. So for the time being, let's stop yelling at each other and work together to find a solution. He expects that I know where he is. We don't have a lot of time."

"How do I know this isn't another trap?" Gant asked her.

"Seriously? If I wanted to kill you, I'd just do it," Mai said.

Gant seemed to sense the honesty and nodded. "Okay, fine. I have no idea what to do, but I guess we don't have much of a choice. We have to go after them," Gant said, an air of desperate strength about him.

"I don't know where they are," Mai said, realizing the difficulty of the task.

"We'll have to find them quickly," Gant replied. "We don't want to miss the opportunity."

"But how?" Mai asked, looking up at him in a brief moment of vulnerability.

"I don't know, but we had better figure it out. You read that note, Long will hunt you down! And where do you think his search will start? He'll kill everyone here while he looks for you. We need to find him first."

Mai put her head back in her hands and screamed. She was ready to be done with this life, this chain of events that had led to her being framed as a rebel. All she had done was what was asked of her. A secret mission to find a relic for the king, only to be outed by a drunk at an inn and bested by a wizard who Long had left alive. Accompanying the king back to Saros to defeat the threat that she had uncovered, only to be left here as a babysitter. Making the most of her situation by attempting to forge a fragile peace between her and the town, only to be betrayed by her own knights to the general, who had apparently found a rebel base. Not two weeks had passed and she had gone from Long's unquestioned right-hand woman to being branded a traitor based on hearsay.

Mai had put every bit of energy into making sure she was the one selected as General Long's second in command. Mai worked harder than every other knight and made a name for herself with her relentless pursuit of glory. Now all that she had built was crumbling. She worried that Long's suspicion of her could cause him to interpret her drive and passion as eagerness to help the rebels gain an edge on the inside. She had to nip this in the bud, before it flowered into a fully blossomed betrayal.

"All right," she responded after a moment. "Maybe General Long will listen to reason, maybe he won't…but I hope for his sake that he does."

~~~

Forbin and Zhira approached the entrance to the cave: a small opening barely large enough for them to walk through single file. If Zhira didn't have Forbin with him, he never would have known the entrance was there. A mere crack in between some rocks, the opening was completely innocent and unassuming. Zhira squeezed himself through the short tunnel until the crevice opened into a dark long hall that appeared to have been burrowed out.

"We got tired of squishing ourselves all the way down, so we hollowed it out. Had to keep the first bit though so we didn't give ourselves away! We left plenty of rock so the front wouldn't collapse either," Forbin explained as the ground began to slope down.

After a few minutes of walking in the cold, damp underground, the tunnel's mouth opened up into one of the most impressive sights that Zhira had ever seen. Before him was a massive cavern that looked like it could house the whole main street of Saros. Jutting from the walls were large and almost unnaturally smooth stones that glowed a soft yellow, giving off light in place of torches. In place of buildings, there were about a dozen dome-shaped structures that were carved from the rock itself, with two to three dozen people buzzing about.

"Welcome to The Cave!" Forbin gave a sweep of his arm.
~~~

Zhira took it all in and gave a small laugh.

"What's funny?" the rebel asked.

"That's the name?" Zhira asked, amused.

"Well, yeah. It *is* a cave. We're rebels, not poets. Why does it need a fancy name? It is what it is," Forbin said.

"Fair enough," Zhira replied. "I'm impressed. This is a serious operation and it's practically right under the king's nose!" His eyes continued to scan the remarkable space. He saw two large openings in the walls on the far side of the cavern that seemed to lead off into tunnels similar to the one they had just come through.

"We have a pretty decent network of underground paths and tunnels that allow us to get in and out without drawing any attention. Some of the openings are hidden in plain sight so we can just hop off the road and disappear," Forbin explained.

"What are those rocks?" Zhira pointed to the glowing stones in the walls.

"Oh, they're called ferrosols. They glow when there is no natural light to be had. When we found The Cave, they were already here! I've never seen anything like them," he replied.

They walked the small main path between the dome-shaped structures until they came to the last one on their right.

"There is someone here I think you should meet," Forbin said as he walked through the archway into the bulbous structure.

Inside were smaller versions of the glowing ferrosols, abundant enough to give the interior a weird look that was devoid of shadows. There was a small table with three chairs on either side, and seated in one of them was a very elderly man with a long grey beard and a bald head. His wrinkles had wrinkles and Zhira was worried that if he tried to stand up, his legs would buckle underneath him.

"Who is this?" The old man's voice was surprisingly strong and authoritative given his appearance.

"Sir, this is Zhira, from Saros. He is an alchemist."

"Your base is impressive," Zhira said.

"It serves its purpose," the old man replied. "What can I do for you, Zhira of Saros?"

"The king has taken my daughter, Mara, hostage. I was hoping the rebellion could help me rescue her."

"He has, has he? Gjanion is not big on prisoners. Why has he taken your daughter?" the wrinkled man inquired.

"Because she is a wizard." Zhira didn't know if he could trust this man, but he had no other option. Letting him know that Mara was a wizard could be the only thing that encouraged the rebellion to help him get her back.

"A wizard? How interesting…I always thought we took them all out…" the old man said thoughtfully stroking his beard.

"We?" Zhira asked.

"Yes, 'we'. My name is Radion," the old man said, smiling.

Chapter Sixteen
Revelations

Mara sat in her dark cell listening to the rats scurry about and the occasional drop of water plummet to its doom with a quiet *drip*. She considered doing whatever magic she could to free herself, but the risk was too great; it would only cause problems, or even death, for her fathers and the people back home. *Besides,* she thought, *I couldn't beat Gjanion back home. How could I possibly beat him here, in his castle?*

Mara sat cross-legged on the floor and meditated, her breathing slow and methodical. Her senses felt amplified in the silent dungeon. Her ears picked up every small sound. Her skin felt every little draft between the stones in the wall. Even her tongue could taste the acrid air full of semi-rusted metal and moldy stone that played host to the rats.

She tried to focus her mind on someone, anyone she could find. Mara had found mild success with mind reading before, grabbing memories from people she could replay for herself; this only worked if they were significantly strong or fresh memories. Her father had done it with a potion the day he had found her. Zhira had seen some of the chaos surrounding her abandonment, describing to her a scene that sounded like someone had been hunting her family down. The details had been hazy, though, due to the fact that she was an infant and her memory was poor. The more details someone remembered, the easier it was to find the memory. Mara had never tried to reach someone over a vast distance; every mind she had ever infiltrated had been cooperatively sitting right in front of her.

The more she tried to search for memories from where she sat, the bleaker the world around her felt. She was truly on her own. Nobody she could think of was within a range that she could grab a memory from. Mara wasn't even sure why she was trying; she didn't know what good it would do if she could pull a memory. It wouldn't help them find her. If anything, she needed to do the opposite: plant a memory. Unfortunately, that had never been done before.

Even the memory retrieval was a skill known only to her fathers and her, as far as she knew, and it was a relatively unexplored one. Before they had adopted her, her fathers had created the potion while trying to create a memory enhancer for some of the older residents of Saros. Later on, as a young teenager, she had successfully imitated the ability. To do it in reverse, however, to plant a memory, was a truly unique and far-fetched idea. First, she had to be able to find someone that could help her.

"One thing at a time," she said to herself as she regained control of her mind and relaxed, focusing on just being able to reach someone.

An hour went by, and then another, and Mara's mind was as empty as the cells around her. Eyes closed, she leaned back and groaned in frustration.

"Are you okay?"

Mara nearly hit the ceiling in surprise as she opened her eyes to see the princess holding her fire and looking through the bars.

"I think my heart jumped into the next cell over," Mara replied, clutching her chest as Rylan gave an apologetic smile. "How long have you been there?"

"Oh, only a minute or two. You seemed busy and I didn't want to startle you."

"Good job," Mara said sarcastically as she got to her feet and stepped up closer to the bars.

"How are you?" Rylan asked her.

"I'm…fine?" Mara replied, motioning to the cell she was in to highlight the absurdity of the question.

"I'm sorry you have to stay down here. I'd ask my father if we could provide you better accommodations, but I'm sure he would just say no and forbid me to come back down here," the princess said sympathetically.

"You're really not used to having prisoners are you?" Mara asked. How could this kind hearted girl be the direct spawn of such an evil man?

"No, we haven't had many."

"Hm, I wonder why," Mara said pointedly.

Rylan's eyes looked at the floor. It was clear to Mara that this was not something the princess wished to discuss. *She has to know how horrible her father is, right?*

"Anyway…" Mara tried and failed to change the subject smoothly. "How was your coming-of-age extravaganza?"

"It was…" Rylan trailed off; a sudden sadness swept across the princess's face that Mara had not expected.

"What happened?" Mara asked, her desire to learn more about wizards more prominent than her concern for Rylan. Furious as she was for being held captive, Mara still itched for as much information about wizards as she could get, and this girl could be a wealth of knowledge.

"I don't think I'm supposed to tell you, but I don't know anyone else who can help me."

The dejected tone Rylan spoke in was disarming. There was an honesty about Rylan, and an openness that surprised Mara. Mixed in with her excitement for new information, Mara felt a sudden wave of pity for the princess. Her longing for whatever secret Rylan was debating whether or not to reveal was starting to be overtaken by a concern for the girl.

"What can I do to help a princess?" Mara asked honestly.

"Well, as it turns out, I'm not a wizard." Rylan was on the verge of tears. Mara could suddenly see this girl's whole world crumbling down around her. In a stunning display of honesty, Rylan had conveyed to Mara that the thing she wanted most in life, her life-long dream, had been shattered by the realization that she didn't have the abilities she so desperately wanted. Mara saw the genuine sadness in Rylan's face. *She is nothing like Gjanion,* Mara thought. Having no idea what to say or do next, Mara went with her instincts.

"I'm...sorry to hear that," Mara said, lamenting the fact that Rylan would not be the source of information she had hoped for.

"I wanted it...so badly. But I never even had a chance of being a wizard, because my father isn't one either." Rylan sniffled and turned away for a brief moment to wipe her nose.

Mara's brain exploded. *King Gjanion wasn't a wizard? How did he do magic? Why did everyone think he could? Am I really the last wizard, then?* Mara's thoughts tossed around like a wagon on a rocky road, filled with more questions than she could process until the tumult in her head came to a sudden standstill with one all-encompassing answer: he was lying. Gjanion was lying to the entire kingdom.

Rylan turned back around and continued talking. "He is more than a wizard, actually. He is a god."

Mara brain hurt; it felt like the horse had finally bucked the wagon of thoughts off, sending it careening down the mountainside.

"What?" was all Mara could manage to ask.

"According to our family history, my father is the reincarnation of Knorr, the god of power," Rylan said.

"How can he be a god?" Mara asked, wondering what this new revelation meant for his powers.

"So, a really long time ago, The Three created a sustainable life for the people and creatures that lived in their world. They made a pact that they would never reveal themselves, for they feared that if the people knew about them, they would try to obtain god-like powers and status. Well, Knorr broke that pact in pursuit of worship from the people; he wanted credit for all that he had done for them. The result was worse than the goddesses had imagined. Factions warred against other factions and created immensely powerful weapons to combat each other.

"The goddesses, Eres and Dazel, were not pleased with their brother for breaking their pact and ruining the prosperous world they had worked so hard to create, so they destroyed what they had made and banished Knorr to a new world with new life that had never known gods: our world. Knorr was doomed to a life without magic and would live out his days in an endless cycle of rebirth knowing nothing of his former status as a god."

Why is she telling me all of this? This is secret and personal information, Mara thought before the realization hit her. *Rylan is lonely.* It made sense. Rylan felt betrayed and didn't have anyone to turn to. Here Mara was, a literal captive audience, and one that had been willing to listen. *I listened for my own benefit,* Mara thought, suddenly feeling slightly guilty. *I wanted to use Rylan for information. Now, she needs a friend.*

"So…you think…your dad thinks…that he is Knorr?" Mara attempted to soak in everything Rylan had said.

"He does."

"And how does he know?" Mara asked.

"Because our ancestors have been keeping track of the lineage since the beginning. I don't know how he figured out who he was, but in one of his lives, Knorr wrote down everything he had learned so that he could pass it down to himself. The first record is of someone named Radion."

"Radion? Like your great-grandfather?" Mara's eyes were wide.

"No, it's a family name. This record goes back hundreds if not thousands of years," Rylan clarified.

"So if Knorr knew he was going to be reincarnated, why didn't he just have kids with a wizard? Get some magic into his bloodline and have some of the powers that had been stripped from him? Wouldn't he come back as one?" Mara asked.

"The cycle skips a generation, so my father is a reincarnation of my great-grandfather. But to answer your question, he did try. My great-grandfather, Radion, tried to have children with a wizard to entwine her magic with his reincarnated self. It didn't appear to work, according to everything I've read."

Mara sat for a moment, thinking about this new game-changing information. The king was a god, not a wizard, but it didn't give him any special powers that she was aware of. *Then how had he done magic? Was he just a really good alchemist?* Mara needed more answers, but the princess had given her more information than she ever could have hoped for.

"So there is no hope of you doing magic?" Mara asked the princess.

"None that I can see," Rylan said, despondent.

Mara saw an opportunity. Maybe Rylan wasn't a wizard, but she likely had access to a plethora of information. If this secret existed, what other information was the king holding back? *This girl has been through so much,* Mara thought to herself. Something about stringing her along for the sake of learning about who she was felt…wrong. Rylan had been open and honest, clearly needing someone to be on her side. *Maybe that's what I need to do…*

"That's not fair," Mara said bluntly. "Your father has told you a lot of lies for a long time. Why would he string you along like that?"

Rylan seemed surprised by Mara's sympathy. "He wants me to carry on his legacy. He'll be reincarnated as my son. It's my duty to teach him who he is all over again and carry on the family legacy."

"So he's using you?" Mara asked, stoking Rylan's emotions slightly.

"He…" Rylan trailed off. Mara saw the realization hit her.

"Look," Mara said before Rylan could formulate her thoughts into words, "What your father has done to you is unfair, but who's to say he isn't withholding knowledge? He's lied to you plenty. I have no idea if I can help you, but what if there was another way to get you powers? I only know what I have figured out on my own, and there are no other wizards I know of to ask. I need to know more about who I am. If you can find me anything else about wizards and how they get their magic or how they control it, I'll try everything I can to get you powers of your own."

Rylan did not respond immediately; Mara's heart beat rapidly to the point of bursting through her chest. She hadn't promised anything to the princess, but Mara feared that there was nothing she could do for the girl. Still, Rylan could be a useful ally, if not just a source of information. Giving her a small piece of hope was all Mara had to ensure their meetings continued.

"Fine," Rylan said after a while. "I'll see what I can find. You're right, my father lied to me for twenty one years. It's time I found out the truth for myself."

"Thank you, Rylan." Mara allowed herself to smile.

"No, thank you." Rylan's smile was considerably underwhelming; she looked almost broken.

"Are you okay?" Mara asked before she knew what she was doing.

"I just wonder what else my father has lied to me about…" Rylan's voice trailed off as she spoke.

"I didn't mean…"

"No, you were right. He misled me…wanted to ensure I was on his side, without him being on mine. There was never any thought for what I wanted. Now…not only am I not a wizard, but I'm never going to be. I never *was* going to be…" Rylan hung her head and dropped her flame, blackening the cell.

"Shit! I'm so sorry!" Rylan panicked in the darkness until Mara's hand appeared cradling a flame and relit the scene in a cool blue hue.

"Wow, yours is blue? That's so cool!" Rylan exclaimed, making Mara blush.

"So do we have a deal? Will you help me so I can help you?" Mara extended her non-flaming hand through the bars.

"I will." Rylan took Mara's hand and shook it.

~~~

Zhira's mouth was agape.

"Close your trap, son, you'll catch flies," Radion said, pointing a knobby finger at him.

"You're…King Radion? The wizard crusader?" Zhira couldn't believe this was real.

"In the flesh! Though I'm not what I once was, I promise you I'm still not someone to be trifled with."

"Why are you here with the rebellion?" Zhira's mind was reeling at the implications of what he was seeing.
~~~

"I'm not *with* the rebellion, boy, I *am* the rebellion!" Radion stood up with strength that surprised Zhira. He wondered how skinny and frail looking the old king actually was underneath his robes.

"You're…I'm sorry, did you say you *are* the rebellion?"

"Did I stutter? Yes, Zhira. I am leading the rebellion against my own grandson." Radion made his way to the door; Zhira and Forbin followed.

"But…why?" Zhira felt like an idiot for asking so many questions, but he had not expected to meet a long-dead king leading an uprising.

"The short answer is that my grandson is a disgrace to the family," Radion said as they walked the short path passing the domed structures in The Cave.

"I don't understand," Zhira said, thoroughly confused.

"You see, my boy, I overthrew the wizards because they meant to rule us, keep us under their thumb. The lives of all of their subjects were miserable. Crops were taken from them, people were taken to serve the castle…the bastards even hunted the last of the unicorns to extinction! They could have helped Kyros. They could have made sure nobody suffered. They could have improved everyone's lives. But they didn't. Their powers were great but they themselves were not."

They passed what looked like a small forge; Zhira made a note to ask later about how that worked underground.

"So what does this have to do with the king?" Zhira asked the old man, feeling he was pestering him at this point.

Radion stopped in the middle of the path and turned toward Zhira, his knobby finger pointed at his chest. "It has everything to do with him! He's no better than they are! Gjanion talks of uniting the territories, but what utter nonsense. He wants to rule them, he wants to be adored, respected, and praised! He takes and takes and never gives, never helps his people. I wanted a kingdom where people felt that they were a part of it, where they could talk freely and be who they wanted to be. My grandson took that away by banning alchemy and taking food. It's the same all over again. I decided I had to return to my crusading ways in order to stop him."

"So you're trying to stop your grandson from being the thing you tried to destroy the first time…"

"I'm not trying to stop Gjanion from becoming the very tyranny that I overthrew. He is already that. I'm trying to stop him from getting worse," Radion replied darkly.

"Why don't you just take him on? If you could defeat several wizards with your magic, surely you could take down the king…" Zhira challenged.

"First of all, when I defeated the wizards, I was not alone. I had help from some of the most talented and dedicated military minds of the age, led by General Geralith, rest his soul. Second, despite what you have heard I do not possess the ability to perform magic. I am not a wizard." The old man paused to allow the fact to sink in.

Not a wizard? Zhira was stunned. "How do you know Gjanion isn't a wizard?"

"Because I am not one, nor were any of my children."

"King Radion was a very accomplished alchemist," Forbin chimed in, "He defeated the wizards because he was the smarter player. It didn't help that the wizards were cocky. They underestimated his support." Forbin spoke as if he had witnessed the wizards being overthrown.

"Those fools didn't even bother hiring more than a few mercenaries to defend them. When we overwhelmed them, they didn't stand a chance. Gjanion, on the other hand, is no fool, and he has help," Radion said. "Geralith taught Gjanion's right-hand man, General Long, everything he knew. Long is an incredibly smart man and my grandson is no slacker either. He figured out the relics."

"What are relics?" Zhira asked.

"Not now, son. That's enough for today; I'm tired. I may be the leader of a rebellion, but I am ninety years old. I don't exactly have the stamina I used to. Forbin will show you where you can stay." He shooed them away and closed the door to a small dome hut they had meandered to.

"Follow me," Forbin said as he walked further up the path.

"What are the relics?" Zhira decided to ask Forbin, his curiosity piqued.

"Items that we know the king uses to make his alchemy stronger. Our spy on the inside provided us with that much. Apparently they're ancient artifacts from a time when wizards were commonplace. They hold special power."

"So anyone can use them and make magic?" Zhira asked.

Forbin shrugged. "We just know what the commander told us. We aren't engineers down here. We don't know how everything works." Forbin took Zhira past the last of the big domes and down a tunnel into a smaller cavern. There were multiple smaller domes peppered around the space. "You can take any of them that are empty. I'll come fetch you for breakfast. Sleep well!"

Zhira sat quietly in his stone hut, lit dimly by the glow of the smooth ferrosols in the walls outside. His head spun as he tried to sort through the information that had been thrust upon him. *So, Radion is alive and trying to overthrow his own grandson. Radion isn't a wizard, which means Gjanion isn't either. The rebellion has a spy who Forbin had referred to as 'the commander' that was working to pass information from high up the chain of command.*

He had to tell someone. This was game-changing information. The rebellion already knew Gjanion wasn't a wizard, and yet that wasn't public knowledge. *Why wouldn't they try and discredit him?* Zhira craved more information. After a while, he got up and walked out to find Radion.

Zhira rapped on his door and the old man appeared more quickly than he had anticipated.

"Back so soon? Didn't I tell you to go away?" he rasped angrily at the alchemist.

"I'm sorry, sir…my liege…erhm…" Zhira stuttered, not knowing how to address the man.

"Do you see a crown on my head?" Radion asked. Zhira shook his head.

"Sorry sir, it's just…I'm worried about my daughter."

Radion gave a deep sigh and beckoned him into his tiny hut. Zhira had to duck under the low ceilings; the elder man was short and hunched so he wasn't bothered.

The old king poured him a cup of hot tea that smelled of raspberry. "Your daughter is the only wizard, I am sure she can handle herself."

"She is being held hostage by a murderous king under threat of death to people she loves," Zhira said.

"Clever man, my grandson, playing to her emotions." Radion busied himself with another cup of tea and sat at the table with Zhira.

~~~
~~~

Following the pigeon Long had handed him, Tren raced over the moors and through the woods towards the castle; he did not sleep, so as not to lose sight of the bird. Two days later he arrived at the foot of the castle and watched as the pigeon climbed into the sky and disappeared into the mail window.

Exhausted, Tren navigated the crowded streets of town and entered the castle gate. Handing his horse off to the stable hand that met him just inside the walls, he walked into the main hall and took the stairs to the aviary. Dozens of birds roosted here every day, but Tren had tied to the pigeon a small strip of purple cloth he cut from the tunic he wore under his armor.

His eyes scanned the roosts until he found the pigeon, sitting in the commanders' mail roost.

"Looks like Long was right," Tren said to himself. "Mai has some explaining to do."

Chapter Seventeen
Strength of Will

Mai had no idea where the outpost was, nor did Gant. Mai wasn't one for breaking rules, but they were desperate so she allowed Gant to use a potion to enhance their strength so they could travel faster. The two of them followed tracks that Gant was sure were Zhira's, and a few others that had to belong to Mai's knights, to a spot on the moor that held their quarry. Luckily, General Long was waiting for them on the open moors, his armor-clad profile unmistakable even from a distance.

I have to convince him that I am not who he thinks I am, Mai thought, desperation setting in as she came face to face with the grizzled general.

Long stood with two knights near a pair of rather large boulders. Mai stepped into view leading Gant, whose hands were now tied.

"Glad to see you showed up," Long sneered.

"General, there has been a misunderstanding." Mai said, trying her best to control her emotions.

"Where is my brother? What did you do to him?" Gant yelled.

"Your brother?" Long asked.

"His brother, Zhira. He went missing so I sent some of my men looking for him. I would have gone myself but I did not want to let this one out of my sight." Mai shoved Gant forward.

"I see…so you claim that your brother simply got lost? That he wasn't giving the rebels more instructions?"

"We didn't know the rebels had a base near Saros. Please!" Gant exclaimed. Mai heard the desperation in his voice.

"A likely story," Long replied.

"Sir…" Mai began, but Long cut her off, holding up a hand.

"Commander, you had the opportunity to scout this place out. You knew the best places to send our attack force so that your rebel friends could ambush us."

"Sir that's not…"

"I don't want to hear excuses! Your men already corroborated the whole thing," he snapped at her.

"Sir, please…have you seen any rebels here?" Mai asked.

"Yes, your men. Why? Worried I would slaughter all your traitorous friends and you'd have nobody left to work with?"

"No! If it was just my men, how can you be sure they are rebels?" Mai snapped.

"How did they know where the outpost was?" Long retorted.

Mai was trapped. She had no proof she wasn't a rebel or that her men weren't either. *It's his word against mine.* She struggled for a moment, and the delay seemed to be all Long needed to drive his accusation home.

"The king will be furious that you were the informant, but relieved that it wasn't me."

A realization struck Mai like a bolt of lightning. Her whole body tensed as she realized what was happening. *He's throwing me to the wolves to save himself!*

"You…you're the spy?!" she asked.

"Don't be ridiculous. I'm no traitor, but after learning of my failure to dispose of all of the wizards, the king is understandably suspicious of me. Knowing you were the spy will make him feel much better about this whole thing."

"You're framing me to save yourself. You would burn me to keep yourself warm rather than help me. After I dedicated my life to you, to the crown…this is my reward? You chose me yourself! You made me your second in command!" Mai exclaimed.

"A decision that will not reflect well upon me, true. However I believe I will be shown mercy if I come back with the head of a traitor," Long sneered.

"What happens when it's not me? When the information still gets passed to the rebellion?" Mai asked him.

"We are close enough to victory now that I don't believe it will make a difference. But we can simply hide that from the king."

"You're a cruel man. I regret it wasn't me passing your plans to the rebels. A self-serving bastard like you deserves to be ruined!" Mai had angered him, but she was prepared.

Long drew his sword and pointed it at Mai. "You're a disgrace."

Mai pushed Gant aside and drew her own. "Then you're a disgraceful teacher."

She charged him in rage and their swords met with a loud metallic *clang*. Long parried and took a step back before swinging his sword at her side. Mai blocked the slice and guided the general's blade over her head, dropping and spinning underneath the two swords and sweeping her leg to try and break the general's balance. Long was not so easily felled. He stood his ground and Mai was caught in a crouch; he brought his blade down on her and Mai narrowly rolled out of the way.

Mai held her sword pointed down in a defensive position awaiting the general's next move. He reached his hand into his belt and in one fluid motion pulled and threw a dagger straight at her head. The hilt of Mai's sword caught the dagger and it fell to the ground in front of her. While the dagger was still in the air General Long came flying at her. He thrust his sword at a weak point in her armor and caught her in the left elbow. Mai yelled in pain and thrashed her sword at the general, cutting him across the face. Long recoiled and regrouped while Mai inspected her wound. She tried to bend her arm but nothing happened.

Shit.

~~~

Gant watched as Long and Mai, clearly two masters of their craft, assaulted each other with a flurry of electrifying strikes and counterstrikes. The two knights accompanying Long were watching as well, looking both impressed and scared.

Why aren't they helping their general? Gant wondered, then it hit him. *They don't know who to support. They're waiting to see who wins.* Gant seized the opportunity to disarm the knights. The strength potions still had some lingering effects, so he pushed against the binds Mai had put on him until they broke and inconspicuously made his way over to where the two men stood. Their attention was entirely consumed by the deadly fight so Gant had little trouble sneaking up behind them. He tied a rope to the first knight's left metal boot then to the other's right boot. Once he secured the knots, he swiped a sword from one of their sheaths.

They turned, surprised to see Gant standing there and made to subdue him. They two knights got one step before toppling over each other in a rather
~~~

comical display of flailing limbs that made Gant chuckle, satisfied with his work. He took a rock in his hand and swung hard against their helmets, knocking both of them out. Gant still wanted to know where his brother had gone, and they probably had other useful information.

Gant turned back to watch the ongoing sword fight. Mai was holding her own well, despite her left arm hanging limp. She exchanged more brutal swings with Long, continuing to hack and slash with desperation. Mai utilized graceful and fluid motions to keep her momentum working for her, and eventually she parried a swing, got behind Long with a rather agile spin, and slashed the backs of his knees. Long's legs buckled instantly and he fell to the ground.

"No…" he said softly as he lay there on the blood-spattered grass.

"I'm sorry, General Long, but if it's my life or yours, I'm choosing mine. If you taught me nothing else, at least self-preservation stuck."

"You traitorous bitch!" Long spat at her.

"I am no traitor. I never betrayed you, and I would never betray my men. *You* were the one who betrayed *me*. I won't stand for that," Mai said with no waver in her voice.

Mai knelt down to be eye level with the general and didn't break eye contact as she shoved her sword through the gap in his leather armor. She stood and put weight behind the sword, thrusting it completely through Long's body. As she removed the blade, the general fell to the side, motionless.

Mai stood over the general's body for a moment. Gant could see the exhaustion in her face from the fight and loss of blood. The wound in her arm was severe, blood dripping down her arm and off her fingers in a steady stream. Mai looked up at him, then at the two knights laying beside him.

"They're not dead," Gant told her.

"Good." Mai walked over and slapped one of the knights in the face.

The man opened his eyes groggily. "Wha…"

"What did you find at this outpost?" Mai demanded.

The knight looked blankly up at her and moaned, "Oh Goddess, my head…"

"WHAT did you FIND?" Mai yelled at him, which seemed to breathe a bit more life into the man.

"N-nothing! Nobody was there besides your men! It was just a table and a pigeon cage!"

Gant watched as Mai's eyes got wide. "Were there pigeons?"

"Y-y-yes, ma'am. There were two. General Long took one and told Commander Tren to follow it."

Mai nodded. Before he had a chance to get up, she plunged her sword through his neck and into the ground, removed it, then did the same to the still unconscious knight beside him. Mai turned and began walking back the way they had come as they bled out in the grass; Gant took that as his cue to leave as well, surprised by the nonchalant nature of Mai's actions..

"Why did you…"

"Because they'd talk. They would tell a story about something they didn't fully witness. Details would get confused and changed. This way, it just looks like rebels killed them," Mai said, suddenly very woozy as the adrenaline wore off.

They made it another ten paces before Mai collapsed.

"Mai!" Gant barely had time to catch her as she fell forward. He undid her armor plating and found that her left arm was still losing blood. There was a huge gash in the crease of her elbow, the source of the several small red streaks running down her arm.

"Shit," he said to himself. They were two days out from Saros. Gant wasn't sure he could make it back in time to save her, but that didn't stop him from trying. He ripped a part of his tunic off and tied it tightly around Mai's arm just above the gash. The blood flow slowed but did not cease. Gant looked around for anything he could use. He knew some of his mother's basic recipes, which he wasn't sure were enough for such a critical wound. *Better than nothing,* he thought.

Gant scoured the minimal shrubbery and managed to find a tumera plant, the leaves of which could be ground into a paste to seal a wound. He had nothing to clean the wound out with however, and sealing the wound could also seal any potential infections inside. But it was a risk he'd have to take, or she wouldn't live.

Tourniquet and paste applied, Gant lifted Mai and began the two day trek back to Saros. Once they were back in the woods, Gant quickly whipped up another strength potion to help him carry the unconscious commander and speed up his travels. On the morning of the second day, they approached the town, and he started yelling for help.

"Help! Help, please someone help!" Gant cried, as he burst onto the main street.

Keylon came running out of her glassblowing shop and met Gant in the street. Seeing the commander's arm, she asked no questions and began to act. They hastily took her into the back room of the forge and laid her on the floor, where Keylon bent over her arm and frantically tied a strap above her elbow to stem the bleeding.

"Gant, I'm afraid it's too late to save the arm." Keylon observed the wound with a worried look.

"I don't care, just save her," he replied.

Keylon nodded and quickly grabbed a nearby saw. She heated the edge in the forge before doing something Gant had hoped he would never have to watch. While Gant held the commander down, Keylon sawed through Mai's arm just above the elbow and below where he had tied off the wound. Mai had been unconscious until now and began to scream the most horrible blood-curdling scream Gant had ever heard.

"Sorry, sorry. I'm almost done!" Keylon said as she turned the hot saw blade and pressed it against the new open wound, cauterizing it immediately. Mai shrieked louder and higher this time before passing out again.

Keylon and Gant leaned back against the crates of scrap metal behind them, blood sprayed on their tunics.

"Thanks, Key," Gant said, drained.

"Why did you help her?" she asked him.

"Because she killed General Long."

~~~

"Okay, talk to me," Mara said to Rylan.

"Well, I found a lot about my great-grandfather that I think might be useful," Rylan started.

"Let's hear it."

"Well, apparently he was one of four born to a rich wizard family. His mother was a wizard, but his father was not, nor were any of his siblings. She died early and Radion took up alchemy to try and keep status amongst the wizards. He failed to do so and became angry with them, so he befriended a rising general and overthrew the wizards in an act of defiance and rage.

"I also read several accounts corroborating the fact that Radion slaughtered all the wizards he could find, claiming that they could not be trusted with their own power. So it makes sense that you're the last one."
~~~

"Yep, that checks out," Mara said.

"Radion passed right before my father was born, so it makes sense he was reincarnated. So we know he wasn't a wizard and he was dead before my father was born. That matches up with what my father said about being Knorr and how all of this is supposed to work."

"Sure, as much as we'll be able to tell. What do you have on wizards?" Mara asked, still a little skeptical of anyone being a banished god.

"Not as much, I'm afraid. There isn't much written information available. My father has a restricted section with a few books on them, and now that I am of age I can access them."

"What did you find?"

"Well for starters, magic is a female trait. Men can be wizards too, but only women can pass it on."

"Okay, so that explains why he tried having children with a wizard; he must have known back then," Mara said, recalling what Rylan had told her last time about the failed attempt to have wizard children. "Anything else?"

"Yes, actually. It's about your powers." Rylan seemed a little more enthusiastic about this information. "They're strengthened by the stars."

Despite this being new information, it made complete sense to Mara. Ever since she was a child, she had always had an easier time of magic at night. She thought back to the logs she had stacked for her fathers and many other times where she felt she had made progress after the sun went down.

"That does not surprise me. I mean, I had no idea, but I have felt it for so long that I just sort of…knew. Does that make sense?"

"Not at all," Rylan replied, shrugging. "Unfortunately that is all I could find. Sorry there isn't anything on why your eyes glow."

"It's all right. I didn't have too much hope," she replied, hiding her disappointment.

"So what do we do now?" Rylan looked at Mara expectantly.

"I need time to think; I wonder if there is some other way to learn about wizards besides books. Let me meditate on this," Mara said.

"Okay," Rylan said, "I'll pray to the goddesses. Maybe they'll have answers."

"Yeah, maybe," Mara replied. She had never truly believed in the goddesses; the story her grandmother had told her about the broken planet to get her to behave floated around in her head.

"All right, I'll be back tomorrow!" Rylan hurried away, plunging Mara into darkness.

Chapter Eighteen
Family

"What do you mean I don't know everything about my daughter? Of course I don't, I found her in the woods!" Zhira exclaimed.

"The morning after a rather large storm, yes?" Radion sipped his tea.

"Yes…how did you…" Zhira was flabbergasted.

"Her mother told me."

Zhira had no words now; he simply grabbed his tea and drank, indicating to the old man that he was ready to shut up and listen.

"I grew up in the capital. My father had married my mother, a wizard in the elite inner circle, in the hopes that he could give his children a better life than he had by making them magical. His family, the previous royal line, had been cast aside when the wizards took over a century before. While my father did not want to return to the throne, he did not want us to live a poor life. He hid his true lineage and together, he and my mother raised us among the magical nobility.

"My mother died when I was young, and as she was our connection to the ruling class, my father hoped us having magical abilities would keep us in the inner circle. My three sisters showed no promise in that area, but I had learned at a young age how to use the resources around me to make magic, which you know as alchemy. My father helped keep my secret to enable us to live the life he wanted for us. He helped convince the rest of the inner circle that our family was still relevant due to my powers.

"I honed my skills over the years, keeping my alchemy under wraps and always carrying enough potions with me to never be caught in a compromising situation. But as I grew up in the castle, I watched the upper class of wizards abuse their power, terrorize their subjects, destroy the lives of so many. They made sure that they alone had the ability to do magic, and if they ever caught wind of another wizard somewhere in Kyros, they snuffed it out. I was disgusted by their disregard for the lives of those they held power over, and felt pity for those who could not stand up for themselves and fight. It was an affront to the life my father wanted for us."

Zhira looked confused. "So you didn't kill off all of the wizards?"

"No. Unfortunately, those details have been conflated over time, and as I am supposed to be dead, I cannot exactly go out and correct the narrative," Radion replied.

"How did you take back your family's throne then?" Zhira asked.

"I befriended a knight in the castle guard, Raynard Geralith, who shared my sentiment against the wizards. We watched as the magical nobility grew drunk in their power, becoming lazier and more lax in their security and preparations, thinking there was nobody left to defy them once they had completed their genocide against any wizards they deemed unworthy.

"Geralith and I spent the next year hatching a plan to take them down from the inside. We built a network of supporters and spies to help form a coup. We relied heavily on the help of the people who the wizards had subjugated, and it paid off. My youngest sister, Lydia, was not a fan of this plan. When I confronted her about it, I learned that she was in fact a wizard. My mother's gene for magic had carried through after all.

"Why did she hide it? Your father's plan had worked!" Zhira exclaimed.

Radion sighed. "My sister had never revealed her powers to anyone, because she had seen what the powers did to people. She had witnessed firsthand what the wizards of our country used their magic for. Not wanting to become one of them, she suppressed her abilities."

"If she hated them so much, then why did she hate your plan?" Zhira asked.

"It's my fault. I resented her for hiding her powers, the powers I had wanted. It did not help that my plan was centered around the extinguishing of magic. Thinking the wizards who ruled us were the only ones left, my campaign was buoyed by a hatred for magic. Lydia saw this as a threat to herself. She saw me as obsessed with disposing of all wizards, not simply the bastards that had ruled for so long and abused their powers.

"I tried to reassure her that despite my resentment, she had no reason to fear for her life. She had done nothing, and I told Lydia I would not harm her. She didn't seem convinced, and so she fled under cover of night. I went ahead with my plan, conquered the wizards, and we settled into a time of peace."

Zhira looked at the old man with a newfound wonder. Every story he had heard had depicted him as a madman, bloodthirsty and hell bent on eradicating the wizards for his own glory. Zhira took another sip of his tea and sat patiently while Radion continued his tale.

"Eventually, I gave the crown up to my son. Feeling that the people would accept him more easily if I wasn't there to shadow over his mistakes as he grew, we decided to push the narrative that I had died in a carriage accident. My wife and I went into hiding by choice, and left my friend Geralith in charge of overseeing my son's growth as a leader. He did a fine job, but unfortunately my son fell ill and never recovered. Gjanion grew up most of his life without a father along with false stories and whispers of my madness that evolved into accepted truths, despite Geralith's best efforts. Gjanion took over as a teenage king and was nothing like his father. To this day I do not know what happened, but he became power-hungry and ruthless.

"My best guess is that he heard the people of Kyros disparaging my name and worried he would be overthrown as I had done to the wizards before me. Gjanion became more militant, spreading his knights across the kingdom to maintain order, or so he claimed. My *personal* opinion is that he had grown power hungry. Geralith's reports got increasingly grim over time, showing concerning signs that Gjanion was on the path of a tyrant, and eventually I realized that my grandson needed to be removed. I began rallying those who felt the same, and we started what you know as the rebellion."

Zhira absorbed the story and came away with one question: "What does this have to do with my daughter?"

"It is important that you know my past, because it directly influences your daughter's future. My sister Heron was the youngest, born eight years after me. She and I were always at odds and the rift we had over my conquest was the breaking point. She thought I had gone mad, and I had not done enough to convince her she was safe. When she left, I was upset, but I figured that if my plan worked, I could give her family a free world to grow up in. It would be my most sincere apology."

Zhira sat leaned way over the table, entranced by Radion's story.

"I searched for her for years after the uprising. I traveled the whole kingdom in what many call my 'victory tour'. I harbored guilt over her departure and I wanted to make things right between us. I wanted her to know she was safe. Unfortunately, in my travels I never found her. If I came across any of her offspring or subsequent generations at any point in my life, they were invisible to me. That is, until twenty years ago."

Zhira was suddenly aware of the relatively childish pose he had taken up. He leaned back and placed his now empty tea cup on the table.

"It was quite a stormy evening. I remember it well. One of my men found her on patrol on the side of the road not far from here and brought her in. The woman had been left for dead by royal knights. We tried our best, but her wounds were too severe; by the time she was brought to us, there was not much we could do except make her comfortable. The woman introduced herself as Heron, and she looked to be the spitting image of my sister Lydia: blue eyes and all. There was no doubt in my mind this woman was Lydia's granddaughter."

"That's amazing! You never found your sister, yet you met her granddaughter. So you know she survived," Zhira clarified.

Radion nodded. "Long enough to have children anyways. To this day, I do not know what happened to my sister. Heron unfortunately did not survive her wounds long enough to tell me. She did explain, however, that her own daughter was in danger because she was a wizard, which confirmed my suspicions. Heron told me about how she had hidden her baby in the woods and fended off half a dozen knights, and her last request was for us to find the child and make sure it was safe. She passed later that night.

"We were unsuccessful in our search when we went to find the baby the next morning. I prayed to the goddesses that Heron's daughter had been found, and it appears my prayers have been answered." Radion finished and looked at Zhira.

"Sir…that's…I mean…" Zhira didn't know how to respond to this story. He sat there motionless for some time while the old man sipped his tea.

"Well?" Radion asked him eventually.

"There is just so much to process. That means that Mara and the king are…" Zhira trailed off trying to follow the family tree.

"What does it matter if they are related?" Radion asked him bluntly.

"I don't know, but—"

"That's not the important part of this story. History is important because without the knowledge of what came before we are doomed to repeat it. I took control of the kingdom to help people grow in a world that did not oppress them. My legacy did not last because I went about it the wrong way. I took control for myself when I should have given control to the people I was fighting for. I looked no better than those I had overthrown. It became nothing more than a power struggle between upper-class families."

Radion paused, staring at Zhira and letting his words sink in, then continued. "Do not let fear reign. The people should be in charge of their own lives. They need no king, they need no royal family. They need their freedom: free will to make their own choices and not be persecuted for it. Every person who is a part of this rebellion had to agree to this. We are not conquerors, we are liberators. We will set people free, not rule them."

"That is very wise," Zhira replied humbly.

"I am ninety years old. I would hope I've learned a few things along the way," Radion chuckled. "Go get some sleep. I expect we will have quite a busy day tomorrow and I fear I've given you enough thoughts to keep you up all night." He winked at Zhira and guided him to the door, shut it behind him, and left the alchemist to wander back to his own small dome with his thoughts.

Zhira was restless and knew that when he returned to his hut he would not be able to sleep. He longed for the sky; the stars were his comfort, a language only he could read. Underground here he was cut off, muted, frustrated. Meandering the caverns, he came across Forbin talking with the blacksmith.

"Evening, Forbin. Ma'am." Zhira regarded the two of them as he walked up.

"What are you doing up?" Forbin inquired.

"Can't sleep. I'm not used to the lights," Zhira remarked, pointing at a few of the nearby glow-stones.

"Ah, yes. They're not an easy adjustment, but you'll get used to it."

"Forbin, I was wondering, is there any chance I can see the sky?" Zhira asked.

"Sure! Let me show you." Forbin bid the blacksmith farewell and gestured for Zhira to follow him. The rebel led him through a series of small tunnels that shot off the main drag of The Cave until they came to what looked like a dead end. Forbin pushed up on the ceiling and it lifted. Zhira wallowed in the rush of the cool fresh night air.

"That's brilliant! Thank you," Zhira said, taking in the sight of a cloudless night sky with gratitude.

"You're welcome! Happy to help."

"Mind if I stay up here a while? The clear air and stars help me meditate."

"Not a problem. You know where the door is!" Forbin showed him how to open the hidden entrance from the outside and then left the alchemist to himself.

The tunnel had left him on top of a small hill, perfect for viewing the night sky. The forest was thin around the top of the hill and got denser further down the slope. Zhira sat with his legs folded and looked up. Stars twinkled and gleamed across the velvety canvas, the Bright One peeking over the edge of the trees. The moon hung high in the sky, half of its face illuminated.

Zhira's eyes scanned the patterns as he had done so many times from his tower. He felt refreshed; his breathing steadied and his body relaxed. He stayed there for some time until his eyes noticed something only an experienced stargazer could have. *The path the moon is taking means that…* Not sure what to make of what he was seeing, he made a mental note and returned to The Cave to get some sleep.

A few hours later, Forbin rapped on the door, startling Zhira. He'd had some trouble falling asleep with the constant glow of the ferrosols, but eventually had drifted off while thinking about this new expansive family tree his daughter was a part of; he wasn't even sure he fully understood it.

"Just a moment," Zhira called out as he pulled on his robes and leather boots. He stepped out into the cavern, lit exactly as it had been when he turned in a few hours ago. The two men made their way back to the main cavern and into the first house that Forbin had brought Zhira to yesterday. Three of the six chairs around the table were occupied by Radion and two women each seeming to be in their late fifties, Zhira guessed.

"Good morning," Zhira nodded to Radion.

"And to you, my boy. I'd like you to meet the rest of The Cave's council, Gladys and Biranel." The two women nodded in acknowledgement.

Forbin placed a plate of fruits in the center of the table along with a pitcher of water and some cups. Each of them helped themselves until they'd had their fill and Forbin removed everything from the table before seating himself.

"Now, Zhira, I believe you have presented us with a rare opportunity," said Radion.

"The king briefed us last night," the woman named Gladys said. "Your daughter may be exactly what we need."

Zhira contained his excitement; he had hoped that this would be the rebellion's response.

"What can we do?" Zhira asked.

Radion spoke with a voice that was trained to give orders. "I believe that with her on the inside, we can cause enough of a distraction for her to get out and remove Gjanion from power."

"How can she do that? She wouldn't know the plan," Zhira replied.

"Actually, we have a spy working directly for the king. We just inform them of whatever plan we devise and have it delivered to Mara," Biranel stated.

"Okay, and how do we get our spy to deliver the plans to her without arousing suspicion? That's a big risk," Gladys asked.

"It's one worth taking, and our spy would be no good if clandestine operations caused problems!" Radion laughed.

"I think I might have an idea, something I noticed while meditating last night…how fast can you get this message there?" Zhira asked.

"Assuming we come up with a plan now, it can be there tomorrow," Forbin said.

"Good, because we do not have long before the moon is eclipsed."

~~~

Rylan sat with her father and stepmother as they finished their dinner of pork roast. The meal had been mostly silent. Rylan was uninterested in engaging with her father, his betrayal and lies still fresh on her mind. Stella had tried to start a few conversations, but after the third failed attempt, she had settled on eating quietly. As the kitchen maids began clearing the table, Gjanion finally spoke up.

"Rylan, I know you've been visiting the prisoner," he said with a stern tone.

Normally one to be fraught over upsetting her father, Rylan didn't even flinch. "And?"

Gjanion was surprised by her tone. "I don't want you near her. She is dangerous! She's a wizard."

"And so are you. Should I be scared of you too?" She stared him down.

"Rylan!" Stella exclaimed. Rylan's eyes did not shift from her father.

"Young lady, I don't know what has gotten into you, but whatever it is you'd better find a way to get it out," Gjanion said, his voice rising.

"Oh, okay, I'll just use my magic pow…oh wait!" Rylan narrowed her eyebrows.

"It is no fault of mine you don't possess the magic gene."

"No, but it is your fault for misleading me my whole life."
~~~

"I don't want you down in the dungeon again!" Gjanion brought the conversation back to its original point in the hopes of ending the argument. Rylan had never defied him like this.

"I am of age, and I can do as I please. Maybe SHE can teach me something REAL about magic!" Rylan yelled.

"And I'm the king! You'll do as I say! You will NOT learn magic from that WENCH because you CAN'T!" His face was red as he finally broke, scaring one of the maids that was walking by him.

Rylan and Gjanion remained locked in a stare down for what felt like ages. Eventually, Rylan broke it off. "Of course, your highness. My sincerest apologies." She stood up and bowed a deep sarcastic bow before departing the dining room.

Rylan went up to her chambers, shut the door, and fell face first on the bed. Since Mara had pointed out that her father had lied to her and manipulated her for her entire life, she'd taken a new view of him. He had always been kind and supportive, caring and loving, but had it all self-serving in the end? *Has he been grooming me to be his secret-keeper? Am I nothing but a method for reincarnation?* It made her sick to think about.

She was also upset with Mara for leading her to these realizations. *Is Mara just using me to sabotage my father?* Her life had been so good until Mara showed up; why had she decided to trust a wizard? Rylan had told this girl so much in the hopes of getting powers for herself. *Am I no better than dad? Using someone to get what I want?* Her head began to spin.

Rylan sat up on her bed and closed her eyes to pray. She had always prayed with her father to the goddesses. *Was that a lie too?* No, she had to believe some parts of it were real; other people prayed to the goddesses, too. *If I waver in my faith, what do I have left to hold on to?* She took a deep breath to relax and began to pray.

Oh great goddesses, thank you for my life and my health. I am forever grateful for all that you have blessed me with. Please guide me through these troubling times. I am lost.

Rylan repeated the prayer in her head again and again before eventually falling asleep. She wandered through several dreams before coming across a small spring full of pink water that was surrounded by reeds and vibrant blue and purple flowers. The surface of the water reflected her face back to her perfectly, with not a ripple on the surface. Rylan smiled at herself, and her mirror image disappeared suddenly. Confused, she looked closer, bending over more and more until she fell into the spring headfirst.

Everything was immediately right-side up again but with no gravity; she felt like she was floating. Rylan's head swiveled as she tried to find something in the darkness that surrounded her. Eventually she found herself staring into a set of dazzlingly blue eyes. A woman of beauty beyond words floated opposite her in the void. Her hair golden and flowing like a waterfall down her shoulders framed a face of silver that held the sapphire eyes. The woman's body was nothing more than a mist of swirling colors underneath her silver shoulders and arms.

Hello young one. I am Dazel, the goddess of magic.

Rylan said nothing; it felt too real to be a dream.

You are lost, and I am here to help you find yourself.

Rylan shook her head as if to wake herself up but there was no change; the misty silver woman continued to float in front of her.

I sense you feel betrayed by one that you love.

Rylan nodded.

Fret not, for there is another that loves you greatly, and will guide you to that which you seek.

Dazel's form changed until Rylan was staring at a silvery version of Mara.

Trust the wizard. She speaks the truth, though she does not know it.

Rylan gave a confused look.

Look to the stars, they will be your guide.

The darkness around them began to lighten, peppered with stars, the moon, and the Bright One. The familiar sky was oddly comforting to her. The moon slowly faded through its phases until it came to a stop at a phase Rylan had never seen before.

Soon all will be clear. We will meet again.

The stars began to melt away in streaks of white as the dream faded. Rylan watched as Dazel disappeared into the widening streaks of light that eventually gave way to reveal her bedroom ceiling. She blinked again and her room came into focus. Rylan still wasn't sure if what she had just experienced was a dream or not, but she knew one thing for sure: she was going back to the dungeon.

Chapter Nineteen
The Plan

Commander Hearth read the note over again, making sure he did not miss a single detail. Despite his weight and lack of physical fitness, he ran as fast as he could to the throne room, pausing several times to catch his breath. Hearth threw open the doors, causing a bit of a scene, and approached the throne. At the base of the stairs, he doubled over, hands on his knees, panting.

"I…apologize for…the intrusion," Hearth wheezed.

"What is the problem?" The king motioned for Hearth to sit in the chair beside the throne.

Hearth nodded in thanks and sat down; beads of sweat still forming on his forehead from his trek across the castle. "There are rebels in the city. My spies tell me they're hiding in plain sight."

"Explain."

"My spies have been watching a man who appears to be scouting a way into the castle. He loiters about in the same place, not selling any wares nor begging for food," Hearth said, fanning himself.

"This is rather daring of the rebellion, and somewhat sloppy. They must feel the pressure of our mounting victories," the king said.

"Fret not, Your Majesty. I will personally see to the capture of these would-be crusaders, and the removal of their heads."

"No, do not kill them," Gjanion replied. "I want to draw the rebellion in. They're getting bold, so let's force their hand. Capture this man and any other rebels your men have identified. They'll know we're on to them, but they'll try to save their comrades. We can make it look like an innocent attack on the castle and use the people, rally them to our cause."

"That's brilliant, sir. Get the people on our side." Hearth wiped his brow.

"Go and do your work, Commander. Report back to me once you've completed your task."

"Yes, my liege." Hearth heaved himself out of the chair and set off.

~~~

"I will never be able to thank you enough, Radion," Zhira said as he mounted a horse with the rest of the rebels.

"You can thank me by disposing of my grandson," Radion said from the ground below him.
~~~

A large group of rebels that included Gladys and Forbin had congregated outside of The Cave, preparing for the trek to the castle town. They had chosen an area near a more secluded entrance in the woods as their staging ground so as not to attract any unwanted attention from whoever happened to be travelling by. More than fifty volunteers prepared horses, finished filling up packs, and sharpened weapons. As the last of the supplies were brought up from the underground fortress, those that were not travelling said their goodbyes.

"Are you sure this is going to work?" Forbin asked Zhira.

"It's the best chance we have. Any advantage we can get," Zhira said with a feigned smile.

Zhira had worked with Radion and the council to compose a cunning plan, but it required precise timing. Zhira had observed the path of the moon and realized that it was on course to pass behind their planet, shielding it from the sun. This phenomenon was something nobody else in the room had ever heard of, confirming what Zhira thought: when people saw it, they would panic. They would use this panic to their advantage, using a large contingent of rebels to help fuel it and attack the knights in and around the castle, while Zhira broke in and found Mara.

In order for their plan to be successful, it required a large group of rebels to leave The Cave and head to the capital, something that Radion was not keen on letting happen. After some convincing, he had relented and allowed Zhira to go ahead with his idea. The key was their inside man in the capital delivering the rest of the plan to Mara, but without their forces in place, there was no point.

"Here, I want you to take this." Radion held out a beautiful ornate silver sword. Zhira took it and tied the sheath to his belt. "In case you don't have time to whip up a potion."

"This is beautiful, but why are you giving it to me?" Zhira remarked, drawing and examining the sword.

"You're going to need all the help you can get, and this relic is the most I can offer you," he replied, admiration in his voice.

"A relic?! What does it do?"

"Nothing now, it's just a good sword. If you can manage to find the ruby that goes in its hilt, then it will become far more powerful," Radion explained.

"Meaning?"

"Meaning that sword will enable you to do certain kinds of magic. It has been a long time since I last used it, so I don't exactly remember the specifics. Just don't let Gjanion get his hands on it."

"I appreciate such a generous gift. I'll make good use of it!" Zhira reassured him.

"It's been in the family for a few generations. Please treat it with care. I'd be far more upset if you came back instead of it!" Radion laughed.

"Understood! Thank you." Zhira gave a nervous laugh; he could not tell if Radion was kidding.

Zhira turned his horse and took off down the hill, signaling to the rest of the rebels that it was time to depart. As they fell in behind him, Zhira took one last look back to see Radion standing by the entrance, hunched over his cane as the sun cast long shadows of the trees through the forest.

~~~

Mai woke up groggy; her surroundings were blurry as her eyes strained to focus. Her head started to spin and she felt sick. Closing her eyes, she took a few deep breaths to steady herself. When she reopened them, things were less fuzzy. Dizziness set in again and she reached up to press against her temples; she rubbed them both and quickly realized she could not feel the left side of her face. *What the hell?* She pulled her hands away briefly and started feeling both sides of her head; the right was totally normal, but she couldn't feel any part of her left. Mai went to sit up and fell awkwardly to her left on the bed. As she turned, she screamed.

Gant came flying through the door, his red tunic stained from some eggs he had been cooking.

"What's wrong?!" he asked in a slight panic.

"MY ARM, YOU OAF!" She held up her left arm, which ended at a rounded off and scarred nub just below where her elbow was.
~~~

"Mai, I can explain…"

"Where. Is. My. Arm." She tried to be as intimidating as possible, but the effort took its toll. She fell back onto the bed dizzy with a frustrated scowl.

"After your duel with General Long, I had to carry you back here. You had lost so much blood and there was too much damage…I'm sorry Mai," Gant said.

"You…you took my arm off." Mai's facial expression changed from frustration to disbelief.

"You were going to die. Something had to be done so Keylon and I acted just fast enough to save your life."

"First my rank…now my arm…" Mai's face contorted as she grappled with recent events.

"Mai, there was no other way…"

"Leave me alone," Mai said, rolling over to face away from him.

Gant didn't say another word; after a moment, he granted her wish and left the room. As the door closed, Mai rolled over and began to sob. What had her life become? Laying in a bed in a stranger's house, missing an arm, likely to be seen as a traitor. *After all I have done for Kyros, this is how it ends.* Tears streamed down her face. *How long have I been here? Has Tren already sold me out? Have they discovered Long's body?* Mai wondered as exhaustion overtook her worries and she drifted off again.

When Mai awoke again, she found enough strength to get up. She emerged from the bedroom to find Gant sitting at the table with some charts she did not recognize or understand; they appeared to be a recreation of the night sky.

"You're looking better," Gant said, testing the waters.

"Still missing an arm," Mai shot at him.

"Are you hungry?" he asked, ignoring her attempt to pick a fight.

Mai nodded slightly, still scowling at Gant. He got up and began preparing two sandwiches for them. He placed one in front of her before taking his and sitting across from her. As the afternoon sun poked through the cabin's windows, the two ate in silence. Mai could tell that Gant was wary of pressing so soon after her trying ordeal, but the worry in his face was apparent. They had not found his brother. *This man could have kept on looking for his brother,* Mai thought as she took another bite. *Instead, he saved my life. Why?* Mai finished her sandwich and looked across the table at Gant.

"So…when will I be travel-ready, doctor?" she asked him dryly.

"Travel-ready? Where do you want to go?" Gant asked.

"Home. I want to go back and defend myself to the king. Word of General Long's death will hit them any time now and my absence will be all they need to condemn me. I need to be able to show my face without immediate assault. I need to explain what happened.

Maybe King Gjanion will let me back into his ranks." Mai was floundering. Her position as Long's second in command had meant everything to her and now she was willing to fight an uphill battle to get back in the king's good graces.

"Mai, I just don't think it's smart," Gant argued.

"This is my *life*. If you don't think I will die to protect my legacy, then you are more stupid than I thought." She glared at him.

"Okay, okay. I'll go with you," Gant said.

"What?" The menacing tone in Mai's voice vanished.

"Well, Zhira should be in the capital. He'll either be trying to free Mara or be captured himself. Either way, I should help him. Plus, I don't think it's going to be smooth sailing for you riding with one arm," he replied.

Mai had no rebuttal. She didn't want to admit it, but until she figured out how to go about life one-handed, she needed help. "Fine. So when should we leave?"

"As soon as you can get on a horse," said Gant.

That task proved to be more difficult than she initially predicted. Getting up on her horse was a challenge with one arm, and controlling the reins was even harder. She worked throughout most of the afternoon with her palomino and by the time the sun set, she could travel at a canter without falling off.

"This will have to do, I don't want to waste time. I'll keep learning as we go," she said to Gant that evening. They agreed to leave first thing the following morning.

~~~

After Mai went to bed, Gant put on his cloak and set off into the cool autumn air. He made straight for the forge and rapped on Sari's door. The sky was a deep twilight purple and most of the stars were already poking through.

"Gant?"

"I'm sorry to disturb you, Sari. I need your and Keylon's help. Can I come in?"

Sari nodded and stood back to allow him to enter. Their home was humble, but decorated beautifully. Keylon's taste had clearly won out as there were glass decorations everywhere, reflecting candlelight so well that Gant almost forgot that it was night. Keylon came into the room and greeted him.

"I'll get right to the point," Gant said to the both of them. "I'm leaving tomorrow with the commander. She wants to return to redeem herself to the king and set the record straight. I figured it would be my best opportunity to find Mara and Zhira. She can get me into the castle."
~~~

"Look for Kei, too, won't you?" Keylon asked. "I know he is capable of looking after himself, but what he did was dangerous and a bit foolhardy."

"I'll find him too," Gant said.

"Thank you." Keylon smiled.

"If we don't make it back," Gant continued, "I need you two to carry on in our stead." He held out a sealed scroll.

Sari took it in his large, veiny hand, and placed it on an empty shelf. "We won' hafta, lad. You'll be back," he said in his gruff voice.

"I certainly hope so, but regardless, everything you need to help grow crops, make potions for the festival, and brew a few other basics are in there. If none of us make it back, I just want you to know how much we appreciate the town's help in raising Mara, and the love you all showed when mother died."

Keylon hugged him. "Shut up. You'll be back."

Gant returned the embrace before turning to address Sari. "I need one last favor."

~~~

The next morning, as Gant and Mai saddled their horses and packed their bags, Gant stopped Mai before she could mount her horse.

"What?" she asked, irritated at any delays.
~~~

"I have something for you." He reached into one of his bags and pulled out a silver dome with a long pointed attachment.

"What is it?" she asked, taking it from him.

"Something to replace your left hand. I had Sari, our blacksmith, make if for you out of some spare parts last night."

Mai examined the new piece. The dome attached to her stub with a strap and sported a six inch blade screwed into the top. She attached it to her arm and gave it a flourish. Gant saw her flash a rare smirk.

"There are a few attachments you can interchange for your needs," Gant explained as he handed her a bag containing several metal pieces.

Mai looked through the assortment and found a curved piece she could use to hook and grip things. She replaced the blade with it and got up on her horse; looping the reins around the curved piece gave her a much more secure grip. Her smirk evolved into a full smile.

"You're quite clever. Hopefully you're as good a rider," she said as she turned her horse and took off into the woods.

"*Hopefully you're as good a rider,*" Gant parroted snarkily as he leapt onto his brown mare and sped off after her.

~~~
~~~

Kei crouched in the alley, awaiting his opportunity. For the last week, he had been watching the comings and goings of the knights; their schedules were regular and predictable. Every day at noon, the morning patrol would return and be replaced by the afternoon patrol. As the latter departed for duty, Kei counted how long he had before the gate closed: exactly ten seconds before it was too low to roll under.

There was a blind spot in the viewpoints of the castle watchtowers that helped give him a decent path of approach. It wasn't perfect, but with all of the guards swapping out their shifts, it would be his best chance to make his break for the castle.

Kei watched the morning patrol come up the cobblestone road to the gate and hail the guards at the top of the tower. The gate was raised and the men walked in as the knights scheduled for the afternoon rounds of the capital walked out. Kei waited until the knights had passed his hiding space before he made a break for the gate. Trying to stay inconspicuous in the crowd, he hurried as the gate fell lower and lower.

As he reached the edge of the crowds, Kei took his chance and sprinted for it. The gate was low and he dove, rolling underneath the spiked metal grate and hearing it fall into its holes in the stone. *I made it!* Kei stood up quickly and looked for a place to hide.

"Well what do we have here?" A commander with a round stomach was standing in front of him, flanked by two knights. There was nothing Kei could do but put his hands up.

Chapter Twenty
Into the Woods

The fire crackled as Mai and Gant sat in an uncomfortable silence. Gant's thumbs traced tiny orbits around each other like a binary star. His lack of knowledge about Zhira's whereabouts had him on edge. Knowing Long had not captured him was a positive, but he couldn't be sure his brother had found the rebellion. *For all I know, he could have been captured by other soldiers, or have already rescued Mara.*

Gant looked up at Mai across the dancing flames, her features distorted in the heat waves. He felt an odd sense of pity for her. Mai's whole world was hanging in the balance as they travelled to the castle and its unpredictable tyrant.

"Are you hungry?" Gant asked.

"No," Mai replied without looking up.

Gant prepared himself a meal consisting of some berries Mai had picked earlier and a small frog-rat he had fished from a nearby pond. They were like rats except their back legs resembled a frog's in structure; they had no tail and were remarkably good swimmers.

Gant took a loaf of bread from one of his saddlebags and tore off a piece for himself. Mai silently held out her hand and Gant obliged, tossing to her the piece he had just torn for himself.

"What do you think you're going to say to the king?" Gant prodded.

"Whatever I have to," she replied curtly.

"Given the situation you're in, I think you might want to—"

"I think you might want to stop talking." Mai cut him off.

An awkward silence followed, but eventually Gant persisted.

"So…how does your arm feel?" Gant inquired cautiously.

"It hurts, but not unbearably so. You know you don't have to force conversation. I don't need to talk to you. We are not friends," Mai said to him across the flames.

"Why are you so nasty?" Gant asked, challenging the commander.

"Excuse me?" Mai asked, taken aback by his aggression.

"I get it. Killing Long probably went against everything you know. You're basically on the run from your own troops, and you are missing half your arm. You have every right to be angry, but why are you taking it out on me? I saved your *life* and didn't turn you in to the king while you slept, in my home by the way, for like three days!" Gant was surprised by himself. All of his anger at the king taking Mara, his mother's death, and the stress the commander had brought on him just by being there was coming out.

"It's not just that," Mai said, turning away from the fire.

"What do you mean?"

"I don't want to talk about it…least of all with you," she said without the biting tone that Gant had come to expect from her.

"Yes, you do. Otherwise you wouldn't bother responding," Gant said, taking a gamble.

"Fine. You really want to know?" she asked him somewhat sarcastically. "I was born to an upper-class family in the city, given everything I could have ever wanted in life, and was slated to be the perfect bride to a boy from one of the families in our social circle."

"That doesn't sound so bad," Gant said.

"It was the worst existence I could have imagined. I never worked for anything. I had no sense of accomplishment or fulfillment. People doted on me like a doll, dressing me and drawing on my face, decorating me like the ornament I was supposed to be. A beautiful girl to accompany a boy from the same group of nobility that my parents grew up in.

"The night before I was to wed, I snuck out of my bedroom window and ran. I'd had enough of it all, and while I didn't know what I wanted to do, I knew I wanted to do it for myself. I never saw my family again. For I don't know how long after, I slept in the alleys. I befriended a few of the other street urchins, we took over a solid chunk of blocks in the western part of the capital, and I realized I was good at leading and good at fighting. We protected the shop owners in our area from other bands of misfits trying to steal or expand their territory. In return, we got places to sleep, food to eat, and clothes on our backs. I had earned the trust of people and they backed me up, supported me.

"One day, as we ran an operation to steal some better food from the slums south of us, a patrol came by. We were always careful not to get ourselves in trouble, but this time we had been caught in the act. I stood my ground to help others get away and took on three knights at once. It took them a lot of effort to bring me down, and instead of arresting me, they brought me to General Long.

"He offered me a choice: join his ranks and prove that my loyalty and self-preservation were traits to be applauded, or be jailed for aiding fugitives and attacking a royal patrol. It was a no-brainer. I had wanted the chance to earn my place and I had been given a golden opportunity. I rose through the ranks and eventually got to where I am…or was." Mai sat back down by the fire, which had started to die down. Small licks of flame toyed with the edges of the burnt logs while embers glowed red underneath.

"I still don't understand why you're so…brutal."

"To get to where I am required tenacity, hard work, and dedication," Mai said. "I wanted nobody to get in my way. I never gave myself an easy out, so nobody else got one either. I distanced myself from everyone so that I would not become attached to anyone I needed to be better than. Less pain that way." Mai stared at the embers.

"Then why are you opening up to me?" Gant asked.

"Because I don't see you as someone in my way. You were tied to me by the king. You're a weight, not a barrier. Make no mistake about what this is, Gant. The moment I can cut you free, I will."

They sat beside the embers until they had all but petered out. Gant got up and grabbed the sleeping sack from his saddlebag when he heard a rustling in the trees above them. He stopped dead and could see Mai had done the same mid-stride towards her horse; he could just barely make out her form in the dying light of the embers. The stars poked through the leaves intermittently but did not offer much light.

Neither of them moved as the rustling continued. After a moment, it stopped and Gant moved as quietly as he could towards his bag where he had stored two potions: one for healing and one for fire. Without warning, there was a *crash* followed by a *thud* sending embers and sparks flying in all directions. A nearby bush caught fire and illuminated the scene. Something had fallen from the trees and landed where their fire had been. Gant quickly removed the stopper from the fire potion, downed half of it, and lit his hands for more light. Between the long shadows, Mai and Gant could make out the form of a tigerdeer.

"Why would a tigerdeer be in the trees?" Gant asked.

"Because it was dinner," Mai said, pointing to several places on its body where the only thing remaining was bone.

"What kind of animal…" Gant began, but was interrupted by a second *crash* accompanied by a low growl behind him.

Gant turned to face the source of the noises and came face to face with a creature he had never seen. Its head was shaped like that of an eagle, with a pair of round golden eyes leering directly at Gant. The head sat atop the body of what appeared to him like a large cat with wings.

"What in the name of Eres is that?!" Gant panicked.

"A griffin," Mai answered, her eyes locked on the monster and her stance aggressive.

The griffin prowled the edge of the camp, flames illuminating its white feathers and giving it a reddish glow. It kept its face turned towards them as it circled.

"We are between it and its food," Mai said, trying to sound as calm as possible. "We need to slowly back away."

Mai took a step back towards Gant and the tiger-deer carcass. The griffin seemed to interpret this as a defense of the food and launched itself at Mai. She sidestepped the attack and exposed Gant. He yelled and threw fire at the beast, but the griffin hardly flinched and ran into Gant, knocking him over.

~~~

"Why do you watch the stars so much?" Forbin asked Zhira.

"They offer a different perspective. Plus they're fascinating! Did you know that some stars are brighter than others, not just the Bright One?" Zhira asked, his head leaned back staring up through the gap in the trees.

"No, I hadn't really noticed," Forbin said.

"I can't quite figure out why, but I am willing to wager that it is because some of them are bigger than others, or closer to us." Zhira leaned all the way back until he was laying in the grass.

Forbin sat beside him, finishing a ration of pigeon stew. There was one fire for the whole camp of rebels so as to keep a low profile. One fire signaled a single traveler or small group, which was much more inconspicuous to any knights that happened to be travelling nearby.

"Why did you join the resistance?" Zhira asked Forbin as Gladys sat down next to them.
~~~

"My village down south was ruined by the king's men. They took everything and made us pledge loyalty to the crown in exchange for protection. From what, I will never know. I saw what was happening and made my way out of the desert without being seen. I didn't want to rebel at the time, just escape. When I happened upon some of the rebels, I figured it would be as safe a place as any and I needed a home. I've been with them ever since."

"What about you?" Zhira turned to Gladys.

"Just wanted to fight, to be honest. A bunch of bastards violently trying to reclaim a kingdom that was already peaceful? Count me in. Gjanion wanted more control so naturally I wanted to cause more chaos." Gladys flashed a mischievous grin.

"A noble effort!" Forbin saluted her.

"So you're sure you don't want to go back to Saros to get your brother?" Gladys asked Zhira.

"We don't have time. Plus, Commander Mai has a grip on the town. We cannot afford to lose any of our men or women and I don't want to endanger him or our friends any more than they already are." Zhira was surprised to hear himself talking so reasonably. Usually, he acted on his emotions.

"You and your brother must be very close, having raised a child together," Gladys said.

"It was a unique situation and we were different enough that I think it worked out well," Zhira replied. "Gant was a far better father than I was though. I was too fun. I made him look like the bad guy."

"Don't beat yourself up! Mara sounds like a wonderful young woman. That is the product of you and your brother raising her right." Gladys encouraged a smile from Zhira.

"Thanks, Gladys. I just hope Gant is okay. I don't know what I would do without him. I am not used to being the rational and reasonable one," Zhira said.

Suddenly, a screech pierced the night, coming from the woods beyond them in the direction of Saros.

"Douse the fire," Forbin commanded from a young boy sitting nearby. The boy scrambled and kicked dirt over it until it was nothing but a smoking mound of earth.

"What was that?" Gladys asked, her hand on the hilt of her sword.

"No idea, but I think we'd better set up an extra lookout," Zhira replied.

Gladys nodded in agreement and went off to organize it.

Zhira looked in the direction of the screech, curious as to what could make such a sound. Eventually, when it did not repeat, he found a patch of grass on which to get some sleep.

~~~

The griffin had Gant pinned down with its talons, but before it could take a bite out of him, he shot
~~~

fire at its underside, sending it flapping off of him. The griffin screeched and took a swipe at Gant in retaliation, leaving a deep gash in the ground as he rolled out of the way. The griffin now stood between Mai and Gant, blocking Mai from getting to her weapons.

"Throw me my sword!" she yelled at Gant.

Gant scrambled backwards while Mai held the beast's attention. The horses pulled against their reigns where they were lashed to a tree, panicked by the sudden assault. He grabbed the sword from her saddle.

"Here!" Gant called to Mai as he tossed the sword. It flew over the unsuspecting griffin and Mai deftly caught it by the hilt. Armed with the hook on her left stump, she grinned slightly and ran at the griffin, sword drawn. The griffin gave an ear-piercing screech and charged her. Mai leaned a little left, grabbed the griffin's wing with her hook, and swung up onto its back. Gant threw more fire in its direction, and nearly hit Mai.

"Watch it!" Mai yelled at him as the griffin tried its best to buck her off. She clumsily unsheathed her sword, nearly falling off the flailing beast and held the sword up high. With all the effort she could muster, she brought the sword down hard through the griffin's neck; after another few seconds, its body went limp and with only her hook for support, Mai went tumbling.

"Mai!" yelled Gant as he rushed over to her.

Mai was stuck under the body of the griffin and with some help from Gant, managed to squirm free.

"Thanks," she muttered as she brushed herself off. Remarkably, she had gotten almost no blood on her clothes.

"I thought griffins were extinct. Weren't the last of them pets for the wizards?" Gant asked her.

"They were, or so we thought. This one was a juvenile, which means there are parents. Supposedly, they can be twice that size." Mai recalled from her studies.

"I am glad it wasn't," Gant replied.

"You and me both. Come on, let's get some sleep. We have a lot of riding to do tomorrow," Mai said as she walked over to calm her horse and grab her sleeping pack.

Chapter Twenty One
The Note

"What?!"

"I'm telling you, I met her! Dazel visited me," Rylan said to a shocked Mara.

"But…isn't that what got Knorr banished? Revealing himself to humans? Enticing them to want his powers?" Mara asked.

"I guess? It makes no sense to me. Why would she risk making contact with a human?" Rylan questioned.

"Are you sure it was real and not just a dream? Maybe you saw what you wanted to see," Mara suggested.

"No, I did not make this up! I've never had such a vivid dream," she replied stubbornly.

"Okay, let's assume your dream or vision or whatever it was is real. What does it mean?" Mara pondered the details the princess had shared: the unrecognizable phase of the moon, the goddess herself, and "looking to the stars" as Dazel had said.

"I feel like we are missing something," said Rylan.

"No shit. What do you think it is?" Mara said flatly.

"We wouldn't be missing it if we knew," Rylan shot back.

Mara rolled her eyes, but let a smile creep over her face. She enjoyed Rylan's company; she was smart and a calming presence in her otherwise dank and lonely cell. Thoughts rolled around in Mara's head. What was it about the stars that was so important? She already knew her powers were stronger at night, but why? *Was this Dazel's doing, somehow?*

"What did you say the moon looked like again?" Mara asked Rylan.

"Well, the moon went through its normal phases quickly, as if she had sped up time, and then it stopped on a phase I had never seen before. It looked like a new moon, but the color was wrong. The new moon is usually just black like the night sky but this one was…red. I looked in some books but there is very little on the moon and its phases. It seems that there are not too many people that look up at the sky."

Something clicked in Mara's head. "My father has! Zhira…he used to stargaze every night, reading messages in the constellations and finding new and interesting things to keep track of. Maybe he knows something I don't. Damn. I should have cared more about this! I wish I had his books." Mara longed for her father's wisdom as she thought back to all the nights she had spent in the tower with him, looking up at the velvety canvas of constellations and the big white moon that danced along it.

"Where is he? Maybe I can find him," Rylan suggested.

"He's likely still at Saros, held captive by your wonderful Commander Mai."

"Mai isn't all bad. After the rebellion assassinated my mother, she was the closest thing I had to one," Rylan said, defending Commander Mai.

"What about your stepmother?" Mara asked.

Rylan laughed sarcastically. "Stella? Please. She's only here because my father wants a son…needs a son."

Without warning, the sound of footsteps suddenly filled the dungeon as a few soldiers came down the spiral stairs. Their patrol turned off in the opposite direction of Mara's cell. The two women froze in silence until they faded away.

"I'd better go! My father doesn't want me down here anymore, but he isn't doing much about it. If I'm caught, I suspect that would change." Rylan took off at a brisk pace towards the stairs. Mara watched until the hallway curved past where she could see from her cell. Hoping the princess had made it back before being noticed, she sat down and began to meditate.

It didn't take long for Mara to drift off. She'd gotten used to the cell's darkness and could easily find a peaceful state in which to exist. The sounds of dripping water, squeaking rats, and scurrying bugs no longer put her on edge the way it did when she had arrived. She was unsure how long she had been down here, but she was positive it would not be for much longer.

Do not be afraid.

Mara straightened up, suddenly alert and startled by the unfamiliar voice she had heard. Her eyes made out the bars of her cell in the darkness as she glanced around for the source of the voice. The calm Mara had found meditating rapidly dissipated as she began to panic; she snapped her fingers and lit a tiny fire to illuminate her cell. There was nobody there.

Do not be afraid, the voice repeated

Mara stood up and whirled around, the ethereal voice filling the cell as if it was emanating from the walls. The small fire flickered in her hand, setting her long shadow against the wall.

"Who are you?" Mara whispered to the disembodied voice. There was no response, only the usual sounds of the dungeon. She remained tense and vigilant for a few moments, but she suspected it had only been a product of her exhausted mind.

A noise from the end of the cellblock where the guard was stationed made Mara quickly put out her fire and return to her seated position on the floor. She heard some scraping and the clanking of chains as light slowly crept along the stone walls until it illuminated her cell and those around her. Two knights carried an unconscious man by his shoulders to the cell adjacent to hers and laid him down on the damp floor, his thick brown hair cushioning his head. They locked his cell and began to walk away. Before their torches had carried the light too far away, Mara got a good look at the man's face and nearly cried.

"Kei?!"

She heard movement in Kei's cell as he came to at the sound of her voice.

"Mara? Is that you? Where are we?" He sounded groggy.

"We're in the dungeons underneath the castle. How did you get here?!"

"Well I think some guards carried me…?" Kei joked. Mara did not appreciate his sarcasm.

"You followed me?" she asked him.

"Yes, Zhira and I tracked you until…"

"Dad left Saros?!" Mara interrupted him.

"Yes, he went looking for the resistance, and when we found them he split off and sent me to locate you. Fat load of good that's done," he said in reference to their current situation. Mara's eyes were readjusting to the darkness; she could just make out his silhouette.

"How did you get caught?" she asked.

"Well, I was looking for a way into the castle, and I found it," Kei said softly so as not to alert the guard. "I think I took too long though, there was a commander waiting for me just inside the gate. I don't remember anything after that. He must've knocked me out and brought me here."

"And what happened to Dad?" Mara was bursting with questions about the outside world.

"I'm not sure, Mar." She could see his fingers on the bars between their cells; her hands quickly found their way to his. "Last I saw him, he was headed off with a member of the resistance. He told me that he was going to convince them to rescue you by telling them you're a wizard. He's hoping they will rally around you as a symbol of hope."

Mara stared through the blackness at Kei. "Me? A symbol of hope? What do they want, for me to go riding in on a cloud of magic and kill the king?"

"Can you do that?" Kei asked playfully.

"All I'm saying is that I've only ever been a girl from a nowhere town that can do some clever things with the laws of nature. I'm not a leader."

"I'm not saying you are, or that you have to be, but the rebels knowing they have a true wizard on their side might help them…and you…live," Kei said.

"I suppose…but how are we going to get out? There is no plan. I thought you'd show up with a plan." Mara said, disappointed.

"No, sorry. I was hoping to make contact with Zhira or somebody once I had located you. Obviously that plan has failed," Kei said dejectedly.

"It doesn't matter. I am so glad you are here," Mara said. She felt for his face and kissed him through the bars. His stubble tickled her lips.

After a moment, Kei continued. "So how is dungeon life? Does the chef take requests?"

"The food is surprisingly not terrible, actually…and the princess is rather nice."

"The princess? You're friends with the princess?" Kei sounded bewildered.

"I didn't say 'friends'…she comes to visit me every so often. It's kind of a long story," Mara replied.

"Seems like we have nothing but time." Kei regarded their cells.

Mara recounted her conversations with Rylan to Kei. She told him all she knew about Gjanion not being a wizard, but believing he is Knorr reincarnated. Mara explained how Rylan was upset about not being a wizard, about the vision Rylan had of Dazel, and most of the details in between. When Mara finally finished talking, she looked eagerly at Kei, waiting for a response. Having someone new to talk to was refreshing.

"Good goddess, that's a lot," he finally said.

"Tell me about it."

"So why haven't you just busted out with your magic? Why not just go take the king down or just escape?" he asked.

"Because if I do, the king or one of his men tells Mai to kill my dads," she explained.

"Oh, right. The deal you made with the king."

"I don't want any more tragedy to befall anyone in Saros on my account." Mara's mind was pulled back to an image of her grandmother laying on the stone in the town square, an image she had tried and failed to suppress. It was an image that was branded permanently into her memory. The last thing she had seen before leaving Saros with the king was Gant kneeling over the body of his own mother. A fresh wave of grief and guilt washed over Mara. "Did…did she get a proper funeral?"

Kei nodded. "She did, and it was beautiful. Everyone came to support your dads."

Mara began to sob, tears running down her cheeks. Kei fumbled a little, and managed to wipe one off her face in the dark.

"So," Mara sniffed, "what do we do now?"

"No idea. I wasn't planning on getting caught," Kei replied.

"Oh, really?" Mara asked sarcastically.

"Any ideas?" Kei asked, ignoring her quip.

"Sort of, but I need a way to communicate with someone on the outside. We need more than just the two of us."

"How about the three of us?" Rylan asked, appearing abruptly in a flick of her fingers. Her sudden and unexpected appearance startled Mara and scared Kei so badly he flopped back in his cell.

"You really need to stop doing that," Mara said.

"But that's no fun!" The princess grinned. "Nice to meet you, Kei. I'm Princess Rylan."

"Hi…" Kei said as he stood up slowly, rubbing his behind.

"How long have you been there?" Mara asked.

"Long enough to know you need some help," Rylan said.

"Why would you help us?" Kei asked, suspicious of the princess.

"Because my father, the king, is a liar. He used me my whole life, grooming me to keep his secret. He had me use potions not for training, but for testing. He'd test my ability to keep secrets, making sure I could handle being the servant he needed. But I can't live that life," Rylan said defiantly.

"What happens when your father finds out you're helping us?" Kei questioned her.

"The way I see it, he has backed himself into a corner by telling me his secret and giving me proof." She held up the book containing the family tree. "If this gets out, he loses everything. His carefully constructed appearance of being a humble wizard comes tumbling down. The rebellion would have legitimacy in the eyes of every citizen of Kyros. I'm untouchable!" She seemed rather proud of herself.

"I don't know, wouldn't the knowledge that he is a god only make the people of Kyros more fearful and submissive?" Kei asked.

"I suppose…" Rylan pondered.

"Catching Gjanion in a lie would be a boon to the efforts of those who oppose him. If he then tries to convince the kingdom that he is a god, people could see that as him trying to cover the other lie," Mara suggested.

"That's a risky assumption," Kei replied.

"It could work," said Rylan.

"We are thinking too far ahead," Mara said, refocusing. "Right now, we need a plan to get us out of here. After that, we can deal with exposing Gjanion's lie."

"How can I help?" Rylan asked.

"Hold on. We don't know if we need your help," Kei said, still unsure of Rylan.

"Kei, right now she is the only chance we have of getting out of here. What other options do we have?" Mara asked him.

"I guess you're right." Kei rubbed his hip again, still hurting from Rylan's surprise appearance, and paused.

"What's wrong?" Rylan asked.

"It's…" Kei reached into the folds of his tunic where it met his pants and produced a single piece of parchment. The paper was folded a few times and had been jammed into his waistband.

"What is that?" Mara asked.

"I'm not sure." Kei opened it and began to read, his eyes growing bigger and bigger as they scanned the lines down the page. When he was done, he looked up at Mara. "It's for you."

~~~

"I cannot overstate how important this is to our cause," Gjanion said as he paced the room.

"I am glad I was able to apprehend the culprit. We intercepted the boy just as he got inside the gate. Unfortunately, he put up too much of a fight and died defending himself from one of my knights," Commander Hearth said from his chair.

"Understood. Obviously that is an unfortunate outcome, but it is better that our men are not dead." The king continued to pace.

"Very true, sire. Now, the rebellion will be frantic, thinking their man may have given up secrets! Still, I believe that the schedules of our patrols are too regular. Despite our success, I believe a small flaw has been exposed. The rebels surely know our routine by now and can predict with ease when they must hide. The boy was able to figure out the opportune moment to take his chance. Had it not been for my spies, he would have succeeded," Hearth stated.

"Observant and clever, I almost wish I could have met him," said Gjanion.

"Trust me, sir, he never would have taken the knight's oath like others have to save themselves. The rebels are desperate and honor-bound. They're dangerous."

"Commander, you have been nothing but loyal and devoted to our cause. You have shown resourcefulness in hunting the rebels inside our own
~~~

walls, tact in handling this information, and efficiency in carrying out my orders. You are an exemplary knight and I will officially be naming you Acting General in Long's absence. Congratulations." The king extended his hand.

"Thank you, sir. It is a great honor!" Hearth got up and heartily shook Gjanion's hand. "I will not disappoint!"

~~~

Mara took the sheet from Kei and her heart stopped. It was from her father.

Mara,

I hope this note finds you. There is so much to tell you, but I'll stick to the essentials. I have found the resistance and we have a plan to break you out. I have seen in the sky that there will be an eclipse of the moon. That will be the signal, and that is when we will take to the streets and cause chaos to cover your escape. Be safe and I will see you soon.
~~~

Zhira

Mara read the note over and over again, then looked up at Kei while handing the note over to Rylan.

"Where did you get this?" she asked him as Rylan gasped when she got up to speed.

"I have no idea. I didn't have that on me. He only gave me your book which I was supposed to deliver when I saw you. My bag was taken from me when I was apprehended," Kei said, confused.

"An eclipse. Zhira mentioned an eclipse. What is that? How do we know what to look for? How will we know when it happens? We can't see the sky down here!" Mara began to panic.

"It's what I saw!" Rylan exclaimed. "The moon phase I didn't understand in my vision! That must be the eclipse. Dazel gave me the answer!" Rylan practically jumped up and down as she spoke.

"Okay, so if you know what it looks like, can you tell us when it happens? Or when it's about to?" Kei asked her.

"Yes, I'll come get you when the time comes. Nobody will know what is happening. I should be able to slip away in the confusion and chaos."

"Any chance you can locate my bag?" Kei asked.

"Oh…yes of course!"

"Okay, so we have a plan. We don't have any idea when this eclipse will begin, but Rylan, when you see whatever you saw in your vision, come and get us," Mara said.

"Okay. I'd better get going." Rylan hastily made for the exit.

"Do you really think we have a shot?" Mara asked, turning back to Kei.

"I think so. We seem to have another friend on the inside. I'm beginning to think my capture wasn't because I had failed," he replied.

"I hate that we can do nothing but wait." Mara huffed.

"I know," he found her hand again through the metal bars, "but we will be ready."

Chapter Twenty Two
Calm Before the Storm

Gant dismounted his horse. Looming in the distance was Gjanion's castle, surrounded by sprawling markets and houses. Clouds moved across the sky, carried by the brisk autumn breeze. Mai swung her cloak around her to combat the chilly air and, with some difficulty, managed to fasten it with one hand.

"Do you really think this is going to work?" Gant asked her.

"Either it does, or we're both dead," she said pragmatically.

"Great attitude," he said under his breath.

"Give me your hands." She held out a piece of rope.

"Do you need—"

"No." She cut off his offer of assistance and began to tie his hands in front of him. Gant was impressed at how capable the commander had gotten with one hand in only a few days. Their travels had been uneventful, and in their downtime around the fire each evening, Mai had familiarized herself with the different attachments Gant had Sari make for her.

"Hop on." She motioned to her horse.

Despite his hands being tied, Mai offered no assistance and watched Gant as he struggled to get up on the saddle. "We really should have tied my hands after I got on…"

"Oh, is it challenging not having both of your hands to help you?" Mai held up her only middle finger.

"Sorry," Gant replied sheepishly.

Mai rolled her eyes and got on with him. "Remember, you're my prisoner. Say nothing, and follow my lead."

They rode out from the trees into the outskirts of the surrounding town. From his perch atop the horse, Gant observed life in the castle town. It was clear to him that money was hardly important to these people. He witnessed a man trading a chicken for fruit, another selling bowls of something steaming to a woman who gave him blue onion-looking roots in return, and a couple of kids playing with a ball that Gant was pretty sure was just an inflated organ from some animal. There was an overwhelming sense of community in what Gant saw, a stark contrast from what he had expected to find here.

Most of the buildings were no more than leather sheets propped up with stilts; they appeared easy to take down and put up each day, providing shelter from the elements while people sold their goods. Gant wondered where all these people slept and lived until they got farther into town. Gradually, the leather lean-tos gave way to more densely packed stone buildings, which in turn provided less space on the street to move about, especially on a horse. Mai navigated her palomino through the throngs of people as Gant's eyes flew from building to building. On a few occasions, he managed a glimpse into some of the open windows and doors to see very tight living quarters; some had half a dozen straw mats in a single room, many of which were no bigger than the room at the top of their tower back in Saros.

Eventually, the streets became less crowded as they approached the castle. Gant noticed that the quality of life seemed to increase steadily as they got closer to the sky-scraping centerpiece of the capital. Buildings were larger and more spread out, and some even had a fence or gate in front to keep unwanted guests from meandering onto their property. Mai turned them onto the main street of this upper-class locale and Gant saw what could only be described as the true center of activity in the capital.

Shop after shop lined the road on such a scale that would make Saros look like one of the back alleys they had ridden through earlier. They walked by blacksmiths, tanneries, pubs, and buildings whose purpose Gant could not even guess.

"Welcome to the Magic Mile," Mai said from her seat behind him. "It's not actually a mile, but it feels that way when you're on foot."

Gant could see why; it seemed like the shops never ended. Florists, glassblowers, an apothecary, and many other shops surrounded the street between them as hundreds of patrons bustled in and out, their arms laden with parcels and bags. As they passed a fruit stand selling some of the greenest cabbages Gant had ever seen, the gate to the castle, which Gant had not noticed until now, opened for them.

Mai rode her horse through and stopped just inside. The wrought iron bars lowered behind them as she dismounted; she pulled her cloak slightly to disguise her missing hand. She pulled Gant rather roughly off the horse and made her way to the entrance hall of the castle without a word from any of the knights nearby, who were staring in disbelief and shock at her arrival.

"Do they not talk to you out of respect or fear?" Gant asked.

"Either way, maybe you should follow their example," she replied.

With Mai shoving him in front of her, the two of them climbed up the steps and into the castle.

"Commander Mai!" exclaimed one of the knights stationed in the main hall.

"Sir Pike, would you please go inform the king that…you know what, never mind. I'll do it myself." Mai forced Gant to walk and directed him to a door on the left.

As they entered the next room, Gant was overwhelmed. Portraits twice his height hung from three of the four walls, interchanged with beautiful floor to ceiling stained-glass windows. On the fourth wall there was an enormous purple banner with a moon behind a lightning bolt. Below the banner stood a single high-backed golden chair and two smaller silver chairs to each side. The hall was framed by pillars of marble and a floor to match; the pillars sported purple banners while the floor was inlaid with gold leafing in an ornate pattern that wound its way to the throne.

Sitting upon the throne and sporting a purple cape that matched the other decorations of the throne room was King Gjanion. He had either not noticed them enter or was more concerned with the conversation he was having with a man in dark blue armor. Mai pushed Gant forward and gained the attention of the king.

"Commander Mai." Gjanion did not sound happy to see her.

"My king," Mai said as she bent down on one knee. Still sporting her cloak, she looked like a small brown mountain with a head at its peak.

"Rise, Commander. I have an urgent need to speak with you," the king said.

"Commander Tren." Mai nodded at the knight next to the king. Tren did not return the courtesy.

"Why are you here? And why have you brought the alchemist?" Gjanion asked.

"I was instructed not to let him leave my sight, sire. I would never disobey a direct order from my king."

"A wise choice. Why have you come here?"

"Because I felt it necessary to clear my name. General Long and I discussed the manner by which you think I betrayed you, but I promise I would never do anything to challenge you."

Discussed? Gant thought. *That was one hell of a 'discussion'.*

"Lies!" Commander Tren burst out. "She's…"

"SILENCE." The king glared at Tren, who suddenly looked like a turtle retreating into its blue armored shell. "There is overwhelming proof that you conspired to ambush me during our incursion to Saros. How do you plan to defend yourself?"

"With this." Mai pulled back her cloak to reveal her missing left arm. Tren gasped and the king leaned forward. "General Long attempted to frame me as a traitor to clear his name. I made sure that did not happen." Mai said stoically. Gant was impressed.

"What are you saying, commander?" the king asked.

"General Long attempted to kill me in order to save his own skin. I returned the sentiment successfully, though not before he took my arm." Mai stared up at Gjanion with conviction.

"What a shame…" the king leaned back in his chair, pondering Mai's story. The silence in the throne room was palpable. For such a large room where most noises echoed, there was nothing—not even a breath— as Gjanion weighed the implications of what Mai had said.

"My liege," Tren began, earning a scowl from Gjanion. "I followed a messenger pigeon here myself. There is no way that General Long would have sent me to do so if it would have outed him as a rebel."

"Or he was playing you too," Mai replied. "I can imagine that the rest of the evidence made it look like it was me, so something that incriminated him could easily be painted as yet more evidence to support his claim that I was the traitor."

"Where is the general's body?" Gjanion asked.

"Somewhere out there," Mai replied, gesturing to the window. "I nearly died from that fight. I do not remember where we were."

"How did you survive, then?" Gjanion asked.

Mai paused, but Gant stepped in. "I saved her, sir."

"You?" Gjanion looked genuinely surprised for a moment before his face turned skeptical. "Why?"

"Because I knew that if you did not hear from her regularly, then you would kill my daughter," Gant said.

Gjanion ran his hand through his long dark hair. "You're right…I would have."

"My king, I swear to you that the oath I took was honest. I have wanted nothing more than to prove I deserve the life I have. You know this. I have dedicated my life to your service, and I will continue to prove it." Mai fell to her knees again in reverence. The honesty in her voice was impossible to ignore, Gant thought. Gjanion apparently agreed.

"Rise, commander. I do not think that you were the traitor."

"Thank you sir," Mai replied.

"What?!" Tren asked, incredulously. "But the evidence behind—"

"ENOUGH. I've made my decision!" Gjanion roared at the young commander before turning back to Mai. "Commander Mai, you have been through much pain and hardship in recent weeks. It is beyond anything I could ever ask of any of my military leaders. Loyalty and bravery have gotten you this far, and I will reward you properly…General."

Mai's eyes widened and locked with the king's immediately; Tren's head whipped around so fast he grabbed the back of his neck in pain.

"I'm sorry, did you say 'General'?" Mai clarified.

"I did. You have shown exemplary leadership and heroic discipline in the face of adversity. Despite your lack of knowledge of the situation, you removed the true traitor from our midst!" The king stood up and clapped his hands together.

"The true traitor?" Mai asked, knowing Long had been no such thing.

"Yes. I had suspected for some time that General Long was the one feeding information to the rebellion. He was the one who was sent to kill the last wizards, and failed to tell me that one remained. He was working for them all along. I suspect that is why he chose the East as the last of our conquests—to keep the sword relic from me and give the wizard a chance to grow into power and defeat me."

Gant couldn't believe what was happening. The king had believed their story.

"Sire, I am honored to accept the role of general. Your confidence in me is not misplaced, though I will need time to adjust to life without my left arm." She held up her stump.

"Of course, General. You deserve a break. Commander Hearth will continue as Acting General until such a time that you are ready to assume the role."

"Thank you, my king." Mai bowed again.

"Please escort your prisoner to the dungeon in the meantime. The west dungeons will do." Gjanion instructed the newly appointed general.

"Yes, sir." Mai grabbed Gant by the collar and shoved him towards the doors.

As they crossed the main hall towards the dungeons, Mai released Gant's collar. "That was swift thinking back there…thanks."

"Thank me by not sending me to the dungeons?" Gant asked her hopefully.

"Not a chance."

"I thought so. What are these dungeons like, anyway?" Gant asked her.

"Dark, gross, and depressing," she replied.

"Fantastic," Gant sighed.

~~~

Zhira pulled the hood over his head and walked down the alley, making sure not to bump into anyone accidentally. He had been here two days and had found that most people here were itching for a reason to pick a fight; if they won, they got your stuff, and stuff was scarce in these slums. If they lost, it was not their problem anymore. The castle took up a good portion of the sky as he weaved through another alley and ended up behind the tannery that he and Forbin had agreed upon. Forbin was waiting for him.

"How are things?" Zhira asked him.

"Good. Everyone is in place, and we've heard no whispers of the rebels in the city. Seems nobody notices a few more bodies."

"How could they? This place is packed like a barrel of fish," Zhira replied.

"I don't know how people live like this, it's so clustered and smelly." Forbin made a face to match the pungent odor of slums.

"You live underground…how is that not clustered?" Zhira asked.

"We all have our own domes, and it doesn't smell," Forbin replied flatly.

"Fair. Okay, so we will not see each other again until the eclipse tomorrow night. Make sure everyone has what they need."
~~~

"Aye aye, captain," Forbin said as he ventured off into the crowds, disappearing almost immediately.

Zhira and Forbin had planned to keep their meetings short and in a different location each time so as not to arouse suspicion. Zhira checked in with Gladys and a few others around the town and once he was confident that everything was as ready as it could be, he set off to find food. The sun had begun to set and gave a strangely pretty glow to the slums as he tooled around browsing the different food carts.

After selecting for himself a particularly large apple, he ventured across the main street to a spot where he had stashed his supplies. Lifting up one of the stones, he pulled out his bag; he then counted seven stones to the right and three stones up and lifted that one to reveal his sword. He tied the sword to his belt under his cloak and went to find a place to get some sleep before the eclipse.

~~~

Mara sat cross-legged on the damp floor of her cell listening to Kei's steady breathing. He was asleep, but Mara couldn't manage it; she was too worried about the plan. *What if Rylan can't get to us? What if we can't get out?*

She sat and tried to match her breathing to Kei's. Maybe she could get into his head and see something he didn't remember from his capture. Mara focused on him for a while, but was far too wound up
~~~

to remain concentrated. Frustrated, she angrily threw a fireball at the wall across from her, scorching the wall and scaring some rats.

The sudden commotion woke Kei, who could smell the lingering fumes of her flame hitting the rock.

"What happened? What's wrong?" Mara could hear him groping for the metal bars between their cells. She lit a small flame, just enough for him to see the bars, and went to sit with him.

"I'm worried, Kei. I'm worried and I'm frustrated," she said, making the flame weave in between her fingers.

"I'm worried too," he said.

"Really? About what?" Mara knew he felt it, but was surprised to hear him say it.

"I'm worried about our friends, our family…I'm worried that this plan might not work. I'm worried about you," Kei said.

Mara sensed his attempt to calm her and smiled slightly. "I'm worried about you too, but I'm also so frustrated at not knowing what happens next or when. Are we supposed to just sit here and wait for the rebellion? How do we know where to go if we get out?" she asked anxiously.

"This is going to work. We have to believe that. The main goal is to get you out of here. If we don't find them when we make our break, I'm sure we will after," he said soothingly.

"You know…I never wanted any of this." Mara's worry was evolving into guilt. "I never meant for anyone to get hurt…or die…because of me. It's all my fault Fiona is gone, all my fault that you and Dad are risking your lives…" Mara began to cry.

Kei reached through the bars and held her as best he could. "It's not your fault. You did not kill your grandmother."

"I threw the knife," she managed to say between sobs.

"At the king. It could have hit anyone. You did not kill her," he said more firmly.

"I killed her by being me. I exposed myself and brought the king to Saros."

"Mara. I am sure Fiona would rather have died than see you not be who you are meant to be."

"And what's that, Kei?" she snapped at him, pulling away.

"The last wizard. You're the hope the rebellion needs to take down that monster and restore freedom to the kingdom," Kei said

"What if I don't want to be that?" Mara asked. "What if I want a nice, quiet life like my fathers had?"

"Do you really think you could just walk away from this? How was that going to work? We get sprung from here and you just disappear into the woods?" Kei challenged her.

"No, but—"

"Why did you save Reg?" Kei interrupted her. "Why did you reveal yourself without a second thought?"

"Because Mai was going to kill him," Mara said without thinking. "I couldn't let him die."

"But you would be okay with ditching this whole fight, letting many more people die?" Kei asked, knowingly.

"No, of course not," Mara said. She laid back against the bars, letting Kei hold her again. She had exhausted herself worrying and holding in all the guilt of her actions. It felt good to let it all go, if only for a moment.

"You're right, I need to embrace who I am," Mara said, her eyes momentarily glowing.

"I am glad you feel this way, but let's bring it down a notch," he said, slightly worried.

"What's wrong?" Her eyes reverted back to normal and her flame shrank back down, she hadn't noticed that it had grown.

"What's going on back there?" The soldier's voice came from down the hall. Mara quickly extinguished her flame and moved away from the bars where Kei was. The guard came to their cells, torch blazing.

"I just watched no less than twenty rats scamper away from here. I don't know what y'all did, but quit it or I'm getting the general." Before Mara and Kei could say anything, he marched back to his post, taking the light with him.

"What did you just do?" Kei asked Mara.

"I have no idea," Mara replied.

"You need to contain your emotions," he said.

"Yeah, I'll just do that after being locked up in a stinky, dark, disgusting cell for goddess knows how long eating table scraps and waiting like some damsel to be rescued!" she exclaimed.

"You told me the food wasn't that bad…" Kei half smiled, though Mara couldn't see it.

Eventually Kei fell back asleep and Mara meditated, still too restless to get any sleep. She focused on breathing steadily, rebalancing herself and calming her mind. Thoughts of failure and disaster flowed through her mind's eye; death, destruction, and so much more sent her into a jittery state of tension once again.

Mara tried harder to force those thoughts out, focusing on Kei holding her, on Rylan's excitement about the eclipse, and on her own elation at knowing that Zhira was coming for her. Eventually Mara drifted off into a dreamless slumber.

~~~

Rylan sat and watched a single cloud obscure a few stars as it slowly trudged across the sky. The moon hung low, illuminating the castle grounds in pale light. The long shadows it cast made the whole scene look strange and distorted from her vantage point in the window. She had been awake all night watching the
~~~

moon and waiting for the eclipse; as it set, her tired mind wandered.

The cool autumn breeze kicked up and sent chills down her back. Rylan relaxed as she leaned on her window sill, thinking back to the times when her father would take her riding into the fields to practice potions with her. *No,* she thought, *to practice his potions* on *her.* Rylan furrowed her brow, frustrated at these recurring thoughts.

Her father had been so good to her, gifting her the most beautiful clothes, taking her to the fanciest parties, giving her the most beautiful horse, never raising his voice at her unless she really earned it. But now the revelations of who he was had undercut all of the kindness. Was he just buttering her up? Had he been playing her the whole time, distracting her so she wouldn't ask questions? Did he feel the need to constantly win her over so he wouldn't lose her in the critical moments? Did that mean he really cared about her?

Rylan pried a small piece of rock from the window frame and threw it as far as she could. It landed in the pond near the center of the garden, and she watched the ripples spread out over its surface, reflecting the moonlight in perfectly circular silver rings on an otherwise smooth black canvas. Rylan stared at the rings until they faded, then closed her window and turned to her bed.

Chapter Twenty Three
Eclipse

"I'm sorry I lost the armor. It really was beautiful," Mara said.

"You didn't lose it, it was taken from you," Kei replied. "There will be others."

"I can't wait to see what you come up with next." She smiled. Mara was trying to take their minds off the eclipse, the waiting, and the tension.

"Hopefully we won't be waiting too long. When we get out of here, when all of this is over, I just want my own forge to create new and unique things. I don't care for conflict; I'm not sure I even want to make weapons!"

"But your father…" Mara started.

"My father was…*is* an amazing blacksmith. But he never experimented. My dad relied on tried and true methods. It ended up being a really good thing, outfitting the town when we had to defend ourselves, but there is so much more to be done with a forge!

Your armor was an innovation. If nobody innovates, how do we grow? How do we get better?"

"That's true. I bet you could make anything you set your mind to…anything you can imagine."

"Hey, by the way…why did your armor glow?" he asked her.

"I thought you would have some ideas." Mara was equally confused.

"I'm as lost as you are. I had no idea it could even do that. I just wanted it to look…pretty!" He blushed slightly which Mara could not see in the dim light of her miniature fire.

They both sat in silence for a few minutes. Mara sat in her meditation position on the floor and stared at nothing in particular, searching her mind for an answer.

"Mara? Why do your eyes glow?" Kei asked after some time.

"I haven't really figured that out either, besides the fact that it happens when I do more intense magic. The harder something is, or the more I have to concentrate, the more they glow. It gets hard to control and the magic feels like it's spilling over." She was grasping at wisps of ideas, but felt there was something that connected them all.

"So what if the gems are responding to that excess magic?" he asked.

"I did feel more in control with the armor on. It almost felt like the armor was moving me," she tried to explain.

"Moving you?" Kei asked.

"I think the gems react to my magic. That's why they glow," she offered.

"And they enhance your abilities?" he questioned.

"Sort of. It's more like they help me control what I'm doing. I feel more…precise. I don't have to exert as much energy containing or directing my magic because the gems will do it for me." She fumbled through her thoughts.

"So the gems don't give you more power, they help you control what power you do have?" Kei clarified.

"Yes, that's about as right as I can explain," she replied.

"So the question is, why?" Kei paced in his cell.

~~~

"What the hell is happening?" King Gjanion looked up at the sky and saw that the moon, which had been full, was starting to wane. He quickly began running to Rylan's room to wake her and get her to safety.

He tore through the castle. Nobody else had noticed the anomaly and did not have the sense of urgency and panic that he had. Gjanion's actions startled the knights on duty as he raced past them and up to
~~~

Rylan's tower. He met her as she was descending the spiral stairs, dressed in all black.

"Dad, what *is* that?" She pointed at the moon through one of the small windows in the wall. The left edge of the bright orb had gone dark as if some monster had taken a bite of it.

"I don't know, Ry, but I need to make sure you are safe."

"I know what to do, and where to go. Go and get Stella and make sure she is safe! She'll need your help more than I will." Rylan sold the excuse to stay out of her father's sight with ease.

Gjanion hugged his daughter and took off to find his pregnant wife. The princess doubled back up the staircase as she remembered what Kei had asked of her. She grabbed a flask for herself and what she assumed was his bag and made for the dungeons. As she raced through the castle, she was careful not to draw too much attention to herself. Her blonde curls had been pulled back into a tight ponytail and her black outfit helped her blend in as people went every which way, now fully aware of and unsure of how to deal with the sudden and unexpected darkening of the moon.

"It's a sign from the goddesses!"

"The end is nigh!"

Exclamations of doom echoed throughout the castle as she slipped subtly down the corridor that led to Mara and Kei. She made it to the bottom of the stairs to find that the knight who had been on guard had left his post. She took a swig from her flask and lit a fire in her hand to guide her down the dark hall.

~~~

"Time to go!" Rylan said to the two surprised faces that greeted her.

"My bag!" Kei exclaimed as Mara, happy to be doing magic again, bent the metal locks until they broke. Rylan tossed it to him and he slipped it over his shoulder.

"We need to get moving!" Rylan said, already making her way back down the cell block.

"Wait." Kei rummaged in his bag and produced an unsharpened dagger with a wooden handle and a purple gem in the hilt. He handed it to Mara.

"What is it?" she asked him, scanning her new gift.

"Your weapon. I didn't have time to sharpen it unfortunately, but I'm hoping…"

Mara could feel her power like she could in the armor. *Yes,* she thought, *the stones do help channel my powers.* She swung the dagger and finished her flourish with it pointed at the stone wall. A bright flash erupted from the tip of the unsharpened metal and a massive hole appeared where the stone had been, scorch marks tracing the edge.

"What…did you just do?" Kei asked, still cowering from the sudden blast.
~~~

"I'm not sure…as soon as I grabbed it, I could feel the stone. I could feel the control." Mara looked down at the dagger.

"Well that's just dandy and all, but we have to GO," Rylan said.

Mara tucked the dagger into her waistband. They took off running and made their way back up to the main hall where the commotion had died down as the lords of the castle went into hiding. They made for the exit when a voice came from behind them.

"Rylan?" Commander Hearth's deep voice froze all three of them. Rylan slowly turned around to address the heavy-set man.

"Ah, Commander Hearth, I was just helping these…" She wasn't ready to lie and Hearth could tell.

"Prisoners?" He finished Rylan's sentence for her. "Tell me, princess…what was your plan?" Hearth stood confidently in the middle of the hall, arms crossed and resting on his gut.

"I…" Rylan began, caught off guard. Kei began to step up to say something but Hearth just held his hand up. Mara was unsure of whether to attack this man or not.

"Your plan will *probably* be to find the wizard's father, Zhira, and help him gain entrance into the castle. Then you *might* meet me in the throne room where I will have corralled the king and the other commanders. Once there, Mara *could* make an attempt to overthrow him, ending with a crown upon your head as the deserving heir to your father's seat."

The three of them stared at the fat commander, mouths agape.

"You're the spy?!" Rylan asked, putting the clues together.

"Indeed, my dear. Did you not wonder how the boy got the note from Zhira? Did you not wonder why there was no guard on duty in the dungeons tonight? Did you ever stop to ask yourself why I was never a fighter?"

"I just thought you were fat..." Rylan said.

"Well that was by choice!" Hearth laughed. "To protect myself, I needed an alibi so I could plan instead of fight!" He slapped his stomach with enthusiasm.

"Where do we find my father?" Mara asked, still overwhelmed from the last few minutes.

"That I do not know. My only information is that they're about to make quite a commotion in the city in order to give themselves a chance to get into the castle." Hearth glanced out the nearest window. "By the looks of the moon, you do not have too much time. Go!" The moon was almost halfway darkened and beginning to adopt a reddish hue as the fat commander turned and headed for the throne room.

Mara, with Kei and Rylan following close behind, left through the large double door. They crossed the courtyard and came to the gate which was guarded by two soldiers. At the sight of the three renegades, the soldiers became confused.

"Princess Rylan? What are you doing?" one of the knights asked.

"Something I hope I don't regret." And without warning, Rylan took a step forward and swiped the spear from his hand. In the same motion, she spun it and swept his leg, sending him tumbling backwards. The other guard charged them with his own spear, which Rylan parried. Mara was impressed with Rylan's reflexes and agility.

"The lever is up there!" The princess motioned with her head as she sparred with the knight.

Kei made for the ladder and scaled it quickly. Mara followed close behind him and they found themselves atop the battlements where several guards were spaced along at even intervals, all armed with bows and swords. At the sight of Kei and Mara, one of the archers got the attention of the rest and began firing at them. Mara instinctively raised her dagger and blasted one of the arrows out of the air.

"Whatever that was, keep doing it!" Kei yelled as he grabbed the handle of the geared lever and began turning it to open the gate.

Mara whisked the dagger back and forth, blasting the arrows off course or breaking them altogether; she didn't miss once. After a minute, Kei had lifted the gate high enough for them to be able to get through.

"That's all we need! Let's go!" He dropped down the hole where the ladder was and slid down without using the rungs. Mara followed him, sending one more blast at the nearest archer for good measure.

"You're not wielding that much like a dagger," Kei observed.

"It's because it isn't a dagger." Mara held it up and noticed that the amethyst was glowing.

"Let's keep moving!" Rylan pushed them towards the half-open gate. They ducked underneath the iron posts and took off into the city.

~~~

Gant sat alone in his cell. A missing stone in the wall had left a small opening that provided a limited view of the gardens behind the castle. He could not see the sky, which he figured would upset Zhira more than him, but could see its reflection on the water of a pond.

All he could think about was Mara, so close and yet so far away from him. He had done all he could to get here and was now stuck sitting here, frustrated. *So close*, he thought. *I know she is here somewhere. How could I let this happen? I'm useless here.* Gant was furious with himself. He had hoped Mai would help him find Mara, but why? She was still loyal to the king, once she got what she wanted, that was it. He was a fool for believing otherwise.

Gant was grateful for the small bit of autumn wind that fought its way through the accidental window; without it this place would be a stagnant, disgusting, vermin-ridden pit of misery. Luckily for him it was a disgusting, vermin-ridden pit of misery with a breeze.
~~~

Gant tried to relax his breathing, calm his mind, and concoct a plan. The opening in the wall was too small and high up for anyone to hear him yell, and he had no idea where he even was in the castle. If he escaped he would have no idea how to find his way out; he needed a friend on the inside. He needed help.

Gant sat for a while until he eventually noticed that his cell was getting darker. He looked through the hole and saw that the moon's reflection on the pond had changed. At first he thought there was a disturbance in the water, but soon realized that the pond was still. The moon looked like it was missing a piece, as if it was going through its phases all in one night. Gant had no idea what this meant and wished he could talk to his brother. If anyone could interpret this, it would be Zhira.

A moment later, Gant heard footsteps approaching his cell. He backed away from the window and stood in the middle of his confined space. The torchlight preceded its bearer, illuminating the disgusting hole they had thrown him in. A metal-clad figure with only half of a left arm came into view.

"Mai?" he asked, shielding his eyes as they adjusted to the sudden change of light.

"Hello Gant."

"What's happening? Why is the moon changing?" he asked.

"I'm not sure, but it is causing quite a commotion," she said.

"Why aren't you up there helping your troops?" Gant questioned.

"I will be, but I had to check to ensure that none of the prisoners had escaped. It's chaos up there, someone could easily have let you out." Mai placed the torch in a nearby sconce on the wall behind her, then pulled out a key. She unlocked his cell door.

"What are you doing?"

"Repaying you. You saved my life, and gave me the chance to save my reputation. Plus, I don't like being indebted to someone. Nobody will know how you got out in this panic. I don't know where your daughter is, and I don't really care. Get yourself out of here. I won't be able to free you again." She stared intensely at him as if to make her point, then grabbed the torch and departed the dungeon.

"Thank you," he called to her as she walked away. Gant spun on his heel and made for the stairs at the opposite end of the block.

~~~

Zhira swung his silver sword at the guard, who parried and retaliated with a stab. Zhira dodged, and Forbin swung his club, striking hard against the back of the knight's helmet. The man fell to the ground before he could take another jab at Zhira.

"Thanks!" Zhira called out. He turned down another alley with Forbin close behind. They spilled out
~~~

into the Magic Mile which was overflowing with panicked townspeople and guards fighting off rebels in the chaos. It was a veritable river of insanity, with rapids of people flowing every which way, carrying other groups with them. Near the center of the street, Gladys was taking on a particularly aggressive knight who wielded two swords. He was overpowering her until she managed to get him to overcommit on a lunge, which she dodged and drove her sword through the gap in his armor at his neck; he crumpled onto the stone.

"Where do we go?" Forbin asked Zhira, yelling above the commotion.

"That way," Zhira said, pointing up the street. "We need to head for the castle."

They pushed their way through the throngs of people and towards the castle gate, which was still out of sight. Zhira glanced up at the moon and saw that half of its face was now black as their planet marched steadily on between it and the sun. He shoved harder, hoping every step brought him closer to Mara.

~~~

Mara led Kei and Rylan into the nearest alley and immediately sat down and closed her eyes.

"What are you doing?!" Rylan asked her impatiently.

"Shut up!" Mara hissed.
~~~

She concentrated all the energy she had into thinking about Zhira. She knew he was close, and this was her best shot of finding him. It hadn't worked yet, but she was desperate; it was now or never. In her mind's eye, she saw a knight fall over and a scrawny but tough looking man wielding a club standing beside where the knight had stood. She had him, she was seeing through Zhira's eyes, but where was he?

Mara followed the memory until he came out into the street and yelled something she couldn't make out. There were so many people that the memory was blurry, but she saw which direction he had gone. She opened her eyes and stood up.

"I know where my father is. Follow me."

"What did she just do?" Rylan asked Kei.

"No idea. I've never seen that before," he replied with a shrug as they took off after her.

Mara ran back to the street in front of the gate, which had been closed once they had escaped. *One problem at a time,* Mara thought to herself. She looked down the crowded street full of people panicking from the rebel assault and the doom-bringing eclipse. Scanning the sea of heads, she realized there was a better way to do this. *Let him find me.* She drew her dagger and gripped tight; focusing, she got the end of the blade to light up in a bright blue and held it high in the air.

The blue light acted as a beacon in the increasing darkness beneath the disappearing moon.

People in the crowd nearest her stopped and stared, shocked by the sight.

"What is this witchcraft?!" someone yelled.

"The goddesses have come for us!" another screamed.

The panic around them increased dramatically, but Mara held her ground; she had gotten the result she desired. She turned and saw Zhira pushing past two flustered women while wielding a brilliant silver sword.

"Mara!" Zhira hugged her as soon as he reached her.

She returned the hug, then pulled away, knowing they did not have much time.

"Dad, how…" Mara began.

"Questions later. Right now we need to get you out of here!" Zhira yelled above the chaos.

"No." Rylan did not move as the rest of them had begun to evacuate down the street without hesitation.

"No?" Mara asked.

"Who is this?" Zhira asked.

"Dad, this is Princess Rylan, she is King Gjanion's daughter."

"Why should we not be fleeing right this second?" Kei asked her.

"Because my father can't be left in charge. You heard Commander Hearth, we need to face him. YOU need to face him. This might be our best chance." The princess's golden brown eyes pleaded with Mara.

"You really want to take him down?" Mara asked her.

"Yes, I do. He has lied to me and the rest of the people for too long. He'll spin this assault on the city in his favor and it will only benefit him. We can't let that happen."

"Rylan, I'm not equipped…"

"Yes you are! Your powers get stronger with the stars. What better time to face him than during an eclipse? No moon, no sun, just the stars!"

Mara didn't know what to do. She had just been reunited with Zhira and Gant was still a hostage. She wouldn't admit it, not in front of Kei, but she was terrified of facing the king.

"Look, there will be other chances! We can come back," Mara argued.

"Come back when? You think it's going to be easy to come back? You think this is going to get easier?" Rylan was on the verge of tears. Mara began to realize that the longer they waited the harder this would be for the princess.

"I agree with Rylan," Kei said. "We attack now. It's our best chance."

"Count me in." A voice came from behind them.

"Gant?!" Zhira nearly dropped his sword in surprise. He embraced his brother. "What are you doing here? How did you—" Gant interrupted him with a hug, then withdrew.

"It's a long story. Right now we need to finish this," he said.

Mara looked at her dads, her new ally, and at Kei. She knew they were right, and their courage was giving her strength.

"Okay, let's do this. What's the plan?"

Chapter Twenty Four
King of Kyros

"We need supplies," Gant said. "Zhira and I aren't going to be much help without potions."

"Speak for yourself, I've been managing fine with my sword!" Zhira held up the relic.

"Where did you get that?" Kei asked. "It's beautiful."

"The leader of the rebellion gave it to me. Which reminds me—Rylan, your great grandfather is alive."

"He's what?" Rylan asked.

"Alive," Zhira repeated. "He's leading the rebellion against your father."

"Rylan, that means he's not…" Mara trailed off, the realization hitting her like an avalanche.

"He's not what?" Gant asked, completely lost.

"We really do have a chance," Rylan said to Mara, ignoring Gant for the moment.

"He's just an alchemist. We can do this," Mara said confidently.

"Can someone please explain to me what is happening?" Gant interjected.

Mara turned to him. "Gjanion is not a wizard. He thinks he is a god reincarnated, but if Radion is alive, then that isn't possible. That means he is nothing but an alchemist with some fancy weapons. Keep up, dad!" Mara winked before ducking out of the alley and into the street.

"Yeah. Keep up Gant," Zhira said, teasing his brother.

"How was I…never mind, let's go," Gant said, running with Zhira after their daughter.

"Kei, you snuck around here for a while. Where can we find an herbalist shop or something?" Mara asked him.

"I'm sorry, I don't know. I wasn't really paying much attention to those."

Rylan chimed in. "I might be able to help. My father's study is full of ingredients and potions we can take. He uses them to keep up his appearance as a wizard, so he always has to have some ready."

"Okay, take us there," Gant said.

"It's usually locked, and only my father has the key."

"Leave that to me," Mara replied.

They ran back to the castle where there were about a dozen knights between them and the closed wrought iron gate. Rylan and Zhira were the only ones with weapons apart from Mara, so she did the only thing she could think of. Drawing the knife, she brandished it the same way she had done in the dungeon; the blast was superb and tossed aside the knights like ragdolls. Their only problem now was the gate.

Kei grabbed an axe from one of the knights Mara had blown aside and took a heavy swing at the gate, but he didn't even leave a mark.

"What now?" he turned and asked the group.

Mara closed her eyes and pointed the dagger at the gate. The amethyst began to glow brightly as the gate slowly rose slowly, allowing them entrance.

"Go," Mara said in a strained voice once the gate had been lifted up enough for them to get underneath it. Mara walked closer to the gate; in one motion she released the gate, dove, and just barely slid underneath to safety on the other side.

"Are you all right?" Rylan asked her.

"Fine," Mara said. "Let's keep going."

They met no resistance in the courtyard that covered the space between the gate and the castle. It was eerily quiet as they followed Rylan, climbing the spiral stairs to the king's study. When they reached the big wooden door, Mara pointed her dagger at the lock, but Kei lowered her arm.

"This one's mine," he said with a slight grin.

They all stepped back as Kei wound up and took a flying swing at the door. The axe stuck just in front of the hinges and cracked the wood; he took a second swing and the door came loose. With a kick, it fell away.

With Rylan's help, Gant and Zhira grabbed some potions as she refilled her flask with a red liquid Mara recognized as a fire brew.

"Here," Rylan said, tossing Kei a potion.

"What is it?" Kei removed the cork from the vial.

"It ups your strength," Zhira answered.

Kei nodded and downed the vial's contents. Once the alchemists had armed themselves, the group hastily made their way towards the throne room.

"I don't know what is about to happen, but we need to be ready for anything. If I tell you all to run, then you run," Mara said to them as they crossed the main hall to the throne room door.

"We will not abandon you," Zhira said, putting his hand on her shoulder.

"I'm not telling you to abandon me. I'm telling you to listen to me."

Zhira nodded that nod that parents give to their children to humor them. Mara recognized it, but didn't say anything further.

"Mara?" Rylan's voice was unusually soft given the situation.

"What is it?"

"Whatever happens in there…please don't kill him," she said strongly, but her eyes gave away the desperate plea lying beneath. Mara could not imagine what was going on inside the princess, or the thoughts that accompanied such turmoil.

"Rylan, I promise I will do everything I can to not kill your father, but please understand that he will likely try to kill me. If I have to kill him, I will."

"Please," Rylan begged, quieter than before.

Mara looked at her golden eyes. She could see herself in them. She could not say no to the girl who had helped her through so much. Without Rylan, she would not be here.

"Okay. I won't kill him," Mara said finally. Rylan gave her a smile before returning to her stubborn, hardened expression she'd been sporting throughout the night.

"Ready?" Kei asked.

Zhira, armed with his sword, Rylan with her spear, Mara with her dagger, and Gant with his fists aflame, all nodded.

Kei kicked the door open and stepped through.

The throne room was empty save for the four figures at the opposite end. In the light thrown from the braziers that lined the hall, the purple banners looked like shadows across the pillars, the gold leafing laid in the floor seemed to dance as the flames leapt, and the stained glass windows were as dark as the night behind them with the eclipse nearing totality.

King Gjanion sat in his large golden high-backed throne and was flanked by Mai and Hearth in either chair beside him; Commander Tren stood behind Mai. All four of them looked battle ready in their armor, armed to the teeth with swords and daggers.

"It appears you were right, Commander Hearth. The rebels have come for me." Gjanion's voice echoed off of the clean, flat surfaces of the room.

Mara stepped forward in front of the group.

"Before you say anything, wizard, let me guess. You want to go one on one because this is 'our fight', yes?"

Mara gave a single nod.

"Well, unfortunately, it isn't just our fight. Without your companions, you would still be stuck in the dungeon. You would be nothing. You…" Gjanion's voice trailed off as his eyes finally found his daughter. "Rylan?"

"Hello, father," she said coldly.

"What do you think you are doing?" His voice was devoid of rage, the genuine surprise taking command of his tone.

"Helping these innocent people be free of your lies." She stepped up next to Mara to face her father.

"Innocent? These people are not innocent! They're attacking our home! Our legacy!"

"You mean *your* legacy. I was just another pawn in your conquest, the same as the rest of them." Rylan motioned to Hearth, Tren, and Mai. "You lied to me all these years. You told me I was going to be great."

"My princess, you are great!" Gjanion exclaimed.

"I am NOT your princess," Rylan's voice rose steadily. "I am not ANYBODY'S princess! I was only a piece in your puzzle. You wanted me to be your keeper, your teacher in the next life, your…your…diary! You wanted me to make sure you could rise to power again in your next life, and so you told me everything I wanted to hear to gain my trust, to win me over."

The king stared at his daughter with such a terrifying calm that Mara was sure he was going to strike her down right then. The air was electric and her heart pounded out of her chest as she watched daughter against father. Eventually, Gjanion broke the silence.

"Rylan…you fool. I have always loved you, even though you never were going to be a wizard. It was a mistake to lead you on. I never should have let that lie get so far, but if you hadn't met *her*, if General Long had done his job, then it wouldn't have mattered." He pointed at Mara.

"What…do you mean?" Rylan asked her father, rage flushed out by confusion.

"I sent General Long to finish off her family, to make sure there was nobody left but us. You see my grandfather Radion had a sister…"

"Lydia," Zhira said suddenly from behind them.

"I see someone has been doing their homework," the king sneered. "Yes, her name was

Lydia. When Radion emancipated the kingdom from the wizards, she took her family and went into hiding. It took generations, but eventually we located them: the last of the wizards. Your mother, Lydia's granddaughter." Gjanion said, now looking at Mara.

"So that's who was looking for you, chasing you," Zhira said in reference to the memory he had seen the morning he found Mara.

"General Long made one mistake in his life, and that was not doing the job himself," Gjanion said to Rylan. "Your wizard companion here managed to be overlooked by the soldiers that killed her mother that night, and as a result she is here to overthrow me."

"You…you had my mother killed?!" Mara yelled. Gjanion pointed his staff at her and she flew back ten feet, landing hard on the marble.

"It's rude to interrupt!" the king wagged his finger tauntingly.

"You're going to regret that," Zhira said, brandishing his sword.

"Is that what I think it is?" Gjanion's eyes fell on the sword. "You've had the relic this whole time?!" Mara could almost feel the king's blood began to boil.

Gjanion wasted no time and launched himself at Zhira.

"No!" Mara pointed her dagger at Gjanion, who took the brunt of the blast in his breastplate; he fell back onto the steps in front of the throne.

"Get that sword!" the king yelled. Tren made to move towards the rebels, but Hearth had already drawn his sword. He held it in front of Tren, stopping the young commander in his tracks.

"What is the MEANING of this, Hearth?!" the king roared as he got up.

"Well, my liege, General Long wasn't the only one who made a mistake. You put your trust in the wrong people."

"Explain yourself!" The king's face was red with rage.

"Lord Geralith placed me on your council to feed information to the rebellion," Hearth said simply, still holding Tren at sword-point.

"Lord Geralith was the right hand to my grandfather! He was protector of the realm after the death of my father. HE was no traitor!" Gjanion roared.

"You're right, sire. *You* are the traitor. Lord Geralith was only acting in the interests of the people." He gripped his sword with both hands and pointed it directly at Tren.

"I'll have your head!" The king shot lightning from his staff and sent Hearth flying across the room and colliding into one of the pillars before falling to a heap at its base.

Mara decided this was her chance. She conjured a blue fireball and hurled it at the king while his back was turned. It hit him squarely in the back, knocking him to the side. He maintained his footing and wheeled on Mara, beginning a flurry of assaults she could barely withstand. Tren made for Zhira, but was stopped as Kei stepped between them.

"I don't believe we have had the pleasure," Kei said, grinning as he swung his axe at the commander. Tren dodged, drew his swords, and the two went to battle.

~~~

Mai looked down at Rylan and Gant, who stared back at her. Mai had cared for Rylan like a daughter, and had a soft spot for the alchemist after he had saved her life. If she didn't act, her rise to the rank of general would be short lived. If she did act, she would be destroying two of the only people she had ever cared about. They weren't bad people. Why were they doing this?

"I don't want to fight you," Rylan said to her.

"You should have thought of that before betraying your father."

"He betrayed his people. You're no better," Gant spat.

Gant's hostility was surprising. Mai latched onto it, giving herself motivation to fight the two of them.

"You'll regret this," she said as she lunged at Gant with the blade attachment he had given her.

~~~

Tren swung his swords in a tornado of attacks that Kei could not keep up with using only his axe. Zhira mitigated Kei's need to move quickly though, as every time Tren had the upper hand on him, Zhira would be enough of a nuisance to the commander that Kei would regain his footing and take some heavy swings with the axe. It would not have been much of a match had there not been two of them. Having worked in a forge for most of his life, Kei had more than enough strength to effortlessly wield the axe, but Tren was exhausting to fight against. Kei was losing stamina and Tren took advantage, eventually the back of Kei's calf. The muscle couldn't handle the tension and snapped, buckling his left leg.

"Kei!" Zhira yelled.

Tren turned on the alchemist almost immediately, and began swinging both swords in different directions. Zhira was proficient with a sword, thanks largely to the cocktail of potions currently powering his every move, but eventually Tren overpowered him. Tren parried a swing by Zhira and thrust his shoulder into Zhira's chest sending him falling backward. He dropped the relic which clattered onto the marble floor.

Eager to be the one to finish the king's mission, Tren left Zhira wheezing on the ground and picked up the sword.

"My king!" Tren called out before tossing the sword to him.

Gjanion looked up from his duel with Mara and deftly grabbed the sword out of the air, catching it by its hilt. Mara did not pause her assault. She launched another blast from her dagger and hit him in the side, staggering him.

"It doesn't matter. You're too late," he said calmly, an unnerving smile spreading across his face.

Gjanion reached up and plucked the ruby from his crown. Hearth had regained consciousness and watched in horror as the king took the ruby and secured it in the hilt of the silver sword.

"No!" Hearth exclaimed as King Gjanion turned to face Mara with all three relics.

"It feels so…strong. With these relics I will be the unstoppable, unquestioned, unequivocal king of Kyros!" He held the sword tightly in his right hand, the staff in his left, and the crown upon his head, sapphire glinting in the firelight of the braziers.

At that same moment, the eclipse hit totality. The planet's shadow encompassed the entire face of the moon, which now looked like it had been painted red with blood. The sight was so magnificent that people stopped in the chaos of the streets to admire it. In the throne room, Gjanion and Mara stared each other down as the sky behind the stained-glass windows went pitch black. The fires in the braziers seemed to get slightly brighter.

Zhira got up from where he had been bested and ran towards Mara. He stood in front of her with sparking hands.

"You will not touch my daughter, you bastard," he said in such a menacing tone that chills ran down Mara's back.

Zhira's eyes were wide and blazing with hate as he began to throw lightning bolts at the king, who deflected them with ease using the staff. There was a weird shimmering effect in the air around the king, almost as if he was protecting himself with pure energy.

"You are a noble man, alchemist. A fool, but a noble fool." The king laughed as he retaliated with a flood of fire from his staff and a tornado-strength gust of wind directed by the sword. Zhira dodged the wave of flames and Mara returned fire which bounced off of the king's protections and hit the ceiling, sending rubble tumbling around them.

~~~

Gant had taken the lead on his and Rylan's assault against the newly appointed general, trying his best to protect the princess. Gant had drawn water from a fountain in the corner of the room and was using it as a whip in an attempt to freeze Mai's feet in place. Rylan sported her fire in unique and beautiful patterns. She sent waves and spirals at the general, forcing her to dodge and dance rather than lunge and attack. Every attack appeared to be slightly off the mark or reduced in power. Gant did not want to kill Mai, and he could tell she did not want to kill him either.
~~~

Mai swung with the blade on her left arm and cut a gash in Gant's robes before dodging a particularly large wave of fire from Rylan. She pivoted and kicked the princess in the leg, sending her stumbling back. Gant brought the water down on the general and froze her right foot in place. With some effort, she managed to pull free and kicked ice at Gant, cutting his face. Rylan got up and grabbed Mai's arm with a flaming hand. She latched on firmly and did not let go as Mai's armor warmed. She tried to throw the princess off, but her grip was strong; Mai howled in pain as the heat became too much under the metal armor.

"I will not lose my good arm!" she yelled as she thrust with her blade arm at the princess, narrowly missing her shoulder as Rylan let go of the general's arm and ducked out of the way. Mai took the opportunity to sacrifice balance for a good shot at the princess; she kicked up both feet behind her and fell to the floor but not before her feet connected with the princess's face; Rylan crumpled instantly.

~~~

Kei, standing on one leg and bolstered by the strength potion he had taken, re-engaged with Tren, this time backed up by Commander Hearth, and together they managed to subdue the wily young commander. Kei swept the commander's leg with his axe and Hearth pinned him down, kicking Tren's swords out of his hands. Kei borrowed a dagger from Hearth and cut a
~~~

piece of his tunic to use to tie Tren's hands behind his back.

"Guard him," Kei said to Hearth before turning to go help Rylan. He hopped over to the princess and pulled her from the clash between Gant and Mai. Once they were safely out of harm's way, Kei looked up to check on Mara, who, aided by her father, was dueling violently with Gjanion.

Gjanion utilized so much energy that he looked like a self-contained storm. Wind whipped around him as he shot lightning bolts from his emerald-topped staff and took glowing swipes with his silver sword. Mara held her ground, but Zhira was no match; Gjanion's alchemy had become too powerful to be matched by her relic-less father.

Mara threw pure energy from her dagger at the king, along with rubble from the now broken ceiling and fire from her own hands, but the king had created a field of energy around himself that seemed to absorb everything Mara threw at it. She sent more debris flying his way, but Gjanion easily cut through the stone with the sword. She tried subduing Gjanion with vines and plants that she forced through one of the nearby windows, but they simply burned away as they touched him. She was beginning to feel helpless despite the extra control she had with her dagger, and she knew Zhira felt overwhelmed even if he did not show it. Mara herself was beginning to get the feeling she could not protect them both. The king was too powerful, despite being only an alchemist.

Zhira tried to get behind the king, but every time he managed to skirt to the side, Gjanion would summon wind from nowhere and send him tumbling backwards.

"You annoy me, alchemist." The king furrowed his brow and sent streaks of pure energy at him.

Mara, with her dagger pointed, managed to redirect them towards one of the stained glass windows, shattering it and revealing the red moon in its perfect eclipse.

Mara looked out the window. *The stars,* she thought to herself. She focused, trying to feel the connection with the night sky like she had done inadvertently so many times before. She breathed deeply, centering herself, and started to feel stronger and less restricted. Mara pointed her dagger at the king and a large purple streak came shooting from the tip, shattering his energy field and sending him sprawling. Having been distracted by Zhira, Gjanion refocused on Mara and went berserk. Among a plethora of elemental assaults, Gjanion threw the sword at Mara, who dodged its initial pass but was surprised by its return and gained a new cut on her right shoulder. In retaliation, Mara magically pulled one of the marble columns loose and sent it careening towards him. Despite his efforts to break it apart, the large chunks battered him, giving Zhira time to rush in and try to pry the staff loose from the king's grip.

Gjanion roared as he tightened his grip on the staff; all three gems in his possession glowed and a shockwave exploded in all directions, blasting the rock apart and sending Zhira spiraling in the air. The rocks clattered to the floor and so did Zhira.

"No!" Mara cried as she made straight for her father. The king interrupted her path with another blast but she redirected it back at him. Gjanion blocked the energy by throwing the sword, which Mara took control of with her dagger. She guided it around herself in a wide arc, adding energy to it as it traveled and directed it back at Gjanion masterfully. The energy was too much for the maniacal king and it shattered his breastplate entirely as he took the attack square in the chest.

Mara did not wait to see how hard she had hit him. She rushed over to Zhira and pulled him to his feet. Standing side by side they stared the king down, exhausted but not ready to give in.

"You ignorant, pathetic, despicable girl!" Gjanion was furious and charged Mara with the sword head on. Mara matched his pace and sent some of the rubble ahead of her to meet him. Gjanion blasted it aside, some of it returning from whence it came and staggering Mara slightly. As the two closed in on each other, Mara braced for impact but met no resistance. She watched helplessly as Gjanion altered his course slightly, sword extended in front of him, and ran it directly through Zhira's chest.

Chapter Twenty Five
The Bright One

The silver handle protruded from Zhira's chest and Mara could feel it in her own. The king stood just past where he had delivered the fatal blow and was admiring his work. Mara rushed to her father and caught him as he fell. The world around her moved slowly as she removed the sword from his chest. With all of her might, Mara tried to summon the same strength she had displayed when she had healed his leg. The wound began to close slowly but not before Gjanion took another pass at her, swinging his staff at the back of her head.

Hearth's sword met his staff just shy of Mara's head, and in the shock of the moment the commander tore the long slender weapon from the king's grip. He turned and landed a heavy roundhouse kick in the king's ribs, accompanied by a loud cracking noise. Gjanion fell over wheezing and Hearth stood between him and Mara. Gant finally saw what had happened and yelled. Mai stopped mid-lunge as the blood-curdling scream brought everything in the room to a halt.

Mara remained over Zhira, oblivious to the world around her and trying to close the massive gash in her father's chest. Despite her best efforts, the wound would not seal. Blood poured from both sides of the wound as Zhira stared up at Mara.

"Mara..." His voice was raspy. "Find...Radion."

"Dad..." Mara was crying profusely as she continued in vain to try to save him. Color drained from his face and his eyes struggled to focus.

"Find...Radion." He was barely whispering.

"Dad, don't leave me!" she bawled as Zhira's head could no longer support itself. He slowly lowered it back until he was lying motionless on the cold marble floor.

Gjanion got up slowly and picked up the staff. He glared at Hearth.

"How DARE you! I'll..."

A sudden burst of light revealed a glowing silver figure. Her golden hair flowed outwardly around her as if she was under water.

Go, child, the figure said, so only Mara could hear.

Mara looked up through her tears as she continued to hold her father's body.

Go, I will protect you, it said a second time, more sternly.

Mara reluctantly got up, knowing that disobeying whatever this thing was would be a mistake.

She bent down and shut Zhira's eyes so that he appeared to be sleeping. Kei hobbled over to Rylan and lifted her up with Hearth's help, supporting her unconscious body between them. Mara grabbed the relic sword and looked around, noticing that both Mai and Tren had disappeared; only Gjanion remained, gawking at the sight of the goddess's silvery form.

"Sir, I do think now is the time to depart," Hearth said to Gant, who did not turn his head at the sound of the commander's voice.

Using his free hand, Hearth grabbed Gant and pushed him towards the door. Gant slowly started to walk, his eyes locked on his brother's body lying on the floor. He changed course and made for Zhira.

Do not worry, alchemist. I will take care of him, the silver figure said, this time to Gant.

Kei and Hearth carried Rylan out the door of the throne room into the great hall. Mara grabbed Gant's hand and guided him out behind them. As they left, she saw a flash of light, leaving Gjanion alone at the base of the stairs leading up to the throne. Zhira's body was gone.

Run. Mara heard the Goddess's voice in her head and took heed. She broke into a run and headed straight for the stables, led by Hearth. They quickly untethered a couple of horses for Gant and Kei, who was still carrying the unconscious Rylan. Mara grabbed a horse with beautiful blue eyes and mounted it, not wasting time with a saddle or bridle.

Hearth mounted his massive steed and they rode out into the night, through the now-open open gate and down the street, which despite being less chaotic than it had been earlier, still featured a few rebels clashing with knights and fires that had broken out in several buildings.

As they shot down the road, someone Mara did not recognize waved them down.

"What are you all doing, Hearth?" she yelled.

"Who are you?" Mara asked.

"I'm Gladys, one of the rebel commanders."

"Good to see you, Gladys. We need to be on our way, immediately." Hearth regarded the woman.

"Is the job done?" she asked him hopefully.

"Would we be running?" he replied darkly.

"Oh…then…"

"We need to go. Now." Mara started intensely and impatiently at the commander until she nodded.

"Okay, follow me." Gladys quickly commandeered a horse left unattended by one of the royal knights and led them out of the city.

They reached the tree line and rode a while longer at full tilt until the horses could no longer go. When they came to a river, they dismounted and let the horses graze and drink.

"Mara, can you…" Gant began to ask, but she was one step ahead of him.

Without much effort, she managed to fell a small tree and roll it over to them. Kei took his axe and cut it into several small logs, and Mara apathetically flicked her dagger this way and that until they were stacked neatly, then lit them on fire.

First Grandma, now Dad… Mara thought to herself.

"We should not stay in one place for too long. I'm sure the king is already looking for us," Gant said as she stared into the fire.

How is he functioning? Why isn't he breaking down?

"Agreed. We need to get you all to The Cave, regroup, and come up with a new plan," Gladys said.

"How far is that from here?" Kei asked.

"About three days' ride," Hearth responded.

"So you were the informant the whole time?" Gant asked.

"Yes, Geralith assigned me to the council at Radion's request."

He seems so…okay. Her father's lack of reaction to Zhira's death was infuriating to Mara.

"He's GONE, and the only thing you can think about right now is this fat bastard being a spy?!" Mara screamed suddenly at her father, who turned in surprise. She felt bad for insulting Hearth, but she had no control over her emotions. The fire suddenly roared to several times its normal size.

Gant turned to the others. "Would you give us a moment?" He wrapped his arm around Mara's shoulder and walked her a little ways away from the camp. The fire turned to its normal state, flames dancing lazily along the logs.

"Mara, I am beyond upset," Gant said, tearing up.

"It doesn't seem like it."

"Trust me, I am. But right now, right this very second, we are still in grave danger. I don't want to lose anyone else. We need to get to safety, then we can grieve."

Mara couldn't believe his words. He was choosing when to be sad? That seemed inhuman to her. Mara shrugged off his hand and turned her back to him.

"Maybe you can do that, but I can't," she said, tears running down her face.

"Patience and practice," Gant said to her.

Mara turned back around. "What?"

"Patience and practice. I can do this because of patience and practice. When I was young, my father died very suddenly. It was the first time I had known loss, and I was devastated. I cried for days. When mom died, we were in the middle of a fight. I was devastated, but I was familiar with that pain and I had to keep my wits about me. Knowing loss doesn't make it easier, but it gives you the tools you need to get through it. And right now, I know that I need to focus on keeping everyone else safe."

Mara looked at her father, then collapsed into his shoulder and sobbed. She had no more words, no more anger. She was just simply sad beyond anything she had ever felt. The trees around them seemed to bow slightly, as if depressed by Mara's emotions. When she had cried out all the tears she had, she looked up at her father.

"I can't do this," she said.

"You have to. We need to get somewhere safe," Gant replied.

Mara nodded and wiped her eyes. Together, the two of them walked back over to the campfire.

~~~

"I can't believe Radion is alive," Rylan said. She had finally woken up and was tending to a severely broken nose that Mara found oddly fitting for her face.

"He is the one leading this rebellion," Hearth replied.

"So my father really is just a masterful alchemist?" Rylan asked.

"It would seem so, if he isn't a wizard," Gladys replied.

Mara and Rylan again took stock of all the information they had learned that night. Radion was alive, which meant that Gjanion was not Knorr reincarnated like he claimed to be.

"He was never a wizard," Rylan said to the group. "That means that the relics must have some inherent magical properties."
~~~

"Intriguing," Kei replied. "I wonder if we could make our own."

Nobody spoke for a long time. Bugs serenaded them in the darkness beyond their circle around the fire, and the moon continued to fade out of its eclipse until it was a full bright white orb in the sky once again. The horses grazed and slowly knelt down to sleep on the soft grass. The fire flickered and threw shadows between the trees.

"We should give him a proper burial." Mara finally broke the silence.

"Agreed," Gant and Kei said together.

The three of them got up and began digging near the river bank.

"Why don't you just use magic to dig a hole?" Rylan asked Mara.

"It would feel wrong, like we cheated," she replied without looking up.

"I understand, but…" Rylan hesitated, unsure of how to bring up what was bothering her.

"What?" Mara asked, irritated.

"What are you putting in the hole?" she asked sheepishly.

"I have an idea," Kei said, walking back to the fire and grabbing a book from his bag. "He handed this to me to give to you, Mara."

Mara thumbed through the sheets that she had made notes in over the years, Zhira's handwriting was interspersed where he had helped her or explained things to her. On the last page, there was a note.

Mara,

I am beyond proud of you. You are a magnificent wizard, a beautiful young woman, and a strong fighter. No matter how hard things may get, you will always have help: your father, your friends, and any others who rally to you. You are the last wizard, the last hope for freedom from Gjanion and his tyranny. You can do this.

Your Loving Father

Mara read the note several times before tearing it out and stuffing it safely in a pocket of her tunic.

"This is perfect," Mara said as she teared up.

Mara stared down at the book and suddenly felt that she had not appreciated her time with him enough. Now she would never get another moment, another second, to cherish him. She regretted all the times she had been bored by stargazing with him. Tears streamed down her face as Gant put an arm around her shoulder.

"He died bravely," Gant said.

"He died because of me," Mara replied.

"Everyone here is ready to give their lives to end this war, to bring about peace," Gant said.

"We are committed to finishing what we started," Kei added.

Mara placed the book into the hole and took a step back, looking down at it.

"I've brought so much pain and suffering to so many people in such a short time just because I am me. I am sorry I couldn't save you." Mara turned and walked back to the fire.

~~~

Three days later, the group arrived at The Cave. Some of the rebels from the fight in the city had already made it back, including Forbin. The group wound their way through the entrance tunnel until they came upon the large main cavern.

"Greetings." An old man walked up to them leaning on a knobby cane.
~~~

"Sir." Gladys and Hearth both said, nodding respectfully to the man.

"Good to see you've returned intact. A fair bit luckier than some of our troops." Radion turned to Commander Hearth. "If you're here, then that means…"

"Unfortunately, it means that our gravy train has come to an end. The king lives, much to the disdain of all of us. Our best efforts got us close, but not close enough," the fat commander replied solemnly.

"Pity. There is still hope, though, because now we have her." The elderly man pointed at Mara. Mara did not acknowledge him.

"Please forgive my rudeness. I am Radion," he said, and Rylan gasped.

"You're…my great grandfather?"

"In the flesh! Or what's left of it anyway." He laughed a little. "Where is Zhira?" The old king looked around with interest at the returning party.

"Dead." Mara finally spoke and she handed the ruby sword to the old king. The smile on Radion's face disappeared as he stared first at the sword and then at the young wizard.

"My child, I am so sorry. My grandson is a horrible man and I regret that you had to suffer loss at his hands," Radion said to her.

Mara made it clear that she was not interested in talking. Gant offered Radion his thanks, introduced himself, and led Mara to the nearest stone hut.

"Before you disappear, Gant, I have something for you. Zhira left it here." The old man reached in his robe and pulled out a scroll.

"What is this?" Gant asked, taking it from him.

"We record all of our plans, in case something happens to any one of us. This is an observation he made while helping plan our assault," Radion replied. "It's not directly related, but I think it could be of interest to you."

Gant unfurled the scroll and read the contents with intrigue.

It has come to my attention that the Bright One may not be a star. In fact, due to its unique path across the sky, I believe it may be a planet. No other star goes back on its path, and none move relative to each other. I conclude that the Bright One is a planet farther than ours from the sun. Additionally, I believe that it may play a part in Mara's strength. Watching her grow up, her powers were always stronger at night, especially the

summers where the Bright One was high in the sky. My notes back at home in Saros should confirm this.

Gant looked at Mara, who understood the gravity of the note.

"We have to go back to Saros," she said with a sudden sense of urgency, desperate to read more of her father's writing.

"This is interesting, but not terribly important at the moment," Gant said, grabbing her by the shoulder. "You always have your powers. Besides, nobody else knows this information, and we are battered, broken, and in need of some rest. We know where his notes are. We can go get them when it is safe and we are ready."

"Safe?" Mara asked. "It'll never be safe. I couldn't save Dad, I couldn't defeat Gjanion, I…I…" Mara's voice succumbed to the cries she had been holding back.

Gant held her close as she cried into his shoulder.

"Everything happened so fast," Mara sobbed into his tunic.

"I know. It's not fair to expect so much of you, and yet you stood up to the challenge bravely. That's all anyone could ask." Gant reassured her.

"I don't know if I'll be ready next time. I don't know if I have the strength that you do. I can't go through this again," Mara said as she pulled back and wiped her eyes.

"I know it seems impossible, but it will get easier over time."

"I'm tired of losing people," she sighed. *I am an omen of death. Why would anyone stay close to me? Two people who loved me are dead.*

"You won't lose me," Gant said.

"I hope not." Mara hugged him and they went inside for some much needed sleep.

~~~

King Gjanion sat with Commander Tren alone in their council chamber. Gjanion was nursing his ribs and Tren paced back and forth in front of the fireplace.

"If Hearth was the traitor that means General Long was innocent," Tren spoke quietly.

"Or they were working together." Gjanion stared at nothing in particular as he sat at the table.

"Regardless, I am glad it's taken care of. Now it's a simpler operation. Just us against them. No spies, no tricks, just our forces against theirs. I like those odds," Tren said.

"Indeed," the king replied. He winced as he breathed in, his ribs clearly bruised if not broken.

I'll kill every last one of them, starting with that fat, traitorous oaf, Gjanion thought. *What was it Hearth had said? That Geralith placed him to spy? Had Geralith truly been working for the rebellion too? Or was that another of Hearth's*
~~~

deceptions? But Geralith had been loyal to my grandfather…who can I trust?

The two sat in silence for a while until a doctor in blue robes came rushing into the chambers.

"Sire, it's time! Your wife has gone into labor!" The small man squeaked.

The king rose calmly and followed him out without another word, leaving Tren by the fire alone.

An hour later, the sun began to rise on the castle. Stella lay asleep in their bed while Gjanion held a bundle of purple blankets.

The king walked over to the nearest window. "Welcome to your kingdom, Karbalion," the king said to his new son sleeping in his arms.

~~~

Mai watched as the last of the rebels entered the crevice in the rock. She had trailed the group all the way from the castle until she had lost sight of them and they had seemingly disappeared into thin air. She set up camp for a day or two and scouted the area before coming across footprints and a trodden path in the woods leading to a spot along the cliff side.

Armed with concrete evidence of the base she had overheard Gant and the rebels discussing over their campfire that first night, she went back to where she had tied up her horse. General Mai mounted her palomino and took off towards the castle.
~~~

* 9 7 9 8 9 8 5 8 1 3 0 0 5 *